My Totally Awkward Supernatural Crush

My Totally Awkward Supernatural Crush

LAURA TOFFLER-CORRIE

Roaring Brook Press • New York

Text copyright © 2013 by Laura Toffler-Corrie
Published by Roaring Brook Press
Roaring Brook Press is a division of Holtzbrinck Publishing Holdings Limited
Partnership
175 Fifth Avenue, New York, New York 10010
macteenbooks.com

Library of Congress Cataloging-in-Publication Data
Toffler-Corrie, Laura.
    My totally awkward supernatural crush / Laura Toffler-Corrie. — 1st ed.
     p. cm.
    Summary: While coping with middle school drama and costuming a teen
production of *Fiddler on the Roof,* fourteen-year-old Jenna falls for Luke, an angel,
and joins him in battle against demonic foe Adam, who wants Jenna's ancient
pendant.
    ISBN 978-1-59643-733-3 (hardcover)
    ISBN 978-1-59643-882-8 (e-book)
    [1. Angels—Fiction. 2. Demonology—Fiction. 3. Middle schools—Fiction.
4. Schools—Fiction. 5. Necklaces—Fiction. 6. Musicals—Fiction.] I. Title.

PZ7.T57317Tot 2013
[Fic]—dc23

            2012034263

Roaring Brook Press books are available for special promotions and premiums.
For details contact: Director of Special Markets, Holtzbrinck Publishers.

First edition 2013
Printed in the United States of America

10 9 8 7 6 5 4 3 2 1

*To Bobby, Ed, Herbie, and Ceil on the
other side of the equinox*

My Totally Awkward Supernatural Crush

A Dream

I'm babysitting David Lipski, next-door neighbor and demon-child extraordinaire, when he crawls out onto the roof of his house.

"David!" I yell, thrusting my head out the window. "You're going to kill yourself! Come back in!"

"Bite me," is his casual reply.

He merely taunts me with an impromptu hula–break dance, sticks out his tongue, makes a "nyeh" face, and does a cartwheel right on the edge of the shingles. Even though I'm one of the most uncoordinated girls in the eighth grade and the only girl to actually foul out of Miss Manley's medicine ball game, I have no choice but to crawl out after him, two stories up over the Lipskis' well-manicured lawn and disturbingly grotesque collection of garden gnomes from around the world. I am trying to save poor David from his death, but I know that if I ever get my hands on him I will totally kill him myself.

Michael Jackson's "Thriller" suddenly begins to play.

"Hee, hee, hee." David sings along in high falsetto. In a Michael

move, he balances on tippy toes and executes a death-defying turn.

He is going to plunge to his death. I can feel it. I have to do something to save his gangly butt, and fast. But as I wobble my way toward him, the toe of my shoe catches a loose shingle and I lose my balance. Swaying back and forth, flapping my arms in windmill circles, I look like some great, geeky bird.

"Hee, he—" David catches sight of me and stops abruptly.

And then, in that slo-mo so popular in dreams, my feet lift up from the gritty shingles and I fall backward. Falling, falling, falling, forever it seems, until . . . two gentle hands lift me and place me back up on the roof. I turn but see no one. I only see David staring at the space near me. His astonished face is bathed in the most luminous white-golden light. A beatific expression washes across his devilish grin, as if he's seeing something remarkable, something otherworldly.

"Oh." He exhales softly, making a big, round O with his mouth.

Then:

There is the loud blaring of police cars. They careen around the corner, swerving recklessly up the gravel driveway, flattening the gnomes from Spain and Guam, sending them to meet their maker.

Within seconds, David's parents, Bernice and Lenny Lipski, in their blue Suburban, careen around the corner as well. I hear the exaggerated loud whir of the passenger-side window and see Bernice's panic-stricken face as she spots David on the roof.

"Oh my God!" she lets loose, with such a glass-shattering shriek that Lenny loses control of the car. He swerves hard into the driveway, taking out gnomes from France, Italy, and the

Czech Republic. He rams right into the back of the police car, activating the lights and sirens that are now blaring at ear-piercing levels.

I lunge for David. He "nyehs" me once again and agilely steps to the side.

"Ahhhh!" I yelp, and teeter in space. I'm gladdened by the thought of finally having some babysitting money for clothes that I like, but then I'm suddenly saddened by the thought of trying to fit a new outfit over a full-body cast.

I look down and see the astonished face of Jared Needleman coming at me. Terrified, he lifts his arms in a cradle position. The gentle hands again slow my fall until:

Thwump!

I open my eyes to find myself face-to-groin with Jared's private parts. I quickly roll over; the sun passes across my eyes, but something is blocking it. And then I know, it isn't something, it's someone. It's a boy, not much older than me, and beautiful, with great white feathery wings. He's so real. He smells fresh, like a pine tree after it rains. I smile. He smiles back. I blink and awake. And he's gone.

1

It's my fourteenth birthday, and my wish is to be someone else.

Okay, maybe not someone else entirely, but certainly someone less like me. For the moment, however, I'm stuck, packed into a booth with the Blooms and Company at Cowboy Clems Chow House, a rustic Western-inspired restaurant, fully loaded with peanut-shell-covered floor and deer-antler-covered walls. It's a place where the servers wear name tags that read: *Hi, I'm Cowpoke (fill in the name).*

Twangy music plays loudly in the background.

You are my angellll . . .

With a pleasant expression, Dad does his usual: turns up his iPod and adjusts the earpiece hidden discreetly around his neck. I can see by the tracking of his eyes that he's going in and out of his lipreading routine, presumably based on the level of his interest in the table conversation at hand. He smiles pleasantly at Mom, who never seems to mind.

Barbecue-type smells invade my nose as I survey the room. Lots of gluttonous badly dressed adults. What do I like about Cowboy Clems? No one I know, or want to know, is ever here.

The thing is that I'd been planning this birthday dinner

for weeks. My parents were supposed to take my best friend, Tess, and me to Manchu Gardens, which is the nicest Japanese restaurant in town: paper lanterns, waitresses in traditional kimonos, lilting Japanese music, and a tinkling koi pond with real koi. And we were going to sit in the back room with authentic Japanese ambience.

But the fates had a different plan.

In the car earlier today, my younger brother, Michael, let loose with a disgusting belch.

"Michael! Stop that belching right now! You're smelling up the car." Mom did a whole-body turn around from the passenger seat. "Daddy! Daddy!" she said to my father because that is, revoltingly, what she likes to call him. She lifted the earpiece from around his neck. "Open the glove compartment and take out that bundle of air fresheners. It's a good thing I bought these in bulk, Mister!" she scolded Michael, unwrapping a fresh one in the shape of a lemon and hanging it on the rearview mirror.

"Buuuuuuurrrrrpppp," was Michael's witty reply.

I often like to imagine that I'm a genetic throwback to some long-lost princess, but that somewhere along the way one of my ancestors fell in love with a stupid, smelly field peasant, thereby sullying the rest of the Bloom gene pool forever. Those circumstances robbed me of my real identity (and legacy), a normal family, social distinction at Arthur P. Rutherford Middle School, and the opportunity to develop an artistically expressive wardrobe.

In the car, I turned to Michael.

"You better cut it out," I said. "No airy bodily emissions of any kind at Manchu Gardens."

An uncomfortable pause ensued.

"Ooh, Mom. You are so busted," Michael said.

"What?! Mom!! No!" I whined. "You didn't get reservations at Manchu Gardens?"

"Well, honey," she wheedled. "We couldn't get an early reservation. You know how Daddy hates to eat late. He gets so agitated."

We all looked over at Dad, who had taken the opportunity at the red light to calmly turn the wheel of his iPod.

"They're taking you to Cowboy Clems." Michael shrugged. "Hey, it's not my fault."

Could this birthday get any worse?

Moreover, I had been hinting for weeks about my birthday present too: a generous gift card to Maude's Chic Fashion Boutique. You see, I call my parents the Bloom family communists primarily because Mom firmly believes that all worldly goods should be (a) purchased in bulk, (b) made of the cheapest fabrics ever, preferably burlap, and (c) distributed equally among the masses (the masses being the Bloom family members).

In keeping with the communist philosophy, Mom prefers to shop at the Bulk Emporium, an all-purpose store where one can purchase clothing and spark plugs at the same time, not to mention oversize grocery items with expiration dates that extend beyond the time that Earth will colonize other planets.

If I want my own money to spend, I have to babysit the

ever-horrible David Lipski. I am planning to be the baby-sitter of choice when David's parents go to a big bar mitzvah celebration in New Jersey in December. It's going to be practically an all-night affair, with an open sushi bar and a retro disco band, and I figure I can make out big time.

As a matter of fact, I already have the new outfit picked out with my earnings and mentally envision myself sashaying down the hall at Arthur P. Rutherford. New Year. New Me. Girls flitting their eyes enviously in my direction, wanting to copy my look. Boys approving my look with a nod and a wink, indicating that I'm someone it would be cool to know.

———◆———

Back at Cowboy Clems, Jared Needleman (neighbor, party crasher, and unrequited crusher) nudges me out of my reverie.

"I have something for you," he says.

Could it be a birthday gift? I wonder. Tess and I exchange raised-eyebrow looks and lean toward him curiously.

He holds out his pink palm and there sitting in the middle of it is my bite plate.

"Remember in Gym, when I was spotting you on the parallel bars and you fell off, onto my . . ." He blushes crimson. "Onto me . . . Miss Manley asked me to return it to you. I've been keeping it in my pocket," he says, patting the front of his pants.

It's my turn to blush crimson. How could I forget? I suddenly remember my dream from the other night—when I fell off the roof and Jared broke my fall. The boy from my dream flashes across my mind. So beautiful, saving me from falling. The smell of pine. A strange prickly feeling comes over me.

"Uh . . . hi . . . hi!" Tess waves her hand in front of my face. "You in there?"

I look over to see Tess's familiar face: pretty, angular, with her large dark eyes and the mass of black curls that frames her face. The dangling silver piano charm she wears around her neck catches the light, causing me to blink and jostling me back into the moment.

She leans in and whispers, "Well, I hope you're not thinking of ever putting that back in your mouth again."

"What?"

"The bite plate."

"And here are y'all's bibs for the evening," says Cowpoke Heather, handing us little white paper dribble bibs, which Michael and Jared happily put on.

"Here's one for you, Jenna," Jared says, passing me a paper bib decorated with a picture of a happy steer eagerly awaiting consumption by some sloppy Cowboy Clems patron.

I shoot Jared the most withering stare I can muster, hoping he'll get the hint to leave me alone, which of course he doesn't.

"I can attach it for you," he offers, making that *thwacking* sound with the Velcro as he opens and closes his bib over and over.

"Thanks, Jared," I say. "But you'll have to kill me first."

"Oh." He looks dejected.

"Kill you? Hey, I'll do it!" says Michael, grabbing two butter knives and swinging them around like a samurai swordsman, all the while honking little samurai noises through his nose.

"Hwaa, hwaa!"

He pretends to cut me up into little pieces.

"Hwaa!"

Then he and Jared rock with laughter like it's the funniest thing either one of them has ever seen.

"Oh just put it on, Jenna," Mom says. "Otherwise you'll stain your shirt."

"So what? I have another twenty-five at home. In the same color. You bought them in bulk, remember?" I say.

"Oh that's right," Mom says.

I can only sigh and grab a chip from the community chip basket that the Bloom communists love to keep having refilled at no extra cost, furthering their belief that everything should belong to everyone.

"And then I heard the cashier at the Bulk saying that tonight was some sort of special night for people interested in astrology. Isn't that exciting, Jenna?" Mom's voice pulls me back into the moment. "Something mystical about the stars being lined up."

"Do you mean the equinox, Mrs. Bloom?" offers Jared.

"I think that was it. Apparently it only occurs every two hundred years or so and opens the door to all kinds of mystical possibilities," Mom says. She makes an *ooh* sound and wiggles her fingers in space. "Something about a portal for good and evil, inhuman visitations from otherworldly dimensions, heightened paranormal activity. Stuff like that."

She shoves a chip in her mouth.

Was communist Mom talking about mysticism? Could it be?

"What kinds of paranormal activities?" I ask.

"I dunno." She shrugs. "Another cashier opened up so I jumped on that line. Daddy, didn't we order the guacamole dip?"

"Well, Mrs. Bloom, when my father and I did our documentary *Debunking the Mysticism of Astrology, or Crackpots with Telescopes*," says Jared, "we discovered that, despite what you read in popular books and see in the movies about vampires and werewolves and the like, most of all this paranormal stuff is just a bunch of hooey."

"Oh, that's very true, Jared. You're an insightful and grounded young man."

Mom shoots me a wink.

"Did you just say hooey?" Tess interrupts, shaking her head. "You worry me sometimes, Jared."

"Would you rather I say something gross like *poop*?"

"Now I know you really didn't just say *poop*." Tess rolls her eyes.

And as Tess and Jared spar and the communists devour their chips, I realize that I'm at an all-time low. I now have a new appreciation for the Emily Dickinson unit we're doing in Mrs. Hanlan's English class, and of Emily's dilemma as a badly dressed weirdo in self-imposed social exile, which she so poignantly examined in her poem "I'm Nobody":

I'm nobody! Who are you?
Are you nobody, too?

It was turning out to be the worst birthday ever.

Until suddenly, from behind the bar, the kitchen doors swing open, revealing a golden-white light. A boy emerges, tying an apron around his waist and pushing back a wisp of hair from his forehead. And he's the most beautiful boy I've ever seen.

2

He ambles toward our table.

"Now who is that fine thing?" Tess asks, drawing in a breath and poking me in the ribs.

I open my mouth to speak but nothing comes out.

It was a spontaneous connection, like a déjà vu dream. It was as if I knew him, but I had never seen him before. Could it be that this waiter was the boy from my dream, the boy who saved me from falling off David's roof? Who I saw hovering over me when I rolled off Jared's crotch? I know deep in my soul that it was . . . but it can't be.

Within seconds, he's standing over me and I'm reading his name tag: *Cowpoke Luke.*

"Hi, I'm Cowpoke Luke," he says, somehow making the greeting sound sultry.

"Welcome to Cowboy Clems, where the beef is dyin' to please you. Can I take your order? And may I suggest our family dinner special, which includes the fresh open salad bar and the all-you-can-eat stuffed-tater-nachos platter?"

"You're the waiter?" I hear Mom sounding skeptical, somewhere in the hazy distance. "Aren't you a bit young? You look about the girls' age."

"Em . . . one of the waiters is sick. I'm filling in. I'm a . . . bus boy. Really," he says.

Then I vaguely hear Tess ordering something vegetarian and the Bloom communists ordering everything with extra sour cream, meat, sauce, rice and beans, and then checking that all the extras are complimentary. But all I can do is stare.

"And put the tangy chipotle sauce on the side, please . . ." communist Mom says.

I feel a breeze. I startle back to the moment to find Tess fanning me with the menu.

"Jenna? Jenna?"

She nudges me in the arm.

"It's your turn, birthday girl," Mom sings.

"I . . . snooklabeep . . . ha-ha," I babble and laugh incoherently.

"Happy birthday," Cowpoke Luke says to me gently. Then he smiles, lighting up the table way better than the dozens of little pin lights that hang from the ceiling at Manchu Gardens.

"Well, howdy there, Cowpoke Luke," Tess says, passing me a sly sidelong glance. "The Bloom family has a birthday tradition. Whenever someone says happy birthday to Jenna, they have to give her a kiss."

For a long moment, Cowpoke Luke stares at me as if he doesn't know what to do.

"Tess is kidding," I sputter. "She's an idiot. Just ignore her."

A slow, shy grin spreads across his face and he comes around to my chair. I feel electrified and horrified, and time seems to wind down. I'm the center of the world. Everyone around me glows and pulses in vibrant colors. The twangy background music turns heavenly, full of harps and flutes, like the music you'd hear in a New Age crystal store or from my Dad's iPod.

And then all I can see is Cowpoke Luke's magnificent face moving toward me: masculine but soft, smooth golden skin, and large, hazel eyes. One wavy strand of his sandy-colored hair comes undone from his short ponytail and dangles over his forehead. He places his palms on the table for balance, leans on his sinewy muscular arms and tilts toward me. I feel as if I'm being surrounded by light and warmth and the heady, invigorating smell of pine.

"Hey, uh . . . wait a minute. Cowpokes aren't supposed to kiss patrons." Jared's irritated voice sounds very far away.

"Oh my God. He is so hot," Tess whispers in my ear. "This is the best birthday present I've ever given you."

And then Cowpoke Luke's lips brush against my cheek, like the soft tickle of a feather. An electric *zzzz* surges through me, much like the sensation I felt when I accidentally picked up my neighbor's dog's electric collar too close to the electric fence.

Luke pulls away. A soft blush creeps across his cheeks.

Holding his waiter pad aloft, Luke once again glances my way.

"Would you like to order?" he asks.

I grab that paper bib, thwack open the Velcro, and throw it around my neck.

Luke collects the menus and I thrust mine at him. Our

eyes meet again. Electricity! At least for me. He leans forward and, as he takes the menu, our hands brush against one another and I freeze, until Jared reaches over, pries the menu from my stiff fingers, and hands it to Luke.

"Here you go," he grumbles darkly to him.

Luke takes the menu and then shoots me a tiny grin. He turns and heads back to the kitchen.

Adrenaline rushes through my veins. Seriously, I can hear it pumping. And everyone around me suddenly looks beautiful. I no longer see just an unwashed mass of eaters stuffing their faces with taters, dribbling barbecue sauce down their chins. Suddenly everyone is young and hip and dressed in a fashion-forward manner. And they're all glancing over at me with big, accepting smiles. And I'm not even thinking about being the worst-dressed birthday loser of all time, or about being with Jared and the communists, or even about all the beans that Michael is about to consume and all the farting that will take place on the car ride home because of it, or . . .

"For God's sake!" Mom snaps me out of my reverie. "Wake up. Jared is talking to you."

"Huh?"

"I said," Jared enunciates slowly, holding a tortilla chip aloft and looking annoyed, "could you please pass the salsa."

And then it's all normal again.

Everyone is back to the way they were, gluttonous and gross. I hate my birthday and what the hell is that red stuff sticking to Jared's chin? I sigh loudly.

"Well, I think this would be a good time to give Jenna her gift. Don't you think so, Daddy? Her *gift*," Mom says slowly.

"Shift?" Dad misreads her lips and slides down the bench a few inches.

Mom sighs and roots through her purse.

Maybe this night is turning around after all. I sit up, happily expectant in my seat as I imagine how important I'll feel after having spent my birthday gift certificates at Maude's Chic Fashion Boutique, floating down the hallway at Arthur P. with Cowpoke Luke on my arm.

I feel a surge of satisfaction at the thought of Sarah Johnson, my ex–best friend, and the way that she and her new besties would stop, slack jawed with bulged-out eyes, to gape at my new look and my new man.

It's hard to think of Sarah without feeling a sting, without flashing back to how she dumped me. We had been best friends from first grade to sixth but then, in the summer before middle school, she went to Europe with her aunt and came back somehow different, somehow stylish and self-assured. In those few weeks, she became sleek, long, lean, and tan. Her smile beamed after her braces came off, and her hair had grown long and silky. She started attracting the attention of cool girls and cute guys. She became self-absorbed, and I felt her pulling away. By that point, I couldn't seem to ever say or do the right thing to pull her back.

And then there was that night at our frozen yogurt place: a group of cool girls asked her (not me) to join them at the movies. And I'll never forget the way she looked at me as she stood to go with a flip of her hair and a careless over-the-shoulder glance, her expression indifferent, her eyes blank as if she didn't know me.

"I'll call you later, Jenna," she lied.

Then she left with those girls and never called me again. It was the big fro-yo dis.

Back in the present, I glance at Tess and realize how lucky I am that she moved to the neighborhood only a few months later.

Mom pulls out a flat square box and gives it to me.

I take it and turn it over in my hand. Don't gift certificates usually come in rectangular envelopes? Do gift certificates ever make a tinkling sound?

"Open it, Jenna." Tess leans in excitedly.

Fighting a frown, I rip open the wrapping paper and lift off the top of the box. Gingerly, I push the thin pink tissue paper aside.

Please be a square, tinkling gift certificate, I chant to myself. *Please don't be some piece of crap jewelry from the Bulk Emporium. Please . . . please . . . pl—*

I look down into the box. There lies a large, flat, round, silver discus-shaped pendant with ridges all around it like an elaborate bottle cap. It's embellished with some strange engraved hieroglyphics.

I pull it up by the chain. The pendant spins and dangles. Essentially, it's a big clunky thing that reflects the light with such intensity that it momentarily blinds a nearby waiter, causing him to stumble and spill a bowl of garbanzo beans over the head and down the collar of a nearby customer. Everyone at our table blinks back from its gleam and mutters a surprised:

"Oh."

"Oh . . . no," I mutter to myself.

Michael snickers.

"I mean . . . em . . . oh wow." I save the moment.

Once it stops spinning, I can see clearly just how hideous it is. It looks like something a middle-aged woman would wear on some tacky book club cruise to the Bahamas.

"Now I know what you're thinking." Mom smiles and leans in. "You're thinking that this necklace is a very fancy piece of jewelry from the Bulk Emporium. But it's much, much more special than that. That necklace has been in our family for at least two hundred years. Can you believe it's that old?"

"Yeah . . . I mean . . . no."

I feel ashamed for being such an ingrate, but I know that this thing will sit in my drawer for another two hundred years until my great-great-granddaughter passes it on to her own disappointed child.

With reverence, Mom carefully takes the chain from my hands and holds the pendant up to her chest.

"Nice, right?" she says.

"You can borrow it," I offer.

"Oh Jenna." Mom chuckles, dismissing me with a wave.

"I was moving Grandma's jewelry box off the top shelf of

the closet," Mom continues, "and it just fell out! I remembered seeing it when I was a little girl, although for some reason grandma never wore it."

"No kidding," I say.

"The jeweler at the Bulk said that it's pure silver. And to think, these big pendants are exactly the fashion now!" she says excitedly. "So I had it cleaned . . . although it looks like they couldn't get rid of these little scratches."

She examines the pendant more closely.

Jared leans over to take the pendant from Mom.

"May I?" he asks.

She nods and hands it to him.

"I think that's some kind of old writing, Mrs. Bloom." Jared squints at the pendant.

Michael leans over Jared's shoulder for a closer look.

"Maybe it's Elvish," he says.

We all turn to stare at him.

"You know, like from the Lord of the Rings. The Elvish writing on the inside of the ring. The one that Gollum murdered his hobbit cousin for. My preciousssss . . ." Michael hisses low.

And the silent stares continue.

"What? It's possible." Michael shrugs.

"It's possible that we're descended from Elves?!" I say.

"Well, how can you be sure that we're not?" Michael nods knowingly, shoving a chip heaped with a load of salsa into his mouth.

"May I?" Jared gestures at me.

He takes the clasp in both hands and leans toward me, indicating that he'd like to place the necklace around my neck.

"How gentlemanly, Jared." Mom beams. "Jenna, lift up your hair."

Reluctantly, I gather my hair and lean back for Jared to fasten the clasp. Is he taking too long or is it my imagination?

"Thanks, guys." I muster a smile and pat the pendant against my chest. "It's awesome."

"You know, Michael," Jared instructs, "all that Middle Earth stuff is just fantasy."

"Yeah, how do you know?" Michael counters.

Just then Luke reappears with some food, namely a steaming, sizzling fajita that he puts in front of Mom and that encases the whole table in a misty facial, causing all nearby patrons to ooh and ahh.

"Well." Jared chortles in a patronizing way. "Name me one instance in real life where you've met elves or wizards, or hobbits for that matter. No, no. Fantasy creatures or even the supernatural creatures that are so popular these days don't really exist."

As Luke sets the plate down with his beautifully sculpted arms, he glances at me and smiles shyly. He glances at the pendant. A look of surprise crosses his face. He leans in a bit as if examining it and then his eyes flash to mine. His expression darkens in a way that I can't quite read. He looks as if he's about to say something but doesn't.

"And speaking of fantasy and the supernatural, Jared," Mom says, blowing on her steaming fajita, "just last week in *People* there was a story about a family whose members were touched by an angel . . ."

Luke reaches in and touches the pendant gingerly with his fingertips.

Instantly, I shoot a glance around the table, but for the moment everyone is preoccupied either with conversation or salsa. Luke quickly retracts his hand, but his eyes continue to be fixed on the disk.

"And then there's that equinox thingie," Mom says, chewing thoughtfully. "What exactly does it mean though?"

"Well, from what I've read," Jared pontificates, "the equinox occurs twice a year when the sun is at one of two opposite points in the celestial sphere. And astrologists often refer to it as the first cusp of Aries and the first point of Libra. Wiccans and neo-pagans often celebrate the event in the fall and spring. It's been said that paranormal things can happen during the equinox but only for a month, from full moon to full moon . . . But of course that's all just nonsense."

"Where did you get this?" Luke whispers hoarsely to me as Jared continues to ramble. "Can I see it?"

While everyone's distracted, I discreetly lift the pendant from around my neck and hand it to Luke.

He holds it up to the large glass doors behind us. It spins, catching a jagged flash of light from the blue/pink sky outside. And suddenly there's an image of a face in the pendant. A boy. With dark, sinister eyes. Pale. With jet-black hair, just long enough to be slicked back into a knot.

Luke and I both jump at the sight of him, and Luke looks frantic for a moment. His eyes dart to the doors. There, on the other side of the glass, the boy stands: chiseled and beautiful in black jeans, slick black boots, a light blue T-shirt, and a sumptuous-looking black leather jacket. He buzzes and shimmers in and out of existence. I smell wood and pine, but not like Luke's pine scent. Not sweet. More like burnt, smoldering logs, like a campfire that's been put out but where the red-hot logs still burn.

For a fleeting moment, the boy looks surprised, as if he doesn't know where he is. As if he's organizing his thoughts. His expression hardens, his head moves around methodically, his eyes seem to be assessing his surroundings, the people walking by, the block, the doors of Cowboy Clems. Then a small smirk passes across his mouth as if he's figured something out. His eyes meet mine. A cold chill creeps across the back of my neck.

3

A second later, the boy's eyes dive to the pendant. A beat. His mouth opens slightly. Confusion. Then a look of recognition.

He lunges toward the window, moving faster than seems humanly possible, his hands a blur of speed. I jump back in my chair. Luke jumps in front of me. The pendant flies from his hand and accidentally swings into Mom's plate of sour cream.

There's a flash of gray light, and the boy is gone.

I look around. No one in the restaurant seems to have noticed that anything strange occurred or was distracted for one second from their eating.

"Um . . . excuse me," Mom says, sounding annoyed.

She lifts the pendant from her dish. Drips of white goo plop onto her beans. "This is quite valuable, you know, young man."

"Gimme." Michael reaches out nonchalantly. "I'll lick it clean."

"You will not!" Mom glares at him.

"I'm sorry. Please excuse me." Luke bows slightly at Mom.

She dips a napkin in a water glass and starts wiping the pendant down. Luke cleans up around her and collects the remains of her splattered plate.

"Luke . . ." I hear a low whispery male voice almost right in my ear.

No one seems to hear it but me.

"Keep your head. Time is short. He's here," the voice says.

Luke passes me a glance.

I know.

But his mouth doesn't move. It's as if I heard his voice in my head.

"And we'd like some fresh chips and salsa, please," Mom says, handing Luke the bowl.

"Luke, Mr. Deets wants you in back," a waiter calls from the bar.

Luke turns to go, but not without flashing me one more inexplicable look.

I feel Jared's suspicious eyes on me, as if he senses a blip on his jealousy radar.

"Did you see that guy outside the window or hear that disembodied voice?" I whisper to Tess.

"What guy? What disembodied voice?" she asks, trying to keep her veggie taco together.

"Humph," Mom says. "What a rude waiter."

"I agree, Mrs. Bloom," Jared says.

"Let's request another table next time we're here," she adds. "Right, Daddy?"

Instinctively, I feel like defending Luke to my mom, but what could I say? The waiter who came to me in a dream and saved me from falling off David's roof may or may not be totally human and just protected me from being attacked by some kind of joint supernatural hallucination?

Another waiter brings Mom a new dish and, fortunately, it isn't long before the Blooms are once again distracted by their food.

Tess and I spy Luke behind the bar, cleaning glasses. He seems to be avoiding our gaze.

"So who is he?" Tess leans in. "He looks like he might be in our grade, but I've never seen him in school or anywhere before. He must be new in town. He's almost as hot as Carlo."

Carlo is a guy from Italy who just moved here. He plays the tuba and Tess is totally in love with him even though he's barely said two sentences to her and she's not even sure what the sentences were because his English is pretty choppy.

"Even with all this food," Mom says, "I just know I'll be hungry in an hour. Isn't that always the way with Tex-Mex food?"

"I believe you mean Chinese food, Mrs. Bloom," Jared says authoritatively. "When my father and I produced the documentary *Food, J'Adore: Why We're Fat* for the cable-access station, we explored the relationship between food and stomach enzymes and how some ethnic-food portions are smaller and healthier, with higher fish-protein content versus high lactose content . . ."

But my eyes and heart are drawn again to Cowpoke Luke. He looks off into nowhere in particular and I'm struck by his faraway expression. Presumably feeling my eyes on him, he glances up and gives me just the hint of a gentle smile.

My face flushes hot and I dart my eyes into my lap. When I look up again, he's gone.

4

That night, I dream again of Cowpoke Luke.

This time, he's standing in a rooftop bistro with vine-trellised archways under the open sky. He stands by a small table covered with crisp white linen laden with porcelain dishes and silver cutlery. A crystal vase overflowing with sweet-scented lilacs is the centerpiece. Luke is also dressed in crisp white linen, and he holds his waiter pad aloft, poised for taking orders. He looks perfect against the backdrop of a sunset and a panoramic view of Paris in the distance. One strand of his golden-brown hair dangles recklessly over his sculpted cheek.

"Mademoiselle." He bows slightly toward me.

Bang, bang, bang.

"Your table and your destiny await—"

Bang, bang, bang.

"How would you like it prepared?" he asks suavely. "Done, not quite done, or up to you?"

With a flourish of his arm, he gestures for me to sit.

Stay away!

I see a flash of our shared vision of the boy from Cowboy Clems. He's gliding toward me, encased in black fog, in that scary horror-movie way where his feet dangle a few feet above the floor. He claps his hands and the sound reverberates like a loud drum beat. He reaches for me when . . .

My eyes fly open.

Bang, bang, bang.

I'm in my bed and someone is banging on my bedroom door.

"Mom says wake up!" Michael grunts, pushing the door open. "You're gonna be late for school."

I lie in bed, stare at the ceiling, and sigh. School. Yeah. Real life. I forgot about that.

After a rushed bowl of cereal, communist Mom intercepts me at the front door.

"Don't you want to wear your new necklace?" she asks hopefully, gesturing for me to turn so she can clasp it around my neck. After it's locked and loaded into place, she turns me back around to admire it and pats it happily.

"It was on the kitchen table. Don't leave it lying around. It'll get lost," she says.

Now there's a thought.

Then Michael intercepts me, half a bagel dangling from his mouth.

"'Keep it secret. Keep it safe,'" he whispers, spraying me with bits of cream cheese.

"What?"

"Get it? Lord of the Rings . . . When they first discover the ring . . . and Gandalf wants Frodo to hide it so he can go to the wizard library to do some research . . . He says to Frodo, 'Keep it secret. Keep it—'"

I slam the front door in his face and tuck the pendant into my shirt on my way toward the bus. It feels clammy and cold against my chest. *Groan.*

Once at school, my presence is more body than mind. I feel dreamy and dazed and disconnected as thoughts of Luke float through my imagination like clouds on a gentle breeze.

In Math, integers have no meaning for me, nor does History or the leaders of the free world. During Gym, I'm hit in the head with the medicine ball so many times that Miss Manley tells me that I'm in danger of the second half of "use it or lose it," and suggests that I pay attention before I cause my own concussion.

I can barely appreciate the whimsical nonsense of my favorite poem, "Jabberwocky." Even though Mrs. Hanlan's Honors English is my favorite class.

Mrs. Hanlan is not like my other teachers, who focus on meaningless regurgitation of facts that I eventually forget. She encourages us to think about our feelings and spends many class periods sharing her own personal emotional journeys. Her poetry belies a tortured, romantic heart, a soul yearning to be accepted and appreciated for who she really is. Since I spend most of my time feeling like a shadow geek in a world full of solid-gold beings, like Sarah Johnson, I can very much relate. In the end, we all just want to feel special.

Plus, Mrs. Hanlan has earned a certain notoriety in the community because many of her poems have been published in the local *Pennysaver*.

But here I am and my life suddenly does feel more awkward than usual. Something is happening, something that doesn't quite make sense. Not to say that the last number of years of my life have made sense. Somewhere between sidewalk chalk, Barbies, and boy-band crushes, I grew boobs and was subjected to serious assemblies about the dangers of drugs and sex. And there were boys I liked who didn't like me back. And Jared stopped hitting me with sticks and started staring at me with soft, shiny eyes.

It's not like there aren't cute boys at school who have caught my attention over the long years of being trapped in Oceanville, where an odd girl who doesn't look good in a bathing suit can't possibly fit in with the inner circles of popular kids.

Dean Gold, for one, is particularly handsome, with a jaunty confident swagger that makes him even more appealing. But Dean is way out of my league and belongs to Sarah Johnson and never says more than hey to me and only if he catches me staring at him in the halls. There isn't even enough raw material for a romantic daydream when it comes to Dean.

But Cowpoke Luke. He actually looked at me! He actually kissed me, albeit on the cheek! Here was finally a fantasy I could work with! The intrigue! The drama! The specialness of that!

By Science, I find myself doodling his name over and over along the borders of my notebook.

Who is he? Where did he come from? And why did he kiss me? Just because Tess said it was my birthday? He could easily just have said "happy birthday," and walked away. No one would have thought any worse of him.

"Watcha drawing?" Jared, who is my Science lab partner, leans way over the owl-pellet vomit lying on the desk like a hairy blob and startles me out of my reverie. I quickly turn the page over.

"Just doodles," I say, but I'm too slow and I can see the flash of disapproval in his eyes.

"Humph," Jared replies, picking up the long silver dissection tool. "I could use a little help here."

Jared leans toward the hairy nest and turns pale.

"Everything all right over there, Mr. Needleman?" Mr. Campbell asks.

"Don't worry, Mr. Campbell," Jared says. "I have no aversion to animals, dead or alive. When my father and I did our documentary *Fowl Friends: Birds Who Give a Hoot* for the cable-access station, I was the one who instructed our stagehand Bob about the correct way to handle the wildlife."

"All right, but if you're feeling queasy just take a break. We're not dissecting human vomit today," says Mr. Campbell.

I sigh, shut my notebook, and try to concentrate on the owl pellet.

"Ew, is that a piece of dead worm in there?" I wonder aloud.

Suddenly Jared turns all white and gaggy and runs from the room, leaving me to pick out undigested food particles by myself.

I don't even notice that the bell for next period has rung until the other kids have pretty much cleaned up and headed out the door. I quickly follow suit, bump my way down the hall, and race into the cafetorium for chorus rehearsal.

"Almost late, Jebba," Mr. Resnick says, getting my name

wrong like he does with everyone. I drop my backpack and rush up to the bleachers, where the class is packed tighter than sardines.

I glance helplessly at Tess, who's down and to the right, with the mezzo-sopranos.

Wiggling my way into the alto section, I accidentally bump Sarah Johnson, knocking her off balance.

"Be careful! Gah!" Sarah exclaims, grabbing the kid next to her, who then bumps into the kid next to him, setting off a chain reaction of bumps and wobbles.

"Ow."

"Watch it!"

"Let go!"

"Hey, chill. It wasn't me, it was that geek!"

"Whooaa!"

"All right everyone!" Mr. Resnick claps for attention, picks up his clipboard, and places his reading glasses on his nose.

"Before we begin class, I have some announcements to make. I'm holding auditions for the teenage production of *Fiddler on the Roof,* which I will be directing at the Old Vic Community Theater, Oceanville's semiprofessional, summer-stock-style musical venue. The show will open the first weekend in December. There will be a matinee and an evening performance on Sunday. But our most important performance will be the premiere, on Saturday night, December 3, so commit that to memory, everyone."

He glances up over his glasses at the rows of wobbling, clutching kids, and frowns.

"Maintain yourselves, please," he says.

Everyone finally regains their balance, and I can feel forty pairs of eyes shooting me withering looks.

"Now I know this isn't a school activity, but since it is a teenage production, you're my main pool of actors and crew," he says, and then throws a supportive glance at Sarah, who straightens and surveys the class with disdain. Melanie, her *new* best friend and wannabe, nudges her with a smile.

"And I've arranged with Principal Bareli for those who participate to get extra credit on their final chorus grade. But now it takes more than talented performers to put on a show. A show needs the talents of backstage helper elves to make it the best that it can be. For example, we need a musical elf to assist Arthur P. Rutherford's own sports guru, Miss Manley, with orchestration and piano . . ."

I glance over at Tess, who brightens and raises her hand.

Mr. Resnick acknowledges her with a nod and makes a mark on his clipboard.

"Mr. Resnick, can you use a tuba player?" she asks.

"Tuba?" he responds uncertainly. "Well, I suppose, but . . ."

"Awesome, I know just the guy. He's very talented. I'll ask him today."

Tess beams me a happy smile and I know she's thinking of Carlo.

"Well, all right," says Mr. Resnick. "Also, I will need someone to assist with costumes . . ."

Tess then shoots me an expectant, prodding look.

Costumes. Well, I've always liked the idea of using clothes to celebrate one's uniqueness, even though the communists keep me from actually having any clothes, unique or otherwise, with which to celebrate myself. And I do have a good eye for what goes, what's flattering, and what doesn't bunch.

Costumes. The word resonates in my brain and suddenly sounds so appealing, like the words *arpeggio* or *sonata* might sound musical to Tess. Or like when you're in the mood for something sweet and someone says, "Would you like a red velvet cupcake?"

It sounds important and glamorous too. I imagine myself standing on a red carpet, swathed in purple satin, posing for photographers.

"Yes, I'm the costume designer for all the movies receiving awards tonight," I would say, with a flourish of my purple-velvet-gloved hand.

—◆—

My eyes dart around and I hold my breath to see if someone higher up the social ladder has responded to Mr. Resnick.

"Come on," Tess mouths frantically. "Don't wait. Say yes."

"No one wants to assist with costumes?" Mr. Resnick asks. "Okay, well let's move on to the next helper-elf position: stage manager. Any takers?"

"Wait!" I hear my own shout. "I do!"

"Jebba?" He peers at me over the rims of his glasses. "You do what? Want to be stage manager?"

"No, I want to be costume designer."

The words roll off my tongue in such a satisfying way, like they had been hiding in those bumpy white-and-pink crevices my whole life.

"I want to make people look . . . fashionable," I blurt out.

I hear Sarah and Melanie snort behind me.

"Well," Mr. Resnick says, "this isn't the MTV Movie Awards, you realize. It's *Fiddler on the Roof*, set in a turn-of-the-century peasant village. And there's very little budget involved. You'll have to mostly make do with what's backstage."

Backstage! Another glamorous word resounding in my ears.

"Do you have a sewing machine?" he asks.

"A sewing machine?" I repeat.

"Yes, dear, that's a machine that sews." Mr. Resnick sighs.

I have no idea how to sew.

"She's a great sewer. I mean seamstress!" Tess volunteers. "She sews all the time."

"All right then." Mr. Resnick looks through his glasses at his clipboard and is about to make a mark. "If you want to . . ."

"I do! I do!" I exclaim.

"I do!" I say one more time in case he didn't hear me.

"OMG." Sarah groans. "Chillax. You're not getting married."

This remark sends her wannabes into spasms of muffled giggles.

"You'll be assisting Lisa Golowski," Mr. Resnick says. "You children all know Lisa's mother, Mrs. Golowski, don't you? She is Arthur P. Rutherford's own school monitor, but she is also a community theater actress of great range. Who could forget her moving portrayal of Annie Sullivan in my Old Vic production of *The Miracle Worker*?"

Mrs. Golowski did indeed give a pretty dramatic portrayal of Annie Sullivan, despite her somewhat distracting thick Long Island accent. Her performance was especially moving during the last gripping scene at the water pump, where Annie is willing Helen to make the connection between the word *water* and the wet stuff flowing over her hands.

"Wauda, Helen! Wauda!" Mrs. Golowski shouted with great emotion.

By that point in the play, there wasn't a dry eye in the house.

"Wauda!" someone from the baritone section says flatly, followed by a ripple of snorts and giggles.

Mr. Resnick shoots him a squinty-eyed shutdown.

"Everyone else, sign the clipboard before you leave today and check audition times for boy and girl roles. We'll be a close little group. You'll see how rewarding entertainment can be! The theater is a place for drama onstage and off. Friendships will be forged, romances will ignite."

At the word *romance*, out of the corner of my eye I see Jared jerk his head in my direction. I know what that look means. I can practically feel him weighing his options in his mind. He doesn't want to be a theater elf, but he does want to ignite a romance with me.

"I'd like to be a stage-manager elf!" He raises his arm and wiggles his fingers in the air. "I mean stage manager!"

"Oh, well, good. You seem like an organized young man, Jerry. You wear your hair very neatly," Mr. Resnick says, and marks his clipboard.

"Thank you." Jared straightens and shoots me a proud look.

Groan.

"Well, I'm looking forward to working with you talented children." Mr. Resnick smiles at Sarah. "And . . . everyone else."

"Now, altos, sopranos, mezzo-sopranos, let's start with Michael Jackson's 'Man in the Mirror.' Everyone."

Mr. Resnick sits at the piano and plays a chord.

"And do try to find your notes this time," he says.

"Hmm, hmm, hmm." He mimics our pitches.

"Hmmmm!" everyone sings loudly off-key.

Mr. Resnick discreetly takes two earplugs from his pockets and twists them into his ears. He plays another chord.

"Now move those lips with feeling."

A mournfully flat harmony explodes with feeling and then is warbling along pitifully when the door to the cafetorium creaks open.

A figure casts a long shadow on the worn linoleum floor. And then I see what looks like two great gray shadow wings emanating from the frame of a boy. I look around, but no one else seems to be alarmed. I blink hard and shake my head. I open my eyes and the strange shadows have faded. In their place a figure steps into the light.

Suddenly the music around me is melodic, perfectly in key.

"I'm starting with the man in the mirror. Hoo . . . I'm asking him to change his ways. Hoo."

The boy moves gracefully, as if in slow motion. He's wearing black jeans, scuffed black boots, and a pressed gray T-shirt, tight, showing off sinewy abs. His hair is pulled back in a short ponytail. He hooks one errant strand behind his ear.

The singing stops abruptly. Everyone seems mesmerized. A pulsing energy sparks through the web of touching elbows and close-knit bodies among the soprano and alto girls, not to mention a few of the high-tenor boys. Sarah Johnson sucks in a breath.

Mr. Resnick stops playing.

"What's wrong? You stopped moving your mouths," he says, turning in the direction of the stares.

"Ah, New Boy," he says, pulling the earplugs from his ears and turning the pages on his clipboard. "I almost forgot. The office told me to expect you. Class, this is—"

"Cowpoke Luke!" I blurt out.

5

All heads snap toward me, and Luke zeros in on me right away. Our eyes lock for a few seconds. My face blushes hot.

Jared jerks his head in my direction and then back at Cowpoke Luke.

"Ahem . . . hem." Jared clears his throat, breaking the moment.

I glance over at Tess.

"Oh. My. God," she mouths.

"Your appearance couldn't have been a more divinely inspired diversion," says Mr. Resnick. "Now, where to put you."

He surveys the bleachers.

"He can stand next to me, Mr. Resnick," Sarah says.

"Yes, good thinking, Sheila," says Mr. Resnick with a hint of sarcasm. "But we don't need a boy in the girl's section."

"Oh we totally do," Sarah murmurs under her breath.

Is Sarah after my man? I think. Wouldn't that just be like her. You'd think that since *she* ditched *me*, I'd be the one acting pissy toward her, but it's just the opposite. Everything I do or say seems to annoy her. And if she thinks I have something she doesn't, she'll totally try to interfere.

Granted, Luke might only be mine in my overactive

imagination, but in my mind's eye, I can still see the luminous golden skin of his well-defined arms when he leaned right over the guacamole to kiss me!

"Can you sing at all?" Mr. Resnick turns to Luke.

"I'm told I have a pleasant voice, sir," Luke responds quietly.

"All right, well sing a few lines here." Mr. Resnick points to the sheet music. "Don't be shy. We're all friends. It's a Michael Jackson song."

"Who?" Luke responds.

Mr. Resnick stares at him for a few minutes, as if he's trying to determine if he's being played, but Luke looks so polite and sincere that Mr. Resnick lets it go. Luke also looks so sexy in his polite sincerity that I can't help but sigh loudly, which garners a dirty look from Sarah.

"That's fine, sir," Luke says. "I can read music."

"You can read . . ." Mr. Resnick repeats incredulously. "Well, let's hear it then."

Mr. Resnick hits a chord, a look of hopeful expectation on his face.

Luke opens his mouth to sing and out comes the most beautiful tenor voice I've ever heard.

"If you wanna make the world a better place . . . Take a look at yourself and then make a change . . ."

Then he makes that change; up to a higher key, in a perfectly pitched, rich tone with a full and satisfying vibrato! Everyone is enchanted and starts swaying in perfectly coordinated rhythm.

"I'm starting with the man in the mirror!" Luke sings.

"Hoo!" everyone shouts in on-key three-part harmony.

"I'm asking him to change his ways . . ."

Mr. Resnick stops abruptly.

Everyone startles and wobbles into one another again.

He whips the glasses off his face, turns to Luke, and grabs his clipboard.

"Luke, is it?" he says.

"Yes, sir," Luke says, without even a hint of conceit.

"Well that was very good, Luke. Very good indeed."

"Scrumptious," Sarah whispers, all growly.

She *is* after my fantasy crush! By publicly making that remark, Sarah Johnson was marking her territory. Just like Beaver, the goldendoodle up the block, does when he pees on my mom's petunias, which she buys from the Bulk Emporium's flower nursery!

And even though Sarah already has Dean Gold wrapped around her finger and will probably get the lead in *Fiddler on the Roof* and everything else a girl could want, it isn't enough. Treating me meanly isn't enough. Nothing is ever enough for a girl like her.

Tess looks over at me and rolls her eyes.

Just then the bell rings. There's a thunderous stampeding of feet as everyone scurries off the bleachers, claims their backpacks, and moves, chatting, toward the door. Sarah slides by Luke, brushing against him in the process.

"S'cuse me," she says coyly.

I idle nearby and fiddle with my backpack, making sure I'm within earshot.

"Well, Luke," Mr. Resnick says. "I hope that you'll consider auditioning for our semiprofessional teenage production of *Fiddler on the Roof.*"

"I'll have to check my schedule, sir," Luke says politely. "If I make a commitment, I want to be sure I can honor it."

"Wait . . . what?" Mr. Resnick startles, and then a big smile spreads across his face. "Did you say honor your commitment?"

"Sometimes I . . . my family and I . . . move without much notice. My, um, dad's in upper management. I don't like to make promises I can't keep."

"Remarkable." Mr. Resnick shakes his head in disbelief. "You're not from around here, are you?"

"No sir," Luke answers, collecting his backpack. He notices me listening and grins. I quickly become very interested in my chemistry textbook, *Helium and You.*

"Not even close," he says, more to himself than anyone else.

Then, as he's heading toward the door, he gently jostles me and knocks my book to the floor. We both lean down to retrieve it but he gets to it first and hands it to me. Our fingertips touch. A jolt of warmth and light courses through me. I wonder if this could be love.

I don't notice that the hideous pendant has slipped out from the top of my shirt and bounced into full view.

Luke sucks in a rigid breath. He leans down close to it.

He's crouched awkwardly like that for what seems like forever, his eyes blazing into my chest.

On their way out the door, Tess and my other friends Sheldon, Bea, and Kayla notice Luke and me in our awkward chest-gazing moment. From the corner of my eye, I see a quick chain of surprised raised eyebrows and quizzical glances. I even hear them giggling. Tess pushes them forward, winks, and mouths, "Later."

"Keep it safe," Luke whispers hoarsely.

"Uh . . . excuse me?" I say.

"The pendant. Don't take it off," he insists.

Sarah sashays past us and rolls her eyes.

"Seriously?" she snarks. "I wouldn't even put it on."

She smirks at Luke, trying to share a moment at my expense. I feel my cheeks heat up and flush a deep crimson of shame. *How could I ever have been friends with that girl?* I wonder. Luke glances up at her and gives her a blank look like she's from Mars. Her expression tightens. She jerks her head away and swings her hips out the door.

Satisfaction.

"What is with you and this necklace?" I say, averting my eyes and nervously fingering the hideous thing. And then I look straight into his dazzling baby hazels.

"Have we ever met before or something . . . like in a past life?" I chuckle stupidly.

"Or something." Luke looks like he's suppressing a laugh.

"Whaddaya mean?" I say, feeling almost hypnotized by those eyes.

The second bell rings. Luke just shakes his head dismissively.

"Let's put it this way"—he jerks his backpack onto his shoulder, breaking our eye contact—"try to stay off the roof."

Then he turns and slips out the cafetorium door.

6

Later that day, in the cafetorium, Tess and I sit at our usual table with our little clique of friends from Chorus. Together, we're perhaps a bit odd, but each one of us has the potential to do something cooler than the think-they're-all-that Oceanville drones.

There's Kayla, who's shy and mousy and has a love for retro punk music, and Bea, who's larger-than-life, peppy, and, even though not cool enough for popularity, ever hopeful. And then there's Sheldon, a tenor of near-transparent thinness and occasional apoplectic pimple breakouts, who dreams of being a star on a Disney Channel sitcom and loves all things supernatural.

I'm eating my usual sandwich: peanut butter and jelly, both of which Mom bought in bulk so that us Blooms would have enough food not only for the rest of our lives, but also in death, to munch on while crossing the river Styx.

And I can't help thinking about the last thing Luke said to me:

"Try and stay off the roof."

What did he mean? How could he know that I had dreamed of him saving me from David Lipski's roof?

Mid—sticky bite, my cell phone rings.

He rocks in the tree tops all day long, hoppin' and a-boppin' . . .

I flip open my iPhone and, think of the devil, I hear David Lipski's (every babysitter's nightmare) voice on the other end. A teacher drones on in the background.

"Herro," I say, prying my tongue from the roof of my mouth.

"Hey, it's me, David Lipski," he whispers.

"I know, David." I sigh. "Whaddaya want? I'm eating lunch with my friends."

"Oh you mean the geek brigade and the skinny guy rocking the uni brow?"

"No, I mean my *friends*. Of which you are not one," I snap.

"Bernice and Lenny need you to kid-sit me," David says.

"I'm hanging up now," I retort.

"What's the problem?" he says.

"Uh, the problem? Well, shall we talk about the last time I babysat? When you snuck out of the house while I was watching TV and Bernice and Lenny came home to find you racing the lawn tractor across the front lawn in the dark. And how in all the screaming, you lost control and mowed down and dismembered half of Bernice's garden gnome collection from around the world?"

David chuckles. "Yeah, that was epic. Good times."

"Or dare I even mention the incident with the tree frog and Bernice's underwear drawer," I continue. "Or the time you climbed to the top of that telephone pole and refused to come down . . ."

"All right, all right, I get it. Yeesh," he says. "You're so trapped in the past."

"I clearly can't control you. I don't even know why your parents still let me babysit you," I say.

"Are you kidding? They love you!"

"Gotta go, David," I say.

"Wait," he says. "That's why I'm calling. I want to talk to you about—"

I hang up the phone and shove it into my sweater pocket.

"So I saw Carlo in band today and asked him if he wanted to play the tuba for *Fiddler*," Tess says.

"How did that go?" I ask.

"I'm not sure." She frowns. "He shook his head like no a lot of times and then said what sounded like 'Nofider.'"

"He said what? Nofider?" I repeat.

Tess shrugs.

"Nofider, nofider, nofider," I murmur to myself a few times. "Oh, maybe he meant 'No . . . fider.'"

"That helps." Tess rolls her eyes.

"No, I mean like as in 'No fiddler.' Like he heard you say the word *fiddle* and was saying 'I'm not a fiddler,' as in 'I'm a tuba player.'"

"Hmm . . . maybe," Tess ponders. "Anyway, I told his ESL teacher. Hopefully Carlo will just show up at rehearsals . . . So, have you seen *your* guy lately?" Tess asks, picking at her usual alfalfa-tofu-egg-salad sandwich made by her cool mom, who shops at the fancy market that doesn't have the word *bulk* in its name.

"You mean the hot new guy?" Kayla leans in with quiet excitement.

"He's so hooooot!" Bea sings loudly.

"Shhh," we all shush her.

"Very," Sheldon adds.

"They kissed!" Tess announces, smiling broadly.

"You did?!" Kayla and Bea turn to me in unison.

"Shhh!"

"Where?!" Sheldon asks. "On the lips?"

"In Cowboy Clems." Tess nods.

"Really?" Sheldon says, wide-eyed. "With all the twangy music and sizzling fajitas?" He fans himself. "That's hot! Spicy food make-out is one of my biggest fantasies."

He leans in.

"Like, I'm at a steamy Mexican resort drinking some frothy white drink in a long-stemmed glass and in walks Robert Pattinson and he's looking all Twilight and sparkly and everything . . ." Sheldon sighs and takes a few minutes to stare happily into space.

"And speaking of *Twilight*"—he shakes himself from his reverie—"did you hear about that unprecedented space-time continuum dimensional anomaly equinox that occurred last night?"

"English, Sheldon," Tess says.

He shoots her a look, flops his backpack onto the table and unzips it, muttering as he roots around and starts pulling out an array of New Age stuff.

"Ah, here it is!"

He pulls out a New Age magazine, opens it up, and slaps his hand down on a page.

"There!"

"'Cure Genital Warts with Dr. Krishna's Healing Incense'?" Kayla reads timidly.

"Sorry. Wrong page."

Sheldon opens to another page.

"Here!" He slaps his hand down again.

It's a full-page illustration with an over-the-top picture of a twilight sky opening up and fierce-looking angels and demons blazing through. Awestruck, timid, cowering humans gaze up from the ground.

The bolded title reads: "The Door Is Open: Are You Ready?"

"Hmm." Bea nods supportively, but then presumably runs out of anything else to say.

"Are those devils?" Kayla asks, pointing to the sinister beings.

"More like impure entities," Sheldon says.

"Ah." Tess chews her lip, trying to sound sincere. "Hmm . . . that's interesting . . ."

Tess then gently rolls her eyes in my direction. Kayla and Bea wait a respectful five seconds before turning away and changing the subject to chat among themselves.

I swallow hard. Why does one of the angels look sort of like Luke and why does one of the "impure entities" look so much like the scary boy I caught a glimpse of at Cowboy Clems?

"So, like, what does this mean, Sheldon?" I ask.

"Humph. Well at least one of my friends takes an interest in my hobby," he says loudly in the direction of the others, who are too engaged in their own conversation at this point to even hear him.

"You see, typically, twice a year there's an equinox, which is basically a changing of the seasons, right?"

"I've heard," I say.

"And many nature-based religions, Wiccans, spiritually enlightened people like myself, etc., celebrate those changes, just like people did at Stonehenge thousands of years ago. But"—he leans in, his eyes gleaming—"once every hundred years or so the planets align in just a certain way and there's a different kind of equinox. One that provides spiritual entities, both pure and impure, a means to travel through our dimension . . . as if a door opens between our world and theirs. It's just like Halloween without the kids, costumes, or candy."

We both ponder this for a moment.

"Well maybe not exactly like Halloween," Sheldon says.

Sheldon runs his finger down the pages of the article as if he's searching for a particular line.

"Ah, here. Listen to this. It's pretty cool." He continues, "Apparently, this door between 'us and them'"—he makes quotation marks in the air with his fingers—"stays open for two months. So it started on October first . . ."

That was the night I dreamed about Luke saving me from falling off David's roof.

"And this year, yada, yada, this particular portal closes

52

on the first weekend of the new moon year, yada, yada . . .
Oh, December third."

"December third," he ponders, ignoring me. "Why does that date sound familiar?"

"Isn't it the opening night of *Fiddler*?" I say.

"Yeah, you're right." He nods.

"What do all these entities come here for?" I ask.

"Hmm . . . Well I guess because they can, but let's see . . ." He skims through more of the article.

"It says here that, for the creepazoid entities, their whole goal is to stay on earth," Sheldon reads, "thereby wreaking chaos and bringing strife and dissension into our world. And the good-guy entities are . . . yada . . . basically chasing the bad guys, trying to coax them back through the portal, where they can be contained."

"So what can you do if, hypothetically," I say, "one or maybe two of these entities . . . like, make contact with you or something?"

"Don't worry, that won't happen." Sheldon waves his hand dismissively. "You'd have to be highly attuned to even sense a cosmic change, but there's a war going on between these entities all the time for sure. Good and bad. Yin and yang. It's about balance. I mean, I guess these beings *could* make contact if they wanted to, but they'd have to have a good reason, I suppose. Anyway, those kinds of cool things only seem to happen to crazy celebrities, recovering alcoholics, losers on reality shows, those kinds of people . . ."

I breathe a sigh of relief. I was being crazy. This thing with Luke. And my dream, and him knowing my dream and those weird *Twilight* mind-reading moments: coincidence. Yeah, that's it. Has to be.

"Oh but wait a minute," Sheldon says while continuing to skim the article. "This is a really cool bit here. It says that certain people are ordained through their ancestry and can act as gatekeepers for this world, preventing the impure entities from gaining admittance forever. Sometimes these chosen ones have a charm or amulet. Ooh, do you think maybe my ancestors passed down some supernatural gatekeeper powers to me?"

"Are there supernatural powers in your family?" I ask.

"No," Sheldon says. "But it certainly would explain a lot of my weird relatives."

Suddenly Tess sucks in a breath, grabs my arm, and gestures toward the large picture window that overlooks the courtyard.

"Here he comes!"

We all jerk our heads toward him.

"Don't look," I whisper, and then we all dive into our lunches, pretending to be distracted, but our eyes drift back to Luke. He seems as if he's floating in slow motion, past the window and around the corner into the cafetorium. His eyes are fixed ahead, his expression is unreadable. Sarah Johnson glides in a few feet behind him, eyeing him hungrily. Dean and some other hot guys bring up the rear of the group.

Luke glances at me as he passes by our table.

"Hi." He smiles.

"Herro, Ruke," I say.

Curse that peanut butter!

Then he hesitates and looks as if he's going to stop, but instead he frowns ever so slightly and makes his way toward the salad bar.

"Invite him to sit here! Invite him to sit here!" Tess pulls at my sleeve excitedly. "He looks like he wants to!"

"He looks like he wants salad," I say, watching him investigate all the little trays on the salad bar and pile his plate with almost everything.

"Ooh and you better hurry," she continues. "Sarah Johnson is closing in."

"Hi, Sarahh! Hi, Deaann! Hi, Melaniee!" Bea sings loudly. She waves in their direction.

They mostly look through her, except for Sarah, who makes an "ugh" face and sways her hips toward Luke until she's intercepted by Dean.

"She's after your man. Look at her walk, that hussy. I wonder how she does that with her hips while carrying a lunch tray," Sheldon says thoughtfully.

"He's not my man, Sheldon," I say.

"If he kissed you, he's your man," he answers. "Although, no offense, and I say this with nothin' but love for ya, but isn't he a little out of your league?"

"Seriously," says Kayla.

"Sheldon!" Tess scolds.

"Shhh!" we snap in unison.

"Get up, Jenna!" Tess urges. "Put down that Yodel and make believe you like salad. Quick, before the bell rings."

It is a moment to grab, maybe the only one I'll ever get. I take a deep breath and approach the salad bar.

Luke looks around as if he doesn't know where to sit and then just starts scarfing up the salad from his plate.

"Hi. It's Cowpoke Luke, right?" I say.

"Just Luke," he says, killin' me with those baby hazels. My eyes are glued to his strong jaw as he chews.

"I just love salad, don't you?" I ask stupidly, grabbing a plate and piling it up. "It's so crunchy. And roughage is good for your intestines."

I glance over at Tess, who is urgently shaking her head no.

I accidentally knock an apple onto the floor.

Luke tries to intercept it with his foot, but then unexpectedly kicks it, sending it rolling until it stops under the feet of some poor freshman with a full tray.

"Whooaa!" The kid does a little whoopsy dance. His tray gets tossed into the kid next to him.

Then:

He rocks in the tree tops all day long . . .

I glance back at my friends, who urge me on.

Hoppin' and a-boppin' and singing his song . . .

"Um . . . shouldn't you answer your phone?" Luke says.

I pull out the phone.

"Hi, it's me, David Lipski," says the voice on the other end.

The first bell rings, signaling that lunch is over. Luke pulls his class schedule from his bag and examines it as the kids around us start packing up.

"I'll just be a minute." I hold up my finger. "It's the kid I babysit."

Luke nods and turns his attention back to his salad.

"Hey!" David yells from the phone. "Hello!"

"What's going on?" I sing.

"It's about the kid-sitting gig," he says.

I cover the mouthpiece.

"He's so cute," I say to Luke, making a crinkly face. "Only nine years old. Just like a little brother."

Then I move a few feet away and turn around and whisper into the phone.

"Listen closely, evil-spawn child, I don't want to kid-sit you anymore. And by the way, do you know you have the worst timing ever? And where are you anyway?"

"Where do you think I am?" David replies calmly. "It's 11:30 on Tuesday. I'm in school. Duh. Math to be exact . . . Huh? I'll be right with you, Mrs. Moore. Try fourth to the tenth power."

"Are you allowed to talk on your cell phone during Math?" I ask.

"No way, but Mrs. Moore loves me. I'm her star pupil. I got her eating out of my—"

I hear a woman's voice screeching in the background and then footsteps rushing toward the phone.

"Ooh, gotta go!" he says.

The phone goes dead. I close it, shove it back into my pocket, and turn. Luke takes a step closer to me.

I suck in a breath. I feel as if I'm falling into a bed of sweet, musty, just-raked leaves.

"How's David?" Luke asks.

"He's—" I start. "Wait a second, how did you know his name?"

"Jenna." Luke ignores my question. "You probably already know this, but the guy we both saw outside the glass doors at Cowboy Clems . . . You need to watch out for him."

"Wait. What? What do you mean? I didn't think . . . I mean, I wasn't sure he was real. I thought maybe it was a reflection on the glass or my mind was playing tricks . . ."

"But I saw him too," Luke says gently.

"Yeah, I haven't gotten around to figuring that part out yet," I say.

Luke hesitates. His eyes dart furtively around. Then he moves closer still and lowers his voice.

"He's real all right. I can't explain now. I'm not even sure I *should* explain, and this isn't really the place anyway. I just want you to be aware. In case you see him again. His name is—"

"Jared Needleman!" Jared yells, appearing at that moment, up in both our faces, his complexion all pink. Reflexively, Luke and I step away from each other. Jared holds out his hand toward Luke for a shake.

"Hey," Luke says. He reaches out and shakes Jared's hand.

"I'm Jenna's—" Jared starts to say.

I shoot him a threatening look.

"Em . . . neighbor." He recovers. "That's right. Up the block and to the left. She's in the red house, I'm in the yellow house. The Blooms and the Needlemans have been neighbors ever since me and Jenna were in diapers."

Diapers!

"Really?" Luke looks amused.

"Nothing like a neighbor." Jared continues to ramble. "No one knows you better than family and neighbors, that's what I always say. Yup. Lived in Oceanville all my life. All these kids"—he opens his arms wide—"we're like one big neighborhood."

"You're lucky," Luke says thoughtfully.

"Where did you say you come from again?" Jared asks, all squinty-eyed suspicion.

The second bell rings and by now almost all the kids have cleared out.

"I didn't," Luke says, throwing his backpack over his shoulder. Then he heads out the cafetorium door and disappears.

7

That night, I once again dream of Luke.

I'm sitting under a canopy of a thousand beautifully colored pin lights and paper lanterns, like the kind at Manchu Gardens, looking swanky in a southwest-inspired Fiddler on the Roof *ensemble: a peasant blouse and skirt embellished with rhinestones, plus expensive leather boots. Cowpoke Luke, dressed in something crisp and white, stands before me, tapping his waiter pencil on his waiter pad.*

Tap, tap, tap.

"Would you like today's special?" he asks. His gorgeous baby hazels are warm, and his eyes crinkle up at the corners when he smiles.

Tap, tap, tap.

"What is it?" I ask.

"Can't you guess?"

"No," I respond densely.

He leans toward me.

"Angel. Food. Cake."

"That sounds yummy," I croak.

Then:

Suddenly he begins gliding away from me.

"Jenna . . ." He grabs for my hands. "Jenna!"

"Luke!" I yell.

I race toward him, but he's moving away too fast.

"No, on second thought, you have to stay back! Stay safe! And try the pecan piiiieeee!" he wails as he diminishes in the darkness.

Tap, tap, tap, tap, tap, tap.

A pebble flies at my window at fifty miles an hour. *Tap.* And then another. *Tap.* And then another. *Tap.*

I bolt up in bed.

Crack!

I rush to the window, open it, and peer down. Down in the center of the wilting Bulk flower garden stands David Lipski, a handful of pebbles cupped in his hand.

A pebble hits me square in the forehead.

"Ow!"

"Ooh, sorry!" David drawls insincerely.

"What is it, David? What are you doing here?" I rub my head, hoping I'm not going to be left with a big red welt.

"Come down and kid-sit me," David says. "It's Saturday. My parents are going out and they want you to take me to the park."

"To the park? You?"

I imagine David dangling dangerously from the top of the jungle gym, or running amok through the miles of open spaces. In the park, there's a million ways for a speedy, agile, horrible child to disappear in a blink.

I glance at the clock. Nine in the morning. I don't have time for David and his games. According to Mr. Resnick, Lisa Golowski is going to be my design supervisor! She is a fashion and design major in college and the daughter of Mrs. Golowski, school monitor/community theater actress. She is going to e-mail me today. That, plus both my waking and sleeping mind are so filled with luscious thoughts of Luke that I want to spend the day with Tess, gossiping about everything he's ever said to me, every inflection, eyebrow wiggle, look, and gesture, analyzing all their imagined potentially romantic implications. The last thing I want to do is spend the morning jerking around the park with David Lipski.

"I don't think your parents really trust me to kid-sit you anymore, David," I say.

"Nah. Not true," he says. "Bernice loves you. She wants you to kid-sit."

"What's the matter? No one else will do it?" I ask.

"Jenna, I'm wounded that you would say something like that," David says, placing his hand over his heart. ". . . Okay, so no one else will do it. Besides, my parents are totally over the lawn-mower-decapitation-of-the-gnomes fiasco. They're even starting a new garden gnome collection. Gnomes with hobbies. They've already ordered golfers, skiers, a racquetball player. There's even a mah-jongg gnome. That one's more expensive because it comes with its own tiles."

"I don't know . . ." I stall.

"And let's not forget the big bar mitzvah in New Jersey coming up. They'll be gone for at least ten hours. You'll really make out. You're still at the top of the list of kid-sitters," he sings.

"How long is the list?" I ask.

". . . Just you. But, hey, they could decide to take me instead."

"Yeah, right." I snort.

From the window, I spy Bernice in the front seat of her car, cell phone tucked under her chin, primping in the rearview mirror.

She spies me back, sticks her head out the window, and smiles before resuming her conversation.

"See?" David says. "Loves you," he mouths. "Come on. Hurry up. Get dressed!"

"Sorry, David. I'm busy today," I say.

"Oh just hurry up and get dressed," he says, exasperated. "How long could it take to choose between two T-shirts. Either pick the one that says *I'm a cutie*, or the one that says *I'm with stupid*, with the arrow that points up."

I slam the window shut.

Curse that miserable David! But then again, there is that little issue of the babysitting money, and as much as I hate to admit it, the demon child is right. I could certainly use a fashionable-shopping infusion into my unfashionable Bulk wardrobe.

I pick up a shirt slung over my desk chair. I'm sure that Luke doesn't want to hang around a girl wearing a graphic tee that says *Kiss Me, I'm from Oceanville*. What's more, I notice a new shopping bag from the Bulk Emporium that Mom must have slipped into my room while I was asleep. Curiosity overtakes me. I peer into the bag and see, much to my exasperation, three pairs of faux blue jeans, decorated with a revolting swirly pattern of stippled rhinestones. And that's not all. There are also three red button-down polyester shirts, all with *Too juicy for words* embroidered on the pocket. And the word *juicy* is dripping.

Decision made.

I open the window and thrust my head back out.

"All right, David," I yell. "I'm coming. But no trouble today." Just as the words leave my lips, a flock of black crows sweeps over my roof, cawing loudly, and for an infinitesimal second, I feel frightened, as if a dark shadow has passed over my heart.

8

Within minutes, I'm in the backseat of the Lipskis' car, drowning in a crinkly sea of David Lipski's superhero comic books.

Bernice, sharply dressed in a very cute white tennis outfit with matching visor and small gold jewelry, is driving like a maniac, swerving through yellow lights.

It's also not making me feel great that she is illegally talking on her cell phone, plus intermittently glancing into the rearview mirror to give David "Mom smiles."

"I just love the park, Mom!" David exclaims. "There's so much to do."

"That's nice, honey," Bernice answers. Then she returns to talking animatedly into her cell phone.

"Hey," David says to me, noticing colored pages poking out from under my butt. He nudges me over and gingerly wrestles them from under me. "You're sitting on my stuff."

"Well, your *stuff* is everywhere," I say. "Why don't you organize these things or something, like put all the Spider-Man and Green Hornet ones with the . . . I don't know. Who's this? Supernatural animes—"

David sighs in deep exasperation. "Seriously? You're so lame." He grabs a Spider-Man away from me. "You don't put vintage with those comics. And gimme that! That's my favorite."

"Yeah, why is that?" I ask, gingerly shoving the pile in his direction.

"Supernatural forces are threatening to wipe out humankind. Duh! This is the one where evil almost wins against the good guys. *Almost!*"

He opens the comic, pushes it close to my face, and taps his finger on the page.

"You see, the good guy almost gets his soul sucked out by this demon here, who looks just like a regular guy, and he and his brother have to call on help from their friend, who's really an angel, who also looks just like a regular guy—"

Bernice hits a bump, sending us bouncing.

"Uh-huh," I say disinterestedly. "And then what happens? You have to buy the rest of the series to ensure that humankind is safe?"

"It's very compelling." He sulks, lovingly flattening out the cover and placing it into the already-bulging mesh bag hanging off the back of the driver's seat.

Bernice swerves around the corner toward Oceanville State Park.

"Listen, David," I hiss at him softly. "I'm going with you to the park, but we're not running all over the place. Just the playground. Maybe an ice cream and then home. I'm busy today."

"Yeah right," David remarks sarcastically. "I want to go

ice skating," he insists. "They opened the indoor-outdoor dome last week."

He pulls a bag with skates in it from under his seat.

"Ice skating?"

Well, I think. It could be worse. At least in the rink, he'll be trapped in one big circle.

"Okay," I say, "but I don't skate, so I'll just sit on the bench and watch."

David shrugs, and I gaze out the window as images of Luke slide happily into my thoughts.

"Hey, look," David shouts. "There's a gross bug on your shoulder!"

"What!" I squeal, and jump to brush it off.

David snaps my picture, aiming the flash into my eyes.

"Ooh, must have been mistaken," David says. "But here, I got a nice picture of you making a really stupid face. I'll tag it *Bug woman threatens Oceanville*."

I grab for his camera, which he yanks away.

"What the—you little—!"

Bernice glances at us in the rearview mirror.

"Cutie pie . . ." I smile through gritted teeth until she looks away.

Finally, after what seems like forty yellow lights, three narrowly missed car accidents, and twenty minutes of my life that I'll never get back, Bernice pulls up to the park and stops just barely long enough for us to tumble out.

"See you later, kids." She waves. "Have a good time! When you're done, call me!"

"Bye! We will . . . Bite me!" David smiles and waves to the back end of the car as it speeds away.

"Okay, David. Skating rink. Let's g—" but before I can even finish the word *go*, David zooms past me at lightning speed, on his way to God knows where, leaving only a *whoosh* in my ears.

David zigzags through the bushes, past the tetherball court, and straight through the softball field. He gingerly hops and prances his way through the bark park, dog-poop minefield.

I pant and trot behind him to try to keep up. Moist beads of sweat gather in the fleshy crevices of my waist; under my jacket my cheap T-shirt creeps up my back, and my faux-denim jeans give me a wicked wedgie, which I try discreetly to dislodge.

"David! David, slow down!" I cry. "Stand still so I can kill you!"

He stops at the rink, pulls off his shoes, and slips into his skates, while I try to catch my breath.

The music blares from the skating-rink loudspeakers.

'Cause this is thrilla . . . Thrilla nights!

David takes a running slide out onto the ice, gracefully breaking into a series of effortless glides, pirouettes, jumps, and turns. A few of the other skaters step back and, clearly enchanted with him, point and smile.

That's when I notice that among the two dozen or so happy swirling skaters is a little cluster of cool: namely, Dean and a few of his friends—Sarah, Melanie, Amanda, and Emma, plus some other wannabes. They're looking all long-legged in cashmere leggings, slim, fashionable jackets, and cheery in multicolored scarves. They huddle and giggle. Their noses are cute and red. Their flippy hair extends out in a sexy tumble beneath their tilted-just-right stylish hats.

Determined to blend in, I smooth my hair and self-consciously try to flatten my puffy patchwork jacket, which I secretly suspect my mother got as a prize for sending in one hundred cereal-box tops to Kellogg's.

It's no use. Who am I trying to kid?

"Come on, Jenna. You can rent skates over there!" David shouts, pointing to the skate-rental booth.

"David, I told you I can't skate," I say.

And suddenly, there's Luke, gliding across the ice, a beautiful vision in worn black skates, dark-wash jeans, and a brown leather jacket that I am positive isn't faux.

He cuts sharp figure eights with a *swoosh*. Every so often he raises his hand over his head as if he's stretching or winning or something and smiles.

And of course, I'm not the only one who's got my eye on him. Sarah's gaze is so red-hot I can almost feel the ice melting around him.

Then, suddenly, there's David, skating around Luke, snapping pictures of him.

Luke seems mildly surprised at first. He smiles humbly down at him once or twice and continues his circles. But then, with a wild twinkle in his eye, he rushes across the ice and does a series of fancy, impressive ice skating moves: backward, forward, jumps, and spins, like those double- and triple-lutz thingies they do in the Olympics, all in perfect time, to the beat of Michael Jackson's "Thriller."

Well, you can imagine the gasps and stares!

David is so mesmerized and busy snapping pictures that he loses his footing and falls back hard on the ice. Slowly, he gets up with a pained expression on his face and limp-skates all the way back to me, occasionally reaching down and touching his left ankle.

"Ow, yow, yow. I think I hurt my ankle. I . . . I don't think I can make it back to the grass. Can you come and get me?" he mews, hobbling in my direction, reaching out pathetically for my hand, as Luke continues to wow everyone with his mini–Ice Capades show.

Curse that David Lipski!

"I told you I can't skate!" I hiss back at him.

"Please . . ." he pleads, looking to be on the verge of tears.

"Oh for God's sake, David. You're almost here. Can't you take a few more glides?"

"No," he whines.

"Just sit on your tush and slide," I say.

"On my tush?" He looks appalled.

I sigh with great exasperation and tentatively step out onto the ice, which is remarkably slippery, even for ice, and start my hunched, little-old-lady shuffle toward him. Thankfully, everyone's attention is on Luke and not me.

"Fine. Grab my hand, David," I say, extending my arm. "I'll save . . . *Whoa!*"

David grabs my hand, loses his balance, and, before I can pull him in, yanks me out.

Just then Luke whooshes to a dramatic denouement, and everyone claps. That is, until everyone's heads snap in my direction as I'm pulled across the ice like some big, weird, patchwork bird, flailing and flapping my free arm, my back arched, my mouth open in a big, wide *O*, my eyes bugging out in what I can only imagine is a very unattractive manner.

That's when I feel David's hand trying to break free of the death grip I have on him.

"David! What are you doing?" I shriek.

"We're gonna crash!" he shouts.

"What?!"

"You're pulling me down! Just sit!"

And at that moment, he jerks free, sending me careening a hundred miles an hour toward the other side of the rink, where an open gate leads to the outside.

"Noooo!" I wail.

Helplessly I grab the air, desperately trying to latch on to any stable object in my path, when in my flailing, I snag . . .

Onto. Dean's. Long. Black. Sumptuous. Scarf!

"Guymph!" Dean barks as I pull his neck forward, practically knocking him off his feet. He snatches his scarf away from me, leaving me clawing at the air.

Still out of control, I spin toward Sarah Johnson and her fiery glare. Gracefully, she steps from my path before I can reach for the safety of her presumably hand-knit and expensive teal-sprinkled-with-flecks-of-sea-blue scarf/ pashmina that totally makes her eyes pop.

"Daviiiidddd!" I scream, praying I'll clear the rink's edge and land softly on the open brush beyond.

"I'm gonna crash!" I shriek. I'm pulling my arms to my chest, squeezing my eyes shut, and bracing for impact, when my head is filled with the smell of sweet pine. But it isn't coming from the woods beyond. It's surrounding me; my clothes and skin tingle with the scent of it. I open my eyes and it feels as if everything is slowing down, my speed, the people in the rink, even time itself. It's a blur of slowness and I feel peaceful.

Instinctively, I turn my head toward Luke. He's breathing deeply, chest rising and falling hard. He stands stone still and stares at me, his expression solemn and concentrated. And what happens next is the strangest, most supernatural thing of all: a luminous yellow-white vapor floats down from the air somewhere above him. The vapor turns to particles and the particles move toward him as if magnetized, first in gentle waves, then building in force and strength. It's as if they're absorbing into his very skin. Luke closes his eyes and lifts his chin upward. His arms hang straight at his sides, but he turns his palms outward. His whole body shimmers with the most startling crisp white light I've ever seen.

I look around. Activities in the rink continue as if nothing unusual is happening. No one notices. Except for me. And then I spot David Lipski, sitting on the ice, leaning back on his hands, staring at Luke, an expression of pure astonishment on his face.

"Oh!" He inhales, making a big round *O* with his mouth. Luke opens his eyes and turns to me.

Time resumes around me. But now I am standing perfectly still and upright. I look down. My feet are balanced easily on the ice.

I look up again at Luke, but he is gone.

9

"What a dork!"

I hear Sarah Johnson's voice ringing out and her wannabes giggling as I clomp the last few steps off the ice and slip into the woods beyond. There, a few feet away, bathed in dappled light, stands David, leaning on a nearby tree, staring into the screen of his digital camera and shaking with excitement. As I approach him, I'm shaking, too—with something . . . Excitement? Disbelief? Fear that I've gone mental? I can't quite name it yet. David's expression dissolves into disappointment.

"Crap!" he exclaims.

David is the last thing I need right now, as I try to figure out what is happening around the hot new boy / not quite a boy in town named Luke.

"What!" I snap, hands on hips, glaring at him.

"I thought I got some videos of that kid when he was skating, and then I thought I got a shot of him when he morphed into whatever the hell he morphed into, but all I got was this picture of you making a dumb-ass of yourself. See?"

He holds up the camera for me to see. Sure enough, there's a gallery of pictures of me, like a little stop-motion movie, flying across the ice in a very unflattering manner, a big *yow* expression on my twisted face.

"I thought for sure I'd get something," David says, "like maybe some kind of supernatural ectoplasm, but look, all these shots just look like balls of overexposed light . . ."

"So you're not a great photographer, so what?" I say.

"Hey, watch who you're insulting," David says. "I can still tag you on Facebook. I can call it *Klutz Capades*. And it's a good thing that I have at least three hundred friends or it totally wouldn't be worth it."

"Leave me alone, David," I say, scanning the ground for a twig. I reach into my pocket for the rubber band I shoved in there this morning, pull my hair into a tight ponytail, lean down, and start vigorously picking at the ice that's collected in the crevices of my cheap Bulk sneakers.

"But seriously, what just happened back there? Who was that guy? Or maybe 'guy'"—he makes quotation marks in the air—"is too strong a word. I see guys all the time. And that was no ordinary guy."

I sigh deeply, stand, and march past him.

"I dunno, David. I don't wanna talk about it. Just skate back across the ice to the bench and get your shoes. You've got one hour on the playground and then I'm calling Bernice to pick us up. Got it?"

David just trots after me. I stop, and he stares up at me in disbelief.

"You're kidding, right? I've been reading comic books my whole life and nothing supernatural ever happened to me. And finally something does, and you're all like, 'Let's go to the playground'?! Really?! Don't you even want to know who that guy is?!"

"I know who he is," I say flatly.

"You do?" David's eyes widen.

"He's a busboy at Cowboy Clems and now he's enrolled in my school. He's new in town—"

David scoffs.

"Yeah, I'll bet. That's what they all say. All those supernatural-being-demon-thingies. Right before they eat your face off. That's the oldest line in the book . . . unless he's a superhero, in which case that makes him awesomely fantastic! And let's face it . . . Anyone who can de-klutzify you must have some kind of power. And he also does that whole thick-white-vapor-from-the-sky-glowing thing. If he is a superhero, then maybe I can call him Vapor Man."

"Your shoes . . ." I repeat, taking him by the shoulders and pointing him toward the rink.

David actually complies for once in his life: retreats across the rink and quickly retrieves his stuff. Once back in the woods, he pulls off his skates, shoves them into his skate bag, and shimmies his feet into his sneakers.

We start down the wooded path. The fallen leaves crunch beneath us, while the leaves that still optimistically cling to the branches block out the weak morning sun, creating a latticework of shadows.

It is, of course, completely undeniable that there *is* something very crazy, very—dare I say it—*supernatural* going on, but I just can't wrap my mind around it and really admit it to myself. First I'm sharing hallucinations with Luke, whatever he is. Now I'm sharing all these stories with David, horrible devil child.

"I think you're getting carried away, David. It was probably all just a trick of the light. Luke is just a guy, okay?" I say.

"Are you kidding?" He looks incredulous. "A trick of the light, my butt. All that glowing? Right in the middle of the skating rink? Everything going in slow-mo, and no one else noticing except us. Tell me you didn't see it."

"I didn't see it."

I shove my hands in my pockets and start walking away from him.

David grabs my jacket and spins me around to face him.

"You did see it!"

"I didn't," I try again.

"You're lying. Your eyes are darting around."

I bend to look directly into his eyes.

"I didn't see it."

"Aha," he exclaims. "You did see it, because your lips are all stiff and thin. More than usual."

Self-consciously, I suck my lips into my mouth.

"The lying." He nods knowingly. "It's always in the lips. Anyway, why are you so resistant to the idea of something supernatural? Life is full of mysteries. Take you, for example. It's a wonder that you're surviving middle school."

In my heart I know he's right about Luke, but how can it be? Once I admit that it's all true, that makes me . . . crazy.

"Okay, I'll fill you in," I say reluctantly, and then I do.

"So, lemme get this straight. First you dream about this guy, whose name is Luke, very biblical, very 'angelic,' by the way," David says, again making quotation marks in the air with his fingers. "Although I'll have you know that angels are not all fuzzy-feathered messengers of God. Sometimes they can be cranky, scary dudes."

"I'll keep that in mind," I say flatly.

"And then, at Cowboy Clems," he continues, "you and Luke both saw this other freakazoid dude staring at you through the glass doors and he lunged at you and then he disappeared . . . And then Luke shows up at school as a 'student' to sing Michael Jackson? And he has a really good voice?"

"So?"

"Well . . . nothing . . . but maybe that's his supernatural superhero talent. Maybe I'll call him Singing Michael Man," David says. "Or S.M.M. for short. Or when I need him, I'll just hum it. Smm," he hums ominously.

"You do that," I say, picking up the pace.

A flock of black crows passes us overhead. They swoop in so close through the branches that I can see their dark marble eyes. A series of howls and barks echoes through the woods.

"Ooh, did you hear that?" David says. "Maybe it's the call of the werewolf. Maybe Oceanville is suddenly attracting supernatural entities, through some kind of paranormal global warming."

"It's the dogs from the bark park, David. That's all," I say, even though something about the woods and the crows is giving me the creeps. I can see the main walking and bike trail up ahead and I quicken my pace. I hear the faint laughter and hoots of kids coming from the playground.

"Do you realize how mental you sound?" I say.

Does he realize how mental I feel?

"I wonder what his kryptonite is," David says. "You know, the one thing that can harm him. And why he's here. It can't just be to save your klutzy behind and sing Michael Jackson songs. Or maybe," he says excitedly, "it's like your destiny to do something special one day, although I can't imagine what. It's like the Twilight series that you girls read: a centuries-old sexy killer with a heart of gold shows up in high school and falls overpoweringly in love with the klutzy girl who thinks he's hot. You know, that sort of thing."

We reach the trail and I feel a strange sense of relief to be out in the open again. I see kids running through the playground across the road that curves through the park.

"Look, aren't those some of your friends from the neighborhood over there?" I say, pointing toward the jungle gym.

"Well . . . yeah," David admits reluctantly.

Finally, I can ditch him for a while. If we can just get through the morning without any more drama, I can find some time to think, and sort this out.

I put my hand on his shoulder.

"Now, David," I say. "You're totally being overimaginative. This is all just silly talk. Why don't you go run along and play with your friends?"

"You don't have to patronize me, Jenna," David says stonily. "My IQ is probably higher than yours. Bernice and Lenny had me tested."

I give him the dirtiest look I can muster, raise my arm, and point toward the playground.

He starts across the road, walking backward as he talks.

"Just don't say I didn't warn you. I have a feeling. Something supernatural this way comes."

"David," I call back. "You've been reading too many comic books and watching too many freaky vampire, werewolf, and zombie movies."

David grins and then darts behind the bushes toward his friends.

But in that split second, I get the feeling that someone is watching me. I snap my head up. Luke is on the other side of the road, staring at me. Our eyes lock for a few seconds, but he doesn't move or gesture hello.

"Hi there," I finally croak, along with a feeble smile and a finger wiggle.

And then, from out of nowhere, I hear the screeching of tires and the blare of a horn.

"Look out!" someone yells.

I spin around. A huge van races at me, swerving out of control.

I don't have time to move, much less jump from its path, even if I was coordinated enough to do that.

I throw my arms up around my head and brace for impact. The tires screech, road dirt sprays into my face. The last thing I remember is the smell of gasoline pushing up into my nose.

Miraculously, seconds before impact, the van swerves back onto the trail. I hold my breath in shock. The driver gains control, straightens out, and keeps driving. The little bumper sticker on the back reads:

If you can read this, you're too close.

Yikes, was I ever! What was a truck doing on the walking and bike trail anyway?

Still trembling, I head across the road toward David, but then I hear the loud, wild tinkling of bells. I spin around and gasp.

A banana-seat bike swings violently out of control. The little girl riding it looks like a scared alien with her skinny body and purple helmet, too big for her head. She desperately tries to regain control, but that two-wheeler is going to mow me down!

"Move! You big clumsy oaf!" the little girl shrieks.

Within seconds, Luke is beside me. He holds out his arm and bends the high handlebars with his bare hands!

10

"You bent my handlebars!" the little girl accuses, pulling up from the ground and brushing herself off. "You are so paying for that! And give me back my tassels!"

She yanks away the pastel-colored tassels that are entwined in Luke's fingers.

I pick up her bell and give it a *brriiiinng*.

"Here you go."

I hand it to her sheepishly.

"Humph." She grabs the bell, shoves it into her pocket, hops back on her bike, and pedals away.

"Y-y-you . . . you were on the other side of the road," I stammer as Luke helps me to my feet. "How did you get here so fast?"

"I was standing right next to you," he says. "By that bush."

He points to the nearby foliage.

"You were right here?" I repeat.

"Yes," he says earnestly.

"If you say so." I shrug, not believing a word of it.

My whole life is making less and less sense by the minute.

"So," I say, fiddling with my jacket zipper while incredibly awkward seconds tick by.

"Well, I guess I'll get going," he says.

"Wait," I say.

He turns to me and his eyes settle on my face in a patient, caring way, as if he really wants to hear what I'm about to say and is not just waiting to get his turn to talk like most people do. And are those golden flecks in his baby hazels?

Crap. Now just to think of something nondorky, interesting, or semisexy to chat about, like was recommended in a recent article in *Teen Glamour* magazine: "Ten Snappy Conversation Starters to Intrigue That Hot Guy." Ugh. If only I could remember what they were.

And what about what happened at the skating rink? Should I mention that? And everything else that wasn't quite 'normal' that's happened since I first met him in my dream? All that talk with David about demons and superheros has me rattled. But there is also something about this guy, when I am with him, that just seems . . . normal.

"So, what are you doing in the park today?" I ask lamely.

"Well . . . I was skating, for one thing . . . I saw you skating too."

He says this with a straight face, but I can see the amusement in his eyes.

"You're an awesome skater," I say, trying to divert attention from myself.

He shrugs and gazes over my head, suddenly looking as if his thoughts are far away.

"I used to be. A long time ago. I still like it. It makes me feel real . . . grounded in time and free at the same moment. Do you know what I mean, Jenna?"

He looks back at me as if my answer really matters.

"Yeah," I lie. I have no idea what he means. "Me too."

"You too, huh?" He raises an eyebrow. "Well, I saw the free part, but you might want to work on being a little more grounded."

"I just . . . I think my blades were dull."

"Jenna, you weren't wearing skates. You were wearing your sneakers."

We both look down.

Oh, so busted.

"Yeah. I forgot." I bite my lip. "Don't get me wrong. I like winter sports. But I think I'm more cut out for bench warming and cocoa drinking."

"You can tell me the truth," Luke says. "It's all right to say you're not athletic."

"I'm not athletic," I say.

He shifts his head down and grins.

"It looks like David is though," he says.

"David?"

I had forgotten all about him. Imagine that.

We both glance toward the playground, where David is happily and raucously jumping all over the equipment.

"Hey, David! Be careful!" I yell. "Your mother would totally fire me this time if you really killed yourself!"

"You like to take care of him, don't you?" Luke says. "Just like a little brother."

"Yeah," I agree absently. "Wait . . . what?"

"When we were at school, in the cafetorium, when he called, you said that you loved him like a little brother."

"I said that? Well, I might have been exaggerating just a

tad," I say, my eyes sliding away from his. I think of that lying thing David was talking about and reflexively suck my lips into my mouth.

"Maybe," Luke says somewhat wistfully. "But you'll miss him when he's gone."

"Yeah." I snort a laugh, although I'm not quite sure what he's talking about.

For a second, his expression seems wistful and sad.

"Er . . . I mean, probably, you know, maybe." I try to backpedal. "Oh, who am I trying to kid? If David moved away or something, I'd never miss him in a hundred years."

"A hundred years is a long time. Two hundred is even longer. Family and community are very important, Jenna— how you choose to live your life and with whom. It's really the most important thing in the end," he says.

I think about the communists, my gnome-filled neighborhood, and the stiflingly boring community of Oceanville, where I don't fit in. If what he's saying is true, then I am in trouble.

"Even people who eventually become like family over time," he continues. "Even if you're not always crazy about what they expect of you . . . this family, over time, I mean . . . Especially when they expect you to give things up, important things, to follow your path of duty and destiny. Do you understand?"

Luke stares at me long and hard. It looks like he wants to say more, but for some reason thinks he shouldn't. I can almost see thoughts forming behind his face. He's sort of striking me as a little stiff and daffy in this moment, but still in a hot way. And what's all this about family who are not really family, duty, and destiny? I have no idea what he's talking about. Then he's so close to saying something else, and I'm so close to hearing it that I actually say, "What? You're not, like, a teenage Marine, are you? Like under-cover?"

Suddenly this seems like a viable theory to me. Top-secret espionage tricks and advanced dream reading, ice skating techno gadgetry that he was trying out, perhaps? Maybe I'm not going mental after all. My spirits lift.

It's his turn to look perplexed.

"What? No, I . . ." Luke looks down. "No." He shakes his head.

And my spirits fall.

He spies a dandelion and plucks it from the grass and suddenly is on to another topic.

"Humph," he says. "You don't see many of these in the fall. Want to blow and make a wish?" He steps in close, hold-ing the flaccid stem and wispy fuzz up to my lips.

"I'm good." I nod, suddenly shy that he's so close.

He holds the flower up to his face. The sun reflects through the white puff. He puts his oh-so-sexy lips together in a kiss and blows, sending the delicate white tendrils into flight.

"So what did you wish for?" I ask.

"If I tell you," he says, playfully, "my wish may not come true."

He steps back and gazes up into the deepening blue-gray fall sky. "But I'd say that being alive and here on a day like today is pretty close."

I follow his gaze skyward.

"You wished for cloudy with a chance of precipitation?" Luke laughs.

"You're funny, Jenna," he says.

The way he says my name tickles the hair on my arms.

"Yeah, that's what I hear," I say. "Except that I don't always mean to be."

"Laughing is good for the soul," he says.

"Not if you're the joke."

"And making people laugh is a gift, whether you intend it or not. Besides, you're not a joke. Don't let anyone make you feel that you are."

We stand quietly as the minutes tick by, just listening to the kids' voices and enjoying the crisp air. I still don't know what to say or where to look, but it doesn't feel so awkward.

Are we friends now? Are we having, like, a moment? What would Tess say about this?!

Then:

"I should go." He steps back abruptly. His mood changes. He seems agitated. His eyes dart nervously back into the woods.

And before I can respond, out of the corner of my eye I see something moving across the playground, glinting in and out of the sun, dodging kids and stray balls and ducking water-gun fire, huffing and puffing toward us. The sun dips behind the tire swings, giving me a clear view.

"Oh crap! Is that . . ." I groan.

"Hey there! It's me, Jared Needleman!"

Jared waves wildly. He carefully steps up to the road and

looks both ways like twenty times, even though, aside from my near miss with the van, there hasn't been a car on this road since 2005. Then he trot-walks toward us.

"What are you doing here, Jared?" I sigh.

"I called your house. Your mom said you were here baby-sitting David. I thought maybe we could find a picnic table and catch up on our science project. See?"

He turns around and tilts his tush.

"It's all in the rear."

Luke and I exchange perplexed looks.

"What?" I say.

"My backpack! I have my books and your mom *entrusted* me with your books," he says, emphasizing the word *entrusted*.

He swings back around, slamming his backpack into Luke and causing him to stumble.

"Because we're *neighbors*." Jared gives Luke a self-satisfied nod. "Oh and some guy over there gave me this."

Jared swings his backpack onto the ground, fishes through it, and places something in my hand.

"Here."

"This is David's camera," I say. "Why would David give this to you?"

"No, I didn't see David," Jared says, zipping up his back-pack and hoisting it over his shoulder.

"I told you. Some guy gave it to me. He told me to give it to you. I never saw him before. He wasn't from the neighbor-hood." Jared throws Luke a smug look. "But he must know you, Jenna. He said to give it to the cute girl with the straight, shoulder-length auburn hair, big brown eyes, and dusting of freckles."

Jared hesitates momentarily, and averts his eyes, a pale crimson climbing up his neck.

"He said all that?" I ask.

"Well," Jared says. "He said to give it to you. And he knew your name."

"Some guy had David's camera? And he knew my name?"

"What guy, Jared?" Luke asks, seeming alarmed.

"I don't know, some—" Jared starts.

"What was his name?" Luke asks urgently. "Jared, it's important. What was his name?"

"Where's David?" I ask. My eyes sweep the playground, taking it in as if in snapshots. I don't see him. I start across the road, but Luke puts his arm out to stop me.

"What guy, Jared?" Luke demands, looking as if he's working to keep his tone measured and steady, as if he's talking to a child.

"I don't know. It was something with an *A*. Allen . . . Avery . . . Alex . . .

"Was his name Adam?" Luke asks.

"Yeah, yeah, Adam. I should have remembered that. That was the name of my first goldfish. I named the other one Eve. Get it, Adam and Eve. Although I was never quite sure if she was a girl, but anyway they went belly-up after a few weeks. Had to give them the three-fish salute, and then I got Captain James T. Kirk. He was a frog, very slimy and a really good jumper, right into space like a rocket, but then he jumped right into traffic. Squash. What a mess . . . He really did boldly go where no frog has—"

"Jared!" I interrupt him. "Think hard. Did you see David? Even for a minute?"

Luke grabs Jared by both shoulders now and leans hard into his face.

"Hey, what do you think you're—" Jared tries to pull away.

"Jared, what else did Adam say?!" Luke asks.

"I don't know. He didn't say much . . . But wait . . . he did mumble something about dogs of hell or wolves of darkness, maybe dogs ripping flesh and drinking blood. Something about vicious beasts with salivating, knifelike fangs. Why? You think that's important?"

Luke and I rush to the playground with Jared at our heels.

"David!" I yell. "David, if you're hiding and this is a joke, it's not funny!"

My racing heartbeat and the clamminess under my arms tell me that this time it's no joke.

"Do you think some pervert kidnapped David?" Jared looks all wide-eyed. "I bet it was one of those pervy Internet things. You know, like some psycho in the state pen pretends to be a hot girl and makes like she really likes you and you send her a picture and then your mother finds out and goes ballistic and takes away your Xbox for like, ten whole days and . . ."

Jared stops, presumably sensing our perplexed eyes on him.

"Not that that happened to me, ya know. I mean it hypothetically."

"Don't help, Jared." I sigh.

We hear faint howls. It sounds like wolves.

"Are there any wolves or wild dogs in this park?" Luke asks. "Quick, Jenna. It's important."

"Well, no. There's just . . ."

"What?" Luke urges.

"There's the bark park," I say.

"Let's go," Luke says. "Before it's too late."

11

Fortunately, the bark park isn't far. The afternoon light is starting to fade and eerie shadows of tree limbs and monkey bars, the slide and swings crisscross the ground. The old clock reads 12:45. Moms are corralling their protesting kids in the parking lot, to go home for lunch.

"I'll go, Jenna," Luke says. "You and Jared stay here."

Jared takes one long sidestep glide over to me.

"I'll take care of her." Jared nods to Luke.

"I'll be back." Luke gives me a meaningful glance.

"We'll be waiting." Jared nods again, authoritatively, placing his arm around my shoulder.

Were these guys kidding or what?

"Hey wait a second." I wiggle from Jared's grasp. "I'm the babysitter, remember. David might be a pain in the butt, but he's my pain in the butt. I'm going with you, Luke."

"Me too," Jared says, suddenly looking piqued, his eyes darting nervously toward the woods as the last of the kids are swept off into minivans.

"Listen, Jared." I turn toward him. "Luke is right. Someone needs to stay here. You know, just in case this is David's idea of a joke and he comes back."

Jared squints suspiciously from me to Luke, then back again.

"What makes you think David would come back here?"

"Because he's like a psycho homing pigeon," I say. "He always comes back to the scene of the prank."

"What about *he* stays here," Jared whispers to me, motioning to Luke. "And I go with you?"

"David doesn't know Luke. He knows you. He trusts you," I say confidentially, thumping my hand on his shoulder.

"David hates me," Jared says.

"Maybe . . . but only in the most trusting way. After all, you are his *neighbor*." I emphasize the word.

"I dunno." Jared glares at Luke. "I still think you and I should stay here together."

"Man up, Jared. You'll be fine." I turn to go.

I smile at Luke, take a brave, martyred breath, smooth down my patchwork coat, and, with nervous jelly knees, walk toward him.

He smiles at me.

Don't be nervous. I'm here.

I stop and blink. Did he just say that? I look into his crinkled eyes and at his mouth, which never moved.

Then he reaches out and actually takes my hand.

I throw a guilty glance back at Jared, but he's already preoccupied, squinting into the trees with jumpy vigilance.

"Let's go," Luke says, giving my hand a gentle tug as we rush in the direction of the bark park and the low, throaty, ominous hum of growling dogs.

12

Stealthily we creep toward the bark park. Luke, like a ninja, dry and calm, barely making a sound through the woods; me, crunching leaves, cracking twigs, and panting, with those clammy armpits.

Finally we reach a sign that reads: BARK PARK. A gate opens into a clearing littered with balls, sticks, and other doggie paraphernalia. Way on the other side of the clearing are a sculpture of big rocks and a tall trash can with a sign that reads: PLACE POOP HERE.

Oddly, the area is deserted, but more oddly, I hear yet another Michael Jackson song, "Billie Jean," playing on the high tinkling ice cream bells. His songs seem to fit every occasion.

The ice cream truck is parked about fifty feet away, by the Frisbee meadow, and is surrounded by a mob of people chatting, eating ice cream, socializing, and flirting, all with empty dog leashes dangling from their hands and arms, seemingly oblivious to where their dogs might be.

"Why aren't they with their pets?" I whisper to Luke. "It's as if they don't even realize that they're not around."

Luke motions for me to keep following him toward the clearing.

"Stay quiet," he whispers.

"Okay." I nod and then loudly crack a tree limb under my foot.

Then, suddenly, we have a dawning realization that something is behind us, grumbling in a low guttural rumble that seems to shake the ground beneath our feet. We both turn slowly. Luke extends his arm out in front of me in an act of protection.

Crunching before us is a familiar furry creature.

"Beaver?" I say.

It's the goldendoodle from up the block who likes to pee in communist Mom's Bulk petunias. But it's not the Beaver I know. This dog looks crazy. His blond shaggy fur stands straight up from his back. His head hunches down low. His gleaming eyes focus straight at us; his teeth are bared. White gunk hangs from them and slops into the leaves below.

"Nice boy," I say, taking a step toward him. "Don't be scared. I'm from the neighbor . . ."

Beaver lurches forward. His jaws snap and his lips recede and twitch above his teeth.

In a split second, Luke is between me and Beaver the demon dog.

Then, moving soundlessly from out of the woods, come dozens of dogs in all colors, shapes, sizes, and doodle breeds. And these "pets" look crazy too. They've all somehow morphed into rabid-looking beasts and they're closing in around us.

From out of the trees swoop dozens of black crows, cawing wildly.

A large black wolf creeps from behind a tree. Then, right before my eyes, the wolf transforms into the same sinister shadow boy whose image was reflected in my pendant, the half hallucination who tried to accost me through the window at Cowboy Clems, the image that appeared in my dreams. The boy who has been lurking just below the surface of real life.

"Adam." Luke nods as if he's just been cornered by an old acquaintance he doesn't want to see.

"I couldn't stay away," Adam says.

He holds his palm out to the circle of dogs and flicks it down.

"Sit," he commands the animals. "Stay."

And with that, all the dog beasts promptly sit.

"Ah . . . could somebody please tell me what's happening?" I squeak.

"Be quiet, Jenna," Luke says softly, never taking his eyes off Adam.

A small breeze blows through my hair. Adam flutters his eyes shut and inhales through his nose, long and deep, as if sucking in my scent.

He steps forward and gives me a once-over as if I'm some pathetic sale item from the Bulk Emporium that hasn't sold and has been reduced twice. Luke is planted firmly at my side, looking like he's primed to jump to my defense if necessary.

"Ah, I see you brought a treat," Adam says.

It's another strange Twilight moment: at the mention of

the word *treat*, the dogs go wild, jumping up like pets again: smiling, panting, wiggling, wagging their butts, and thumping their tails.

"*Sit!*" Adam commands.

Looking ashamed, the dogs crouch down into a sit, then look all rabid and morose and snarly again.

Adam steps closer and his eyes slide down, resting on my chest for just a little too long. His expression is lewd and creepy.

"Um, eyes up here," I say, meeting his gaze.

"Where's the pendant?" he says.

"Where's the boy?" Luke counters, stepping in front of me.

"What boy?" Adam responds in a psycho-playful way. "The park is filled with boys."

"You know who I mean."

"Oh that boy," Adam replies. "About yay high?" He places his hand at the middle of his rib cage. "Dirty-blond hair, blue eyes? Skinny? Mouthy? Smart-ass?" Adam grins. "Never saw him."

"Look, I don't know who or what you are, but I need that kid," I say.

Adam turns his full attention on me.

"I don't care about the boy. He was just convenient bait to get you here. And by the way"—he leans in and wiggles his eyebrows—"I know who you are, girl who smells like a treat."

The dogs pant and howl with delight.

"Down!" Adam commands, and they all sit down again.

Adam grins and then steps in close to look, provoking Luke with his eyes, only a few inches from him. Luke is smoldering but a slight fear passes across his baby hazels. It feels as though Adam has something on him, which scares him ever so slightly. Adam grins and it's as if he senses it too. He places his hand on Luke's chest and gently pushes him back a few inches, as he circles me menacingly.

"It's remarkable," Adam says. "The similarities. What do you call it now when someone looks so much like an ancestor from the past? I guess now they attribute it to DNA or something, right?"

"But this one's not so toned." He addresses Luke. "Not as cute as that blond one that you were with."

I have no idea what Adam is talking about, but I know that I am somehow being dissed and can feel my face creep red with heat and shame.

"Well at least I'm not a psycho wolf . . . boy!" I blurt out.

"She's a feisty one though. What's your name, plain girl?"

"I'm David's babysitter," I say.

"Okay, David's Babysitter, just give me the pendant and then I'll go."

"Leave her alone." Luke pushes Adam out of the way and snarls with anger, his whole body throbbing with white light.

Adam raises an eyebrow. He looks from Luke to me and back again.

"Oh, it's like that, is it?" He smirks. "Looks like I'm not the only one who wants to stay. Well, this makes the whole affair a lot more interesting now."

That pendant again. What does it mean? Why is everyone so interested in some ugly necklace?

"For God's sake, take the damn thing," I say, placing my hand to my chest, where the pendant is lying under my shirt. Except I don't feel it. Despite its hideousness it's been incredibly light to wear, except now it's not there at all.

13

Adam sucks in an expectant breath.

I feel around my neck for the chain.

Luke's hand flies up in a blur of speed and pushes Adam back.

"Uh . . . guys," I say.

"You can't have it," Luke growls at Adam. "She's the keeper. It was destined so."

"You know I'll have it," Adam says, leveling a smoldering look at Luke.

Panic rushes through me. I pat the pockets of my jeans. Not there.

"Guys . . ." I say, scanning the ground with my eyes.

Adam's face softens for a moment.

"Luke, just think of what we could have if we stayed in this time period forever. Things are so different now from when we were here."

"Fellas?" I bite my lip.

I start making little circles and kicking the dead leaves over with my shoe. Yesterday I would have given anything to lose this hideous necklace and now I'm sure that losing it probably is a bad thing.

Adam's eyes glisten as he surveys the bark park with all its mangy devil mutts.

We follow Adam's gaze to the group of oblivious dog owners, talking among themselves.

The tinkling ice cream bells turn to Michael Jackson's "Bad" and take on a very eerie tone.

"If we stayed, we could have anything!" Adam says, as if thinking out loud. "And everything. This is a whole population of people who are waiting for me to guide them, manipulate them. As long as they have their cell phones, their ice cream, their designer dogs in expensive bark parks." He spits the words with sarcasm. "They won't care.

"This time period was made for me," Adam continues. "And you could have what you didn't get to finish. You could have David's babysitter." He looks me up and down, bored. "Or anyone else you want."

Luke looks away. His expression is unreadable, except for what looks like a flash of sorrow. Is he considering whatever Adam was proposing? Adam certainly doesn't seem like a good guy to make deals with.

I retrace my steps, bending over and fishing through any glistening leaves with my fingertips. How could I not find this? The other day I found my contact lens on Miss Manley's soccer field, which is full of cleat marks, flattened grass, and clumps of dirt. Why can't I find a silver pendant the size of a small pancake lying on top of a bunch of leaves?

"If you could just break away from . . ."

Luke shoots him a dark look.

Adam grins. "Never mind."

I look up and see Luke's uncertain eyes dart away from Adam's face, nervously turn to the ground.

Who is Adam talking about now? I wonder.

Adam barks a short, malevolent laugh.

Luke rallies.

"No!" Luke says. "I won't let you. You can't stay without the pendant, and you can't get it as long as she wears it!"

"Uh, dudes." I try again. "About that—"

"I can't have it as long as she's alive," Adam states matter-of-factly. "But that could change."

"Not while *I'm* alive." Luke reaches back, presumably to protect me, but his hands feel around for nothing because I'm not there. His head snaps around.

"Jenna?"

I give him a nervous finger wiggle from where I'm standing way over by a tree.

In a blur of speed Adam is on me. Behind me. His arm crooked around my throat.

He reaches down under my T-shirt.

"Uh, excuse me!" I protest.

He pushes me hard so I land on the ground with a *thwump*.

"Ow!"

"She doesn't have it!" Adam says, his face filled with a rage unlike anything I've ever seen before.

He grabs my hair and pulls me to my feet. His monster dogs have suddenly surrounded me.

Luke bolts forward but Adam has a knife to my neck.

"Where is it?" he demands.

"Where is what?" I stall stupidly.

He pulls my hair up tighter, exposing more of my neck and, I'm supposing, a cleaner cut.

"Don't play with me, plain girl." Adam's breath is hot in my ear.

"Is this what you're looking for?"

Suddenly David Lipski pops out from behind a tree. My hideous pendant dangles from the chain clutched in his hand.

Adam releases my hair and shoves me out of his way.

"Give me that!" he demands.

"Come and get it," David goads playfully.

Then:

"Don't worry, Jenna," David says. "I'll save you!"

"David, don't!" Luke yells.

Adam bolts after him, but David is too quick. He tosses the pendant at me and as it flies through the air, it's almost as if everything has gone slo-mo.

"Caaaaatch iiiit!" I hear David's voice sounding suddenly far away.

And all I can think is: *catch it, catch it*. The million times balls have been thrown my way flash through my mind's eye. Big volleyballs, small softballs, enormous medicine balls. I hear a cacophony of echoed choruses of

Catch it!

Followed by the dozens of groans when I don't.

From the corner of my eye I see Adam and Luke's shocked faces. I see the pendant on its descent into my waiting hands.

"Puuuut iiiitttt oooonnnn!" I hear Luke wail.

It's coming. It's coming. I hold out my hands and squint. Luke is rushing toward me.

Adam is rushing toward me.

"Caaatch it!" David yells again.

The pendant brushes my fingertips and . . . I drop it.

"Piiiiick iiit uuup!" David yells.

I snatch it from the ground and throw it around my neck.

Time returns to normal speed. Adam is at me again. The pendant bounces on my chest for a moment. The silver color catches a flash of sun and Adam blinks from the reflection, his expression ecstatic. He reaches for it, but at his touch the pendant sparks wildly in blue and gold and burns the tips of his fingers. And I do mean burns. Bright red, singeing. I catch a whiff of burning flesh. An image of the wicked witch trying to snatch Dorothy's ruby slippers flashes through my mind.

Adam yelps and jerks his hand away. His eyes fill with what look like stinging tears. Pain and anger momentarily morph his face into something grotesque, something between a wolf, a crow, and a boy. He lunges at me again but this time with two hands aiming for my throat. Luke is fast and shoves me out of the way. Then he grabs a stick from the ground and pitches it hard. It goes far and wide.

"Fetch!" he yells, and all the frenzied monster dogs bolt after it.

Adam throws back his head and lets out a piercing wail of rage and frustration.

"I'll get you and your little pendant too!" he says to me.

"Ha!"

We all turn to see David by the tree where he has been hiding.

"That's funny," he says.

Adam's expression turns black.

"You don't want to make an enemy of me, vile boy," he intones low.

"Nyeh!" David taunts, and then he takes off.

Suddenly Adam just vanishes. We hear a great flapping of wings on the wind. And then nothing. Silence. Luke and I stand, listening, looking. We stand like that for a few long moments. Nothing, except for the soft tinkling of Michael Jackson's "Bad" from the ice cream bells.

Then suddenly:

He rocks in the tree tops all day long . . .

It's my cell phone.

Hoppin' and a-boppin' and . . .

I flip it open.

"Jenna. It's me. David Lipski."

I snap my head around wildly.

"David, where are you?" I shriek.

"On the rocks!"

I turn, and there's David on the far side of the bark park, at the very top of a rock sculpture shaped like a giant hydrant. There's a pack of at least a dozen mangy, angry wolves snarling at his feet. He's holding a long tree branch and happily lunging at them like a swordsman.

"Aya! Back!" he shouts.

He sees us and waves.

Adam reappears at the bottom of the rock hydrant.

"The pendant or the boy," he bellows at us.

Before we even have time to respond, Adam morphs into a black wolf. His clothes fall to a heap on the ground. He scrambles up the sculpture until he is on top, inches from David. He lowers his wolf head and growls low.

"Uh-oh," says David, realizing he has nowhere to back up.

"We're coming, David!" I shout.

"I got it!" David yells.

Then he makes an amazing nimble jump at the nearest tree branch, swings himself forward and up in the nick of time.

"It's a bird, it's a plane . . ." he cries out. "It's . . . I don't have a name yet."

Adam throws back his grizzly head and howls in what sounds like frustration. Suddenly Luke appears on top of the hydrant, leaps onto Adam, and wrestles him onto his back. All I can see is the furious flashing of teeth and hair and white throbbing light.

The dogs, stirred by the frenzy, snap and bark and lunge at the branch where David holds on for dear life. There's an overlap of snarls and yelps and screams.

Then what looks like an enormous expanse of wings erupts from Luke's back. He lifts Adam by the scruff of his neck and hurls him off the rocks, sending him cowering. Within seconds, Adam recovers, throws back his head, and releases one long plaintive howl. The dogs encircle him and howl in kind.

Then the whole pack bolts into the woods and is gone.

And one black crow rises up from behind the trees, caws loudly, and flies out of sight.

Luke stands on top of the rocks, glowing white, enormous light gray feathery wings splayed out behind him. He looks over at me with an expression of sadness and shame.

I hear his voice again in my head.

You've been chosen for this. This isn't over by far . . .

"What?" I shout.

He vanishes, and all I see is the green and brown of the woods and the sun throwing winks of light through the branches of trees.

Then:

One by one, all the dogs, normal again, race back through the brush. Beaver galumphs toward me, sits, pants up into my face, and nudges me with his nose so I'll pet his head. The dog owners head back to collect their dogs. The ice cream bells of Michael Jackson's "Bad" have switched over to his earlier "Enjoy Yourself," and the sound fades into the distance as the ice cream truck heads up the road.

He rocks in the tree tops all day long . . .

I flip open my phone.

"Hi Jenna. It's me. Jared Needleman."

"Kinda busy here, Jared," I say.

He ignores me. "What the heck are you doing out there? Did you find David or not? I'm freezing and it's past lunchtime and it's getting rainy and . . ."

"Can't talk now, Jared."

I flip the phone closed. David climbs down from his tree.

He walks over to me. We are both perplexed.

"I am so stoked." David grins. "Because that was the slammin'est supernatural thing I've ever seen in my life."

14

The car ride home is pretty intense. David is jabbering on hyperspeed about what happened in the park, while I'm trying to tune him out so I can process what happened myself. Plus, I'm distracted by trying to prevent Bernice from mangling the car around a tree or flipping over the guardrail.

Every ten seconds, I'm like:

"Quick! Mrs. Lipski! Tractor trailer at 1:00!"

"Oopsy!"

She swerves away just in the nick of time.

Once back home and in my room, I head straight for the computer and type in the word *angel*, which at this point is the best conclusion I can draw about Luke. About a billion religious references glow back at me.

According to Wikipedia, an angel is a celestial being sent by God. No reference at all to skating angels who can magically summon Michael Jackson's music and moonlight as waiters at greasy-spoon restaurants.

And I have no idea what the hell Adam is, other than some kind of wolf-crow boy.

Am I going crazy? There is no denying by now that Luke and Adam are something other than human, of course.

Did the two of them slip through the equinox thingie that Sheldon was talking about? If so why are they here? What is their relationship to each other? How does my hideous pendant play into everything? What did Adam mean about me being like my ancestors? What was that business about me being a "keeper"? What the hell was that? Does it have anything to do with what Sheldon found in his article—about some families passing down a supernatural gift?

Feeling desperate, I decide to enlist the help of the communists.

First stop, my brother, who's playing some kind of loud, violent video game and intermittently shooting canned Cheez Whiz directly into his mouth.

"Hey Michael," I say. "I know you like fantasy and the supernatural. Maybe you even have an interest in, oh, I don't know, angels or werewolf-type thingies or—"

Michael stops playing his game and turns toward me.

"I can't believe it," he interrupts. "That is so way cool that you said that, 'cause I was just thinking about werewolves."

I sit down and pick up the box from his video game.

"Well, maybe that's because you're playing Werewolves: The Demon's Lexicon."

"Yeah, but you came in here to ask me about werewolves at the exact time I was playing the game. Isn't that a coincidence? Like we have ESP or something," he says, moving his hand back and forth between us.

"Michael," I say. "If I thought we thought alike I'd have to gouge out my heart with an ice pick."

"Ever wonder exactly how you become a werewolf?" he asks, pondering.

"I think the lore is that you have to be bitten by one to become one, but that's not what I wanted to tell you . . ."

He leans in close to me, Cheez Whiz on his breath.

"'Cause remember last week when I had that assembly at school?"

"No," I say.

"And those hippie guys with the stinky pits brought in those wolves," he says.

"You mean the wolf conservationists?" I say.

"Yeah, and they let us touch them but said don't feed them anything?"

He looks around furtively.

"Well, I gave one of them a piece of gum," Michael says. "And he accidentally bit my finger. Drew a little blood."

"You gave an endangered species a piece of gum?"

"It was all I had," Michael says.

"Okay," I say, sighing deeply and heading toward the door. "I gotta go."

"'Cause remember that other night when the moon was full?" he continues. "Well, I was feeling kind of itchy and scratchy and like, kind of mean. And by the morning, I could have sworn that my finger and toenails got scraggly and pointy."

He kicks off his sneakers and starts taking off his socks.

"Wanna see?"

Needless to say, that conversation was over.

On to Mom and Dad, sitting on the couch in the den—

Mom watching TV and Dad plugged into his iPod, staring at the screen presumably reading lips.

"This is so sad. It's a terrible, terrible movie." Mom sniffles.

"What's it about?" I ask.

"It's a long story," Mom says. "I can't keep track."

"So," I fish, "why don't you turn it off?"

"But it's not over, why would I turn it off?" Mom says.

"No reason." I give up.

"Oh, by the way, Jared called before. He sounded upset. Something about leaving him starving in the woods with howling wolves nearby . . . He's grown up to be such a sensitive boy. He'll make a nice husband. Just like Daddy."

We both turn to Daddy.

With a maniacal gleam, his eyes follow a spider inching its way across the coffee table. He picks up a magazine, thwacks the spider hard, and then flicks the carcass away with his foot.

"Killed the bastard!" Dad explodes with sadistic delight.

"You should call Jared back," Mom says.

"Er . . . maybe later," I say.

"Did you want something?" Mom asks.

Then they both turn toward me, my dad's gaze settling on my lips, presumably so he can join the conversation without unplugging.

"I was just wondering," I begin. "Do either of you believe in the supernatural? Like, for real?"

"You mean like werewolves?" Mom asks. "Werewolves are the new vampires, you know. There was a whole article about it in *People*. And zombies are the new werewolves. And fairies, well, they haven't hit yet. It was very interesting."

Dad nods in agreement.

"What I mean is," I continue, "do you believe in angels? Do you believe a person can actually interact with an angel?"

"You mean like in a dream?" Mom asks.

I take a deep breath.

"No, for real," I answer.

"I don't see why not." Mom shrugs.

"Really?" I exclaim excitedly.

"Sure," Mom says. "If someone is dying or—"

"Taking crack," Dad interrupts.

"Or taking crack." Mom nods.

"But what if they're not dying or taking crack?" I ask.

"And they're talking to angels?" Mom asks. "Then they're nuts."

So much for the illuminating contributions of the Bloom family communists.

That night, I dream of angels walking dogs, David doing the moonwalk in trees, and Jared morphing into a giant werewolf who turns over the ice cream truck and then licks up everything in sight.

———————

Monday morning at school, I'm so distracted that in Gym, during a rousing game of dodgeball, I'm not dodgey enough and find myself on the wrong side of the line when Sarah Johnson is looking for slow targets to eliminate.

Thwump.

The ball whizzes right into the side of my head.

In Nurse Nolan's office, with a compress pressed up against my temple, I try once again to make sense of an experience that I don't really believe did, should, or ever could happen, especially to me. I try to approach it analytically and make a mental list of more unanswered questions:

- Is it possible that I am going insane?
- Can insanity be brought on by years of being a social outcast?
- Am I having these experiences because my life is in danger or is someone secretly feeding me crack, as the communist Blooms suggested?
- Why does this compress smell like feet, and can I catch lice from it?

And:

- Why does Nurse Nolan dress like a character from a Grimm's fairy tale (long brown skirt, big brown billowy top tied over it with a woven belt, plus brown flat-soled scrunchy boots)?

So many questions. So few answers. So many kids trying to ditch class by pretending to be sick in the nurse's office.

Finally, by fifth period, I catch sight of Tess making her way up the crowded hallway to the cafetorium.

"Excuse me, s'cuse me." I elbow my way through the

throng and bump into some kid precariously balancing a volcano project on a wooden board.

"Hey, watch out!" He tries to swerve from my path, but I accidentally flatten it into his chest.

"What the . . . !"

"Sorry, s'cuse me, s'cuse me . . ." I weave and squeeze my way toward her. She's at the head of what looks like an amped-up conga line of kids trying to push through the one small open cafetorium door.

"Hey, Tess, wait up!" I shout.

She sees me and stops dead, causing a pileup of the kids behind her.

"Omph!"

"Gah!"

"Hey, move it!"

The kids yell.

"Oh no you didn't." Tess turns to me, raising one eyebrow and putting her hands on her hips, oblivious to the bodies piling up behind her. "Weren't we supposed to hang out yesterday? You totally ditched me and then you didn't even answer your . . . Hey!"

I grab her arm and yank her into the lunchroom.

The throng of kids lurches forward through the door and stumbles into the lunchroom behind us.

"I've got something to tell you that you won't believe," I say.

"Well, you don't have to pull me." She struggles against my grip.

"Yeah I do," I say, finding our seats by the door. "Before everyone else gets here."

She plops into her seat, I plop into mine, and I lean way forward.

"Just listen and don't say anything until I'm done, okay?"

"Yeah, okay." Tess shrugs.

"Do you believe in the supernatural? Angels disguised as humans? Demons disguised as humans . . . or wolves?"

Tess stares at me dead-on, and I lose heart as I can practically *see* the gears of her bullshit barometer kicking into place.

"And . . . um . . . crows . . ." I mumble halfheartedly.

Tess stares at me blankly for a few more seconds and then blinks.

"Crows?" she says, and starts to unwrap her lunch. "What are you talking about?"

"Well, it's like . . . You know how you love music? Like you play it and compose it and really feel it in your soul?"

"Yeah," she draws out, as if trying to figure out where I'm taking this.

"Well, it's like music. Like how music is almost supernatural," I say. "Like it doesn't exist until you imagine it or play it."

"Yeah," Tess says skeptically, biting into her eggless egg salad sandwich.

"So if music is transcendent and not real, in a way," I continue, "isn't it possible that things that people don't think are real or don't believe could be real, could really be real too?"

"Wait . . . what?" Tess chews.

"Like love. Or romance. You believe in those things. But love is not a thing you can touch. It's not real until you experience it."

"I'm not following you. What do angels and demons and birds have to do with music or love . . . Wait a minute," Tess sparks. "Now I'm getting it."

"You are?" I ask expectantly.

"Does any of this love talk have to do with . . ."

She glances around.

"Luke," she mouths excitedly.

"Well, that's what I'm trying to—"

"Did you see Luke on Sunday?" she interrupts. "Is that why you didn't call? Oh my God! I want to hear everything. Start dishing right now!"

Bea and Kayla arrive at the table.

"Who are we dishing about?" Kayla asks, sitting down and gently unzipping her lunch bag.

"I bet I know!" Bea sings, banging her lunch tray down on the table.

"Shhh!" the rest of us all snap in unison.

"I bet I know!" She beams. Then, just a few decibels lower, "But I don't think he's in school today. I didn't see him in Math."

Sheldon arrives carrying a lunch tray, completing the group.

"Oh you mean that supernaturally hot Cowboy Clems hottie," he says, swinging into his seat, placing his tray down, shaking out his napkin, and placing it on his lap. "I know why he's not here."

"You do?"

"Sure. It's too sunny and he's too hot and sparkly."

"Huh?"

"Sparkly . . . hot," he says, exasperated. "The Cullens always skip school when the sun is out."

Tess rolls her eyes.

"So now Luke is a vampire?" she says. "First it's angels and crows, now vampires? Has everyone gone crazy today?"

Kayla tilts her head.

"Angels and crows?"

"I think *blood challenged* is the new politically correct term for vampires," Sheldon says. "And no, I don't think Luke is one anyway. But there is something different about him. Something . . . I don't know . . . spiritual."

"Sheldon," I say, abandoning the stale crusts of my PB&J, "do you have your tarot card deck with you today?"

"Sure do," Sheldon says. "It's a great icebreaker. You never know when someone cute will want his future told."

"And let me guess, you're always a part of his future," Tess says.

"Only if he's on my astral plane," Sheldon says. "Why? Ooh, Jenna, do you want me to read your cards?"

"Just tell me if you see anything . . . strange," I say, feeling like I have nothing to lose and maybe something to gain.

"You can't be serious," Tess says.

"Strange?" repeats Sheldon. "Could you be a little more specific?"

"Er, not really."

"Well," he says, "I think the spirit guides prefer places

with atmosphere, more like with candles and incense. Less like the smell of brown Betty—"

"Get on with it, Shel," Tess interrupts. "The period's almost over."

"Not a problem," he says, jumping into action. He pushes the lunch tray aside, fishes in his backpack for his tarot deck, and places the cards in front of me, facedown. Everyone is attentive.

"Ooh, I love this. I feel just like a character from the CW Network," he says. "Okay, spread out the cards and pick one."

Tentatively, I pick a card and hold it up. It's a picture of a skeleton in a graveyard, holding a scythe and preparing to chop off the head of a hanging ghoul.

"Ewww." Kayla wrinkles up her nose.

"That can't be good," Bea announces.

"Er . . . how's this?" I ask.

Sheldon frowns.

"Em . . . don't get nervous," he says nervously. "It's not what you think. It doesn't mean you're going to get hacked to death by an evil entity or anything."

He snatches the card from my hand and places it at the bottom of the deck.

"The cards are symbolic," he says. "It just means . . . um . . . you're going to embark on a pleasant journey."

I eye him suspiciously.

"Pick another one," he instructs.

I pick one of a grimacing witch flying over a house that's going up in flames. I hold it up.

"Another pleasant journey?" I ask sarcastically.

"How about we lose the cards," Sheldon says. "Here, give me your hands. I'll do a reading by sensing your palm energy and vibrations."

"Ooh, he's so talented," Kayla gushes, wide-eyed.

"Yes, there's definitely an angel near you," Sheldon continues. "He's an older gentleman. Very grandfatherly. As a matter of fact, he is your grandfather. White hair, small, but kindly. His angel name is Claude."

I pull my hands away in exasperation.

"My grandfather was Sidney. He was fat, bald, and cranky."

"Nice," Tess says sarcastically. "You're a big help, Sheldon."

"No, wait, wait . . ." He grabs for my hands again. "I'm just messing with you. No, seriously. I'm good at this."

"Fine. One more time," I say.

Hesitantly, I offer my hands up again to Sheldon. He closes his eyes. I sigh and wait as all the colors, sounds, and smells of the cafetorium swirl around me. Bea, Kayla, and Tess, having lost interest in Sheldon's theatrics, have their heads together and are gossiping about hot guys . . .

When suddenly I feel a jolt of something electric.

"Ow, Sheldon. What the hell was that?" I say, trying to pull my hands away.

Sheldon's eyes flutter open. And I know in an instant that it's not quite Sheldon staring back at me.

"Hello, Jenna," says a voice that I recognize as clearly not Sheldon.

"Sheldon?" I try.

"Not Sheldon," he answers, his eyes now as black and empty as a pit.

"I can be a friend to you," he says.

"Uh, I don't think so. Can I have my hands back, please," I say.

"Jenna," he cajoles. "You don't like your life. And why should you? You don't fit in. Your family doesn't know you. You have a couple of strange friends. Your best friend deserted you for something better."

His eyes travel over to Sarah Johnson, at a nearby table, laughing and flirting with her large group of wannabes and admirers.

"You're plain and you're clumsy. You'll make a terrible costume designer. And what's more . . ."

He twists Sheldon's expression into a malevolent smirk.

"Your pathetic life will never get any better."

"And your point is?" I sniff.

"I can do so much for you! You have no idea what I'm capable of." Not Sheldon leans in. "But I have to have the pendant in order to stay."

I try once again to pry my hands loose from his grip.

"I have a pretty good idea of what you're capable of, crow-wolf-psycho boy," I spit. "And besides, Luke likes me . . . sort of . . . I think . . . although I'm not sure why."

Not Sheldon barks a laugh.

"You think Luke really cares about you? He's a puppet."

"Well, I have the pendant, and I'm not giving it to you. So just go back to where you came from."

Not Sheldon grips me tighter, cutting off my circulation.

"This is not a joke, plain girl. Beware . . ."

"Let go, Not Sheldon." I struggle.

Then suddenly I hear a gentle, familiar voice.

"Let her go."

Not Sheldon loosens his grip, and I yank my hands away from him.

Luke comes up behind Sheldon.

"So, what was I saying . . ." Real Sheldon pops back into his own body again. "Oh yeah . . . um, I don't know. I thought I felt something, but I got nothing. Sorry. It's totally so much better when I've got patchouli incense and candles."

Sheldon follows my gaze behind him and twists around in his chair.

"Oh, hi there!" he says. "I didn't see you."

He smiles and pretends to slap Luke's arm.

Just then, the lunch bell rings, sending everyone around us into a frenzy of loud scraping chairs, goodbyes, and general shuffling toward the door.

Luke clears his throat.

"We need to talk."

My friends beam up at him expectantly. He hesitates, looking like he's hoping that someone, including me, might get the hint.

No movement. We all just lean in closer.

"Em . . . alone. Maybe," he says politely, "just you and me."

"Oh." I startle and blush. "Alone. I thought you meant . . . Oh never mind."

My friends all exchange grins and hustle to gather their things.

"No problem. We're gone. Don't want to be late for class," they mutter over one another in unison.

I grab my backpack and pull up next to him as we head out of the cafetorium and up the hall.

"I have a free period next. What do you have?" he asks.

"I have a Gym makeup," I say. "But I can miss that."

"Are you sure?" he says. "I don't want to get you in trouble."

"No worries. I'll just tell Miss Manley that I had to go to the nurse. She'll be relieved. It'll save her the trouble of sending me there herself."

"Isn't there anywhere in school we can go?" he asks urgently.

"Well, I . . ."

From the corner of my eye, I notice all of my friends conspicuously following a few paces behind. I turn. They see me, suddenly scatter and look busy.

I lead him around the corner toward the auditorium and there's Jared. He catches sight of me and waves. Then he catches sight of Luke. His face pinches tight. He starts moving toward us, but a cluster of kids emerges from a classroom and intercepts him. I grab Luke's jacket and swing him out the door.

"The beach is just a few blocks away," I say. "Why don't we go there?"

15

I've done the short walk from school to the beach a million times, and it's pretty ordinary, but for Luke it seems almost extraordinary. He notices everything and, through his eyes, I see things that I have never noticed before: the angular cut of someone's roof, the gargoyle on someone's door knocker, the way one tree came up from under a grate and then grew upward around it because, in Luke's words, "it had that much will to live."

I wonder what Luke needs to tell me so badly. After all, even though I have many unanswered questions, I feel like I've gotten TMI in matters supernatural lately.

Near the beach, we trudge past the wispy dunes and walk gingerly down the little slated walkway that leads to the sand. The ocean waves are rough, the water dark blue and green. The blue-gray sky is streaked with fingers of white clouds reaching across the horizon. Luke stares out at the water for what feels like many awkward minutes.

Then:

"Oh." He exhales in reverence.

He exuberantly pulls off his shoes and socks, kicks them to the side, and rolls up the bottoms of his jeans, exposing his cute, tan, well-groomed feet.

"Let's go." He grins.

I hesitate. Have I recently trimmed my toenails? (Whew, okay, yes.) Am I wearing holey socks? (No, whew again—I put on a new pair this morning.)

"Well," he coaxes.

I bend over to slip off my faux-leather fashion boots from the Bulk, but when I glance up and see him smiling over me, I'm shy about exposing my pale, naked feet. I stand up awkwardly.

"I'm good," I say.

And instead of teasing me or scolding me about how I'll ruin my shoes, he says, "Okay," and steps out onto the sand. "Come on." He reaches for my hand.

A millisecond of connection and understanding! *Is this what love feels like?* I find myself wondering. I can't help but notice that his baby hazels reflect the beach light with flecks of gold.

Tentatively, I take his hand and there's that electric-dog-collar surge again as we tromp across the sand toward the briny smell and cold spray of the water. I can only hear one word pulsing in my brain: *love, love, love.* In response, the voice in my head shouts back:

He reads your mind! Stop thinking of love, love, love*!*

Okay, brain says,

How about sex, sex, sex.

Shut up! my head voice screeches in reproach.

I force myself to sing the first Michael Jackson song that I can think of, silently, over and over, until I stop thinking about love and sex.

Because I'm bad, I'm bad, I'm bad, bad, bad . . .

"What's that you're humming?" Luke asks.

Ooh . . . *Shut up, brain voice!*

"Nothing," I say, but my brain keeps singing:

And the whole world's got me dancing like that . . . Who's bad? . . .

You don't have to be nervous, Jenna.

In another Twilight moment, I hear Luke's voice in my head interrupting my crazy and suddenly I do feel calmer, what with the water nipping at the tips of my boots, leaking through the cheap pleather to my toes. The rhythmic, hypnotic sound of thunderous waves breaks up my thoughts and pulls them away, like the waves sucking at the sand.

"Man," he says, sitting down and pulling in a deep, luxurious breath.

He holds out his arms as if he wants to give the ocean a big hug.

"That salty air!" he pronounces dramatically. "Don't you love it! I mean, just love it?"

"Well, yeah, I kinda like it." I shrug. "I live just up the block, but I don't come to the beach much 'cause I burn in the sun. And sometimes it's cold living near the seaside and in a storm our basement floods, which smells, and . . ." I ramble.

"Jenna." He ignores me and motions for me to sit down next to him, suddenly all intense. "I don't have much time to explain everything. And I'm not even sure I should be telling you anything. Well, actually, I'm kind of sure I shouldn't be telling you anything. It's really against the rules. I know he's not happy with me already. But it's kind of too late for secrets."

"Who's not happy with you?" I ask.

"The boss," Luke says.

"You mean . . . God," I whisper.

"No, not God exactly," Luke says. "That's not how the system works. Think army, with its chain of command. My boss is more like a . . . decorated field officer," Luke says. "You know what I mean?"

"Oh yeah," I lie. I totally am not sure what he means.

"I know you have a lot of questions," Luke continues, "but I'm in a rush because I've got a meeting with *him* soon to discuss issues, like"—Luke makes quote marks in the air with his fingers and gently rolls his eyes—"'matters of great spiritual importance for the future of the human race.' Plus, I've got an algebra quiz next period, so let's just move quickly through the obvious things you need to know."

"Okaaay." I hesitate.

And suddenly I'm nervous. Suddenly I don't want to be here. Suddenly I realize that once it's all actually said, then the crazy is out of the bag. And my life will change forever.

He leans in closer and looks piercingly into my eyes. I wonder if my breath smells. I wonder if he can see the two little blackheads on the right side of my nose or if he has noticed that I have two or three rogue eyebrow hairs that just won't flatten.

"The most important thing I wanted to say, that I wanted you to be sure of right now is that . . . Well, you know what I am by now, of course," he says.

I look down into my hands, which I'm anxiously fidgeting into "here's the steeple."

He leans in even closer. His awesome pine scent fills my head.

"Say it," he gently coaxes.

"You're incredibly fast," I say. "You're a great skater."

"Say it," he coaxes again.

"You like the beach . . ."

"Say it." He smirks.

"You're being pursued by a supernatural wolf-crow-guy. You have big wings. You vanish at will. You have big wings . . ."

"You said that part."

"Sorry."

"Just say it, Jenna," he says, starting to get exasperated.

"Angel," I say. "You're an angel."

"Good." He smiles and places his hand on my leg.

Places his hand on my leg!

Who cares about the angel part?! *On my leg!*

"Okay, so now we've gotten that out of the way." He lifts his hand. "Do you feel better now?"

"Not really," I say, my leg still tingling. "I feel weirder."

"But at least you know you're not crazy." He smiles.

"That's true," I concede. "But there's still a lot I don't know and there's plenty of time to feel crazy."

"Also," Luke says, looking all serious again, "and this is

important. I hope you know that Adam is, well, let's just say don't underestimate him. We have a history together in earth time and I know him pretty well."

I'm not quite sure what Luke means by "earth time" together, but before I have time to explore that further, somewhere in the distance, sounding dull and far away, the Arthur P. Rutherford late bell lets out a shrill *briiiiiinnnngg*.

Luke stands and brushes the sand from his jeans. He reaches his hand out to me and pulls me up. The air suddenly chills. Gray clouds wash over the sun. A great white, fat seagull with one blue eye and one green swoops down onto the nearby rickety lifeguard stand.

"Caw!" it screams angrily, seemingly at us.

Luke sighs deeply and kicks some sand into the loamy foam washing around our feet.

"Guess we better go," he says.

With that, the seagull takes off and swoops up and away and behind the dunes.

"Was that . . . your boss?" I ask reverently.

"No, just an officer in the chain of command," Luke says.

"He runs an infantry of seagulls? What's with you supernatural people and birds?"

Luke laughs.

"Cheap labor." He shrugs.

We return to the top of the beach. He pulls on his sneakers and we walk quickly back to school.

At Arthur P. Rutherford, packs of kids mill around the track and field, gather gym equipment, and head inside. I even spot Jared Needleman by the low chain-link fence. He pretends to be stretching, but he's really eyeballing the road. He catches sight of us.

"Needleman!" Coach Manley shouts. "Get some balls!"

Someone throws a ball right at him.

"*Oomph,*" he exclaims as it bounces off his chest. Then he pathetically chases it around the grass.

I stop Luke a few feet away from the school steps.

"There's still a lot I don't understand," I say.

"The less you know, the safer you'll be. Getting close to you would be selfish," he says, invading my personal space again.

Be selfish, be selfish! my head voice shouts.

"But I'm already involved," I say, wondering if he can actually hear my heart thumping. "I'm the keeper, remember? Whatever the hell that is. You know, the girl with the ruby slippers stuck around her neck."

I pat the pendant under my shirt. "With the psycho wicked witch on her tail."

"Locking the doors! Late bell's about to ring!" shouts Jared Needleman, eyeballing us suspiciously from the front door.

Luke hesitates. Another fat seagull swoops around, lands on a nearby garbage pail, and starts gnashing up a strand of pasta.

"Another one of the recruits?" I ask.

"Dunno," he says, squinting toward it. "I think that one really is a bird. But I have to go anyway."

Luke hesitates. "How about we meet up again later this afternoon? Where will you be?"

"It's the first rehearsal of *Fiddler* at the Old Vic Theater," I say. "I'm supposed to meet Lisa Golowski. I'm helping her with costumes. And didn't you promise Mr. Resnick that you were going to audition?"

"Ah! The theater!" he announces with a flourish. "I wouldn't miss that. I love the theater. And I've missed so much already. I'll be there and I'll tell you more."

Then he turns, bolts up the steps, and disappears through the doors.

16

After school, I'm determined to get to the Old Vic Theater early so Luke and I can meet up. I manage to slip away from my friends and make my way up Main Street. I stop in front of Maude's Chic Fashion Boutique. This is, hands down, the cutest store in town, where all the fashionistas shop. Mom refuses ever to go because, according to her, you can find more value at the Bulk. Besides, as she likes to say, "Expensive doesn't necessarily mean high quality."

Apparently the crap they sell at the Bulk meets her criteria for high quality because, unlike cashmere or wool, it lasts forever. I'm guessing that the Bulk clothes are made of some kind of titanium that prevents fading and stretching in the washing machine.

But I'm in a hurry and, after all, what's really the point of going in, so I'm just about to move on when I catch sight of Melanie, Amanda, Kara, and Emma coming around the side of a clothes carousel, talking, holding clothes up against themselves, and admiring one another.

Even through the glass, I can hear their muted chorus of: "OMG!"

"That is *soo* cute!"

"That would look *awe*some on you!"

Followed by outbursts of laughter:

"Ha-ha-ha!"

After a few minutes, it all blends into a cacophony of noises and letters and cackles which sounds like:

"OMG, *soo, awe.* Ha-ha-ha, OMG, soooo, awe. Ha-ha-ha, OMG, soooo, awe. Ha-ha-ha!"

And suddenly I feel as if I'm observing an animated living diorama exhibit at the Museum of Natural History, and their gibberish sounds like the primitive language of an ancient race of nincompoops.

I'm about to move on, when suddenly Sarah flounces from the dressing room. She's wearing a totally OMG, soooo awesome, ha-ha-ha outfit. She does a turn and all her fan girls practically faint from admiration.

She steps up to a full-length, three-sided mirror, which makes it look like there are hundreds of her that go on into infinity. Her expression is adoring as she cocks her head and pivots to admire the reflection of every single one of herself.

I can't help thinking back to when Sarah used to be my best friend, and how we did share some close moments and good laughs even though there were so many signs along the way that she was on the lookout for ways to trade me up: looking bored when we were together, starting conversations with other kids but not including me, being busy when I called and then not calling back, things like that.

And how, after she ditched me, it was only a matter of weeks before she ascended to Oceanville elite status.

Now, I can't pull my eyes away from all those Sarahs in the mirrors: long tan limbs, trim waists, flippy dirty-blond hair ironed straight, wearing the coolest outfit ever, and I wonder, *Where did I go wrong?*

And even though I know some people are born con-formists and can only be validated in the reflections of other people's envious gazes, for a millisecond, I long to be part of Sarah's beautiful infinite reflections. She really is OMG, soooo awesome ha-ha-ha. Would I feel perfect if I were part of her crowd?

Sarah looks up and catches my gaze through the window. I smile and, presumably forgetting herself for a moment, Sarah smiles back. Within seconds, however, her lips tighten, her expression turns into something I can't quite determine, and her eyes slide away from mine.

I can't help but feel that old pang of hurt again. But it's time for me to go. I console myself with the thought that I have more important things on my mind now, as I rush past Anderson Street onto the theater's property, past the pond, past the small buildings that dot the acreage, and up the cobblestone path to the theater.

Tires screech up behind me, nearly scaring me out of my wits. Bernice's car skids to a halt, idling only long enough for David to hop out.

"Hey Jenna, wait up!" he yells, trotting toward me.

Bernice waves goodbye, hits the accelerator hard, and speeds into the dwindling afternoon light.

"What are you doing here, David?" I ask.

"By the way, Bernice says thanks," he says.

"For what?"

"For keeping an eye on me," he says.

"What?!"

"She signed me up for the show."

"She wants me to babysit you during rehearsals?" I say, exasperated.

"Kid-sit," David corrects. "She'll pay you," he sings.

I start up the path to the theater and he trots after me.

"Actually my mom was really excited about my being in the play. She thinks I should channel my need for attention in a more productive way. That and she's busy taking this afternoon aerobics class called Shake Your Funky Groove. You ever see a bunch of porky suburban women in spandex trying to find their funky groove?"

David shudders.

"It isn't pretty. Anyway, the women didn't like me hopping around the back of the room imitating them. So here I am!" he exclaims.

"Fine." I harumph. "But you're going to have to behave. I'm here in a professional capacity."

"Yeah? What's that?" David asks skeptically.

"I'm a costume design intern," I announce proudly.

"Uh-huh . . ." David raises one eyebrow and gives me the once-over. "Is that why you're wearing a costume? What's the play called? *Bulk Emporium, the Musical*?"

"Shut up, David." I storm away from him and pull open the heavy outside door. David scurries in underneath my arm, probably afraid I'll lock him out.

At that moment, someone opens the lobby door and I'm jolted into the world of the theater: actors rehearsing onstage, the clanking of auditorium seats as extras await their scenes, stage crew jostling around, and the tang of greasepaint as stagehands put touches on Tevye's house, a large plywood structure that has been erected against the back of the stage.

The village people/chorus are rehearsing in a corner. I wave to Kayla and Bea and spot Tess's back at the piano practicing the songs. She grins and motions with her head over to Carlo, who is sitting nearby, cleaning out his tuba and smiling and nodding.

"How's it going, Carlo?" Tess shouts in his direction.

"Zip!" he responds enthusiastically, and then gives her a thumbs-up.

Tess thumbs-ups him back and shoots me a perplexed look.

Nearby, Sheldon tries to inject some life into Miss Manley's disturbingly awkward choreography moves (mostly box steps and jazz hands).

Luke is still nowhere to be seen.

"I hear they built a catwalk along the back of Tevye's house so that Mary Beth O'Churney can really sit up there and play the violin." David points to the stage. "'Cause she's the fiddler. Fiddler on the roof, get it?"

"Hmm . . ." I respond distractedly, and then head to the middle seats where I have a good vantage point on all that's going on, plus the lobby door. I deliberately plop my backpack and jacket on the seat next to me so David can't sit down.

"So are we gonna talk about what happened at the park or not?" David asks, moving my things over and sitting down next to me anyway.

"Not."

"I tried calling you *and* texting you *and* e-mailing you," he says.

"Really? I didn't get the messages."

My eyes dart away from him.

"You're gonna have to deal with it sometime." He shakes his head as if I'm the kid and he's the teenager.

"Not now, David. I'm still processing it," I say. "Luke and I are going to talk some more. He's meeting me here."

"Okay, but don't spend too long processing it," he says. "That psycho Adam wolf-crow guy is not gonna stay away forever."

Don't I know it, I think.

"And I hate to admit it," he says solemnly, "but I'm not sure exactly what my superhero powers are yet, other than extreme likability and athletic spryness, of course. But the more I know about my foe, aka Adam the psycho, the more I can protect the innocent."

"Mmhmm," I answer absently, checking the door to see if Luke has arrived yet.

"Anyway, do you want to know what part Mr. Resnick gave me?" David continues. "I'm in the chorus. I'm Boy #3."

"Boy #3?"

"It's a good part as far as anonymous boys with no talent go. I even have some bits."

He holds up his palm and pulls a couple of wrinkled pages from his backpack.

"Let's see," he says. "I get to laugh heartily in act 1, scene 3. I'm a rampaging Cossack in the wedding scene, and I actually have a line. Wait. I'll find it . . . I'm leaving the little town of Anatevka, and I'm holding a chicken and I say: *We're going to America.*"

He looks up at me expectantly.

"Nice," I say flatly, glancing at the door again.

"Although I was thinking of improvising here," David continues. "You ever hear that joke where a man goes into a restaurant and orders chicken soup? Then the waiter tells him that the pea soup is better. So the man changes his order, and the waiter goes into the kitchen and yells, 'Hold the chicken and make it pee!' Make it pea . . . pea soup . . . make it *pee.* Get it? It's funny, right? It's a really old joke, but it still has legs. Whaddaya think?"

I roll my eyes and glance to the door again.

"Um . . . I think you're being stood up," David offers.

"Shut up, David!"

"Ahem!"

Sarah Johnson glares down haughtily from the stage, where she is rehearsing the lead role, Tzeitel, Tevye's oldest daughter.

"Could all you *crew*"—she spews the word out like it's something foul on her tongue—"keep it down, please. The actors are trying to rehearse here."

"Tzeitel, I'm your father and I won't let you get with your boyfriend, Motel. You have to marry the old butcher," Walter Allevio says flatly, and then yawns.

"No, no, no!" Mr. Resnick comes striding down the aisle from the back of the auditorium.

"What are you saying? That isn't even a real line from the

play, Waldo! Besides, you have the motivation of wanting your daughter to marry the man you chose. *Feel* the guilt. The anxiety.

"Testing, testing. Crew! Can you hear me?"

There, of course, is Jared Needleman, playing stage manager, on the side of the stage, holding a clipboard and being authoritative into his headset.

"Crew! Why aren't you wearing your headphones?"

A whistle shrieks from Jared's headset, so loud that we can hear it in the seats. He yelps and snatches the headset off his head.

"Very funny, crew!" he barks.

This causes the techies, mostly smart-ass geeky boys wearing gangsta pants, to double over laughing, giving the rest of us a gross flash of their butt cracks.

Jared squints into the seats. I hunker down, but too late. Spotted. He adjusts his headset, proudly rests his clipboard on his chest, puffs himself up as if he's pledging allegiance to the flag, and waves at me.

"Hey, isn't that your boyfriend? The kid from up the block whose family owns the Frosted Pig bakery?" David asks.

"He's not my boyfriend," I snap.

"I'm not getting anything from Walter here, Mr. Resnick." Sarah rolls her eyes and sighs dramatically.

Mr. Resnick rushes up the side stage steps to Sarah and collapses on one knee.

"Now you have to plead to Tevye, your father, Sheila," Mr. Resnick pleads.

"Please, Daddy. Let me marry the man of my dreams, the poor but good-hearted tailor, Motel."

Silence.

"Good-hearted Motel," Mr. Resnick begs louder.

The actors on stage cough, sigh, and shuffle their feet.

"Wonderful, darling . . . Who knows his cue? *Motel!*" Mr. Resnick says through clenched teeth.

"Oh, me?" says Duncan, the boy playing Motel. "Is it my cue?"

Sarah moans in disgust.

"Doogie," Mr. Resnick addresses him, "you have to be passionate. You're here because you love Tzeitel, even though everyone around you thinks you're a bad match. That your love flies in the face of convention. Of tradition! But you're willing to break all the rules!"

Duncan shuffles toward Sarah and awkwardly places his hands on her shoulders.

"Um . . . Sarah, you're really hot and I love you," he says.

"It's Tzeitel! Tzeitel!" Mr. Resnick bellows. "What the devil are you saying? You have to speak the lines and then feel the torrent of not being able to be with her because her parents don't approve."

I glance back at the theater door. Still no Luke.

Tzeitel and Motel's romantic dilemma speaks to my heart. What if Luke likes me as much as I like him? What if Luke and I have an ill-fated love that defies not only the laws of the community, but also the laws of the natural universe, what with him being not a real person exactly, and all. And what if, like Tzeitel, who is expected to marry Lazar, the old town butcher, a man she doesn't love, I am expected to date Jared Needleman?

Reluctantly, I glance across the stage at Jared, authoritatively directing the stage crew.

"To the left! To the right! Lower. Lower the scenery, fellas. That's right. Slow!"

Jared, presumably sensing my eyes on him, turns proudly and nods in my direction.

The stage-crew elves exchange malevolent grins behind his back, and then release the pulleys, which release the unraveling backdrop, which hits Jared in the head and knocks him off his feet, engulfing him in yards of fabric. This sends the crew into gales of unbridled laughter. Jared, like a turtle on its back, struggles to stand up.

"Your boyfriend is smooth." David snorts.

"How many times do I have to tell you? He's not my boyfriend," I snap.

"Ugh . . . Hopeless! Hopeless!" Mr. Resnick shakes his head. "And Jerry, for pity's sake, get out from under the scenery. Community theater, good Lord!"

He strides dramatically into the spotlight, throws back his head, and shakes his fists at the rafters.

"Angels in heaven! I would sell my soul for a talented boy!" he bellows.

For a moment, all is still, as an eerie silence fills the theater.

Then:

There's a great whooshing of wings and great cawing screams.

A flock of black crows swoops down from the rafters and skims wildly across the stage and through the seats.

"Caw!" the birds scream.

"Ahhhh!" the people scream.

Everyone runs, shrieks, and ducks. Bedlam ensues as the birds circle and flap wildly.

"Good Lord, what now?" Mr. Resnick exclaims. "Jerry! Quickly! Open the front door and chase out these confounded birds!"

Jared flails around until he's extricated himself from the scenery. He runs, arms outstretched, flapping after the birds like some great boy bird himself.

"Shoo! Shoo! Shoo!" he shouts at the flock, all the while also shouting into his headset at his crew.

"Hey guys! Testing, testing! A little help here!"

David rocks with laughter.

"Your boyfriend is such a dumb-ass!"

Then the stage-crew elves race from the stage up the aisle and toward the lobby doors, waving their arms in the air, shrieking in high C like a gaggle of little girls, their pants slipping down, revealing more of their butt cracks.

And before I can even move, or tell David for the grillionth time that Jared is not my boyfriend, I hear Adam's voice, low, inside my head.

Watch out, I'm coming for you.

A great dark shape enshrouded in gray mist hovers high in the rafters. It has the vague form of a person, a person with large, black wings. The creature swoops down across our heads, laughing, dark and sinister. A heavy scent surrounds it, like a smoldering fireplace, like something burnt.

Reflexively, I clutch at the pendant around my neck.

"Go away, Adam," I say softly. "You can't hurt me."

"Yeah, you can't hurt us!" David shouts.

"Uh, David," I say. "You should probably stay out of this. This one is a little out of your league, no offense."

David holds up his palm.

"Don't worry. I've got it," he says.

He scrambles for his backpack and pulls out a few rocks.

"Here, take some," he says.

"What?" I say.

One by one, he pitches them at crow/Adam.

"Throw one!" he says.

"I . . . but my aim is terrible. I can't throw."

I take one in hand, pull back my arm, close my eyes, grunt, and toss.

"Ow!" I hear some kid yelp from under a seat about twenty feet to my left.

David continues to throw his rocks. He misses but he's close.

"Uh . . . David." I grab his arm nervously. "You don't want to make him mad."

"Take that!" he yells.

One of his rocks skims the crow's wing. In turn the crow yelps and swerves.

"Score!" David pumps his fist in the air.

Within seconds, crow/Adam swerves straight back toward us, vengeance in his beady birdy eyes.

"Uh . . . David." I gulp, reaching for his arm again.

"And of course, fleeing is a hero's only and best option sometimes too. There's no shame in it," says David.

"Let's go," I yell as we race up the aisle for the doors.

But before we can make it, the crow glides low. Its long, slender talon skims the top of David's head.

We hear Adam's voice: "A prick of blood."

"Oww!" David yelps. "I think it bit me!"

David touches his head and there's a small bit of blood on his fingers.

"Oh crap, rabies shots, here I come," David says.

Then, suddenly, he pales, and his expression turns strange, disoriented.

"What?" He turns to me.

"I didn't say anything," I say.

"Not you," David snaps.

"What?" he says to no one again.

Then, without warning, David turns and bolts toward the stage.

"Hey!" I grasp at the corner of his jacket, but he's already out of my reach. "David, get back here!"

The crow/Adam swings around and glides after David.

"Hey!" I scream after him. "Leave David alone!"

I look frantically for help. Luke is still nowhere to be found.

Mr. Resnick dashes up the aisle past me and into the lobby.

"Someone call 911! Take cover, theater elves!"

He swerves into the coatroom and slams the door shut.

Chaos ensues as the rest of the kids rush to the lobby or out the side exit doors.

David bolts up the side stage steps and onto the stage.

"Yes, master," he intones flatly.

"Don't talk to him, David!" I shriek. "Stranger danger! Just say no!"

I crouch-run up the aisle after him. The crow/Adam flaps to the top of Tevye's house and perches, staring out like a sentinel with ominous, glowing eyes.

"But master, I'm afraid," David says.

"David!" I yell, sliding around on bird poop and trying to keep my balance. "Stop! Be afraid! Be very afraid!"

Then the crow/Adam lifts its neck and expands its wings, growing to enormous proportions, casting two black shadows across the length of the stage.

"*Caw!*" it screams.

"Yes, yes, yes!" David shouts out exuberantly to the perched crow.

"No, no, no!" I shout.

I sprint up the side stage steps after him. But David has already disappeared behind the thick, tacky blue curtains, into the dark shadows of backstage.

17

Backstage, all is shadowy, dark, and quiet.

"David," I whisper. "Where are you?"

It's like another world, a haunted, timeless world of old pulleys, ropes, and gears that lead all the way up beyond the theater lights to the impossibly high catwalk. Almost every inch of floor is littered with dusty furniture, boxes of props, and racks of clothes from shows and eras gone by.

"David?" I whisper, creeping deeper into the shadows.

I can't bring myself to leave David at the mercy of this humanoid-type polymorphic thingie who has invaded our regular lives, and that I now know simply as *Adam*. But I have to fight my overwhelming cowardice and impulse for self-preservation, ditch David, and run for my life.

Disoriented, I bump against the CD player and activate it. Michael Jackson's "Bad" blares out.

Startled, I'm totally reeling all over the place, bumping into everything, causing all manner of props to crash onto the floor.

I'm desperate to calm myself, and force my mind to recall an article from a recent issue of *Teen Glamour* magazine, entitled "Ten Ways to a Cheerful Attitude: Letting Go of the Negative Feelings That Threaten to Ruin Your Look."

But while straining to yoga breathe, I spot Adam from the corner of my eye—in his human form, his mere presence heady and alluring in that dark way of his. One of his arms hangs stiffly at his side and there's a stain of blood on his brown jacket. I guess it's where David hit him with the rock when he was crow/Adam.

He grins at me.

"Hey there," he says.

"Hey there?" I snap. "That's what you have to say?"

Adam stops grinning and moves toward me. I back up until I'm flush against a pile of props.

"Where's Luke?" he asks.

I'm starting to tremble as a deep fear grips me.

"Afraid?" he asks. "I have that effect on a lot of people. It's cool, isn't it?"

"Luke's . . . coming . . . He should be here any minute," I say.

"Really." Adam leans in and flicks my hair. "I don't think so."

Then he turns, walks a few feet away, and turns back to face me.

"I think he's . . . at a meeting," Adam says. "Preoccupied. You know, with bigger, more cosmic responsibilities. He's like that. You'll find out. A good soldier."

Adam clicks his boots together and performs a mock salute.

"You like him, don't you?" Adam barks a laugh.

"You can't take the pendant," I say, my mind racing for

an escape route. My eyes dart around for a weapon of any kind. The only thing nearby is some sort of worn-out lace-up boot that looks like a prop from *Oliver!*

"No." Adam casually half sits on a pile of boxes. "But you can give it to me."

He tilts his head upward.

"Up here!" a small voice calls out.

David is on the catwalk.

Suddenly the CD plays Michael Jackson's "Thriller." And David breaks into his best imitation Michael-zombie dance. Except he's still in some kind of trance and stumbles and teeters out of control like a marionette whose puppeteer is mercilessly jerking the strings.

"David! Hang on!" I yell up to him.

"Yes, master!" He continues to dance, teetering dangerously close to the edge.

Another crow swoops across the rafters and lands on David's head.

"Shoo!" He flails wildly in an attempt to bat it away.

In the process, he teeters forward.

"Whoaa!" Adam mocks. "Hang on there, buddy. Wouldn't want to fall and crack open your head."

Adam touches his fingers to his wounded arm and levels a blank, malevolent look at me.

"I told him not to make an enemy of me," he says.

David leans way over the catwalk.

"*No!*" I scream.

The CD suddenly switches to Vincent Price's laugh. It plays over and over again:

Aha-ha-ha-ha-ha-ha-ha . . . Aha-ha-ha-ha-ha-ha . . .

"The pendant?" Adam casually holds out his hand.

What should I do? My mind races. Should I release Adam permanently into the world just to save one boy? A horrible, annoying, pesky boy at that? What should I do? What would Luke want me to do? What can I do to stop Adam even if I want to?

My hand rests on the pendant.

Adam jumps up, a gleam of expectation on his face.

"That's a good girl," he says.

Suddenly I realize I have David's rocks in my pocket. With the other hand, I pull one out.

Adam looks down and raises an eyebrow.

"Seriously?" he says. "You're kidding, right? You're gonna throw a rock at me? When I'm two feet away?"

"No," I say, looking defeated. "I'm not gonna throw it at you. I'm gonna throw it at him!"

And before Adam can respond, I pull back my arm, close my eyes, grunt, and mentally aim about ten feet to the left of David.

"Ow!"

Bull's-eye!

I open my eyes. I hit David right in the arm, rousing him from his trance.

"What the—" He grabs for his arm with his other hand. "Are you crazy? Whoa . . . What am I doing up here?"

At that moment, Jared rushes backstage.

"Jenna, are you all right?" he says. "Oh, hey, you're the guy I met in the bark park."

A rock lands at his feet, and he looks up.

"Whoa, David, what are you doing up there?"

"Climbing down," David says.

"Hey there, Jared," Adam says. "Nice theater you have here. One of the things I always loved about this world. And it's all a stage, right? Maybe I'll get involved. Are there roles available?"

"Um . . . Well, actually, you could talk to Mr. Resnick," Jared says. "I'm not sure all of the parts have been cast. He's in the closet right now, but I'm sure he'll be out shortly."

"Jared . . ." I say warningly.

Adam levels a dark expression my way. "Great. Well, toodles," he says. "Till next time."

Then he sashays out the backstage door.

Hesitantly, the three of us creep toward the stage. The birds are still circling and cawing, which now sounds disturbingly like laughter.

Jared, presumably sensing an opportunity to be heroic, rushes up the aisle to the lobby. David and I hurry after him. Jared reaches the front doors, props them open, and presses himself against them as all the crows escape out the door, past the misty pond, flying on until they become black dots and blend into the dusky afternoon sky.

"And stay out!" Jared declares, quickly shutting the door behind them.

Then he scuttles over to the coatroom and gently raps on the door.

"Er . . . Mr. Resnick?" he says, placing his face by the keyhole. "You can come out now. The birds are gone."

The door creaks open and Mr. Resnick pokes his head out; he's holding his handkerchief against his face.

"Are you sure?"

"I'm sure, Mr. Resnick," boasts Jared. He shoots me a proud glance and pulls himself up to his full height of five feet five. "I'm glad I solved *that* problem. Those birds could have been rabid. When I coproduced my father's cable show *Birds, They Do Give a Hoot*, I—"

"Yes, I have no doubt that you were invaluable, Jerry," Mr. Resnick interrupts, gingerly stepping out of the coatroom and poking his head out the front door, where the group of students are standing around on the lawn.

"All right, people!" He claps his hands. "Rehearsal isn't over. Let's try to collect ourselves, and . . . Eeeoooiii . . . What on earth?"

He places his hand on the doorknob, lifts it, and then examines the white-and-green smeared wiggles smooshed into his palm. With great disgust, he wipes them off with his handkerchief.

"Um . . . I think that's bird droppings, Mr. Resnick," Jared offers.

"Thank you for that enlightenment, Jerry," Mr. Resnick says sarcastically. "What would I do without you?"

"No need to thank me, Mr. Resnick." Jared blushes proudly. "I'm just doing my—"

Mr. Resnick rushes past Jared.

"Backstage elves, where are you?"

A few of them meekly rise up from under the seats.

"We need some paper towels, pronto. Steal them from

the restrooms and pass them around. No one leaves until every last bit of crow droppings is wiped away. And . . . you, costume elf." He looks at me.

"Me?"

"Tomorrow in class, remind me to call the exterminator. Thank God this ordeal is over," he says, zigzagging cautiously up the aisle in poop-avoidance mode.

Suddenly, a single spotlight beams onto the center of the stage and into the light steps Adam. Admittedly, he looks striking, having changed from whatever nondescript jeans and T-shirt he was wearing backstage into a sleek black outfit with, most prominently, his usual badass attitude. His presence has a bewitching effect on everyone; people gasp and stop short in their tracks.

"Oh no." I exhale slowly.

"You there, son!" Mr. Resnick calls out as he dashes up the side steps to the stage with Jared, David, and me at his heels. "Do I know you?"

"I'm here to audition." Adam smiles.

David and I exchange grimaces.

"Well, regrettably, you're too late. Our show is cast, but you do have a lot of stage presence for a teenager. It's really uncanny," Mr. Resnick says, looking a bit trancey.

Just then Sarah enters from stage right.

"Mr. Resnick, Duncan gave me this note—"

She catches sight and scent of Adam.

"Helloooo." She sashays over to him, and I can tell by her suddenly bedazzled expression that he's working his woodsy mind-bending spell on her as well.

"Do I know you?" she asks. "You seem so familiar."

"No . . . I would have remembered you," he says, his eyes clamping down on hers with an intensity that actually causes her to blush and take a step back.

Mr. Resnick rips open the note Sarah gave him and reads it aloud:

"Dear Mr. Resnick,

I'm sorry, but I can't do the role of Motel. I'm a scientist, not an actor. I don't like to sing or dance. I like helium. My mother is just going to have to accept that.

Best wishes,
Duncan."

"What?" Mr. Resnick exclaims. "Who's Duncan?"

"Doogie," I offer.

"What?" he exclaims again. "Where am I going to find another Motel?"

Adam clears his throat.

Mr. Resnick paces up and down the stage, careful to zigzag out of the way of bird poop.

"Do you know how many teachers I had to bribe and blackmail just to get some tone-deaf boys in the chorus?! I'm not even allowed in the teachers' lounge anymore!"

Adam clears his throat again.

"Do you know how hard it will be to find a boy who can sing and dance"—Mr. Resnick declares—"without looking like bad Elvis?! Do you?!"

"Umm . . . No. Not really. Hadn't thought of it, must be tough," we all murmur in unison.

"A good-looking boy with stage presence, who's a quick learner, with just the right amount of chaste sex appeal, like Zac Efron? Who can sing! In Oceanville?"

Adam clears his throat very loudly.

Finally, Mr. Resnick swings around to Adam.

"What am I saying? These bird-dropping vapors are clouding my judgment. I've just been presented with a divine intervention! You—"

"It's Adam, sir," Adam says.

"Adam," Mr. Resnick says, "you have all the qualities I'm looking for. Looks, *and* appeal. Plus you exude this intriguing aroma of earth. Has anyone ever told you that? No matter. Can you sing? Oh, who cares. You couldn't possibly be any worse than Doogie!"

"I've been told I can howl a tune," Adam says. He shoots me a sidelong wink.

"I'll say," remarks David under his breath.

"But, please. It's only fair that I audition," Adam says smoothly.

He clears his throat, walks upstage, and sings a cappella. His voice is perfect: melodic, rich, and smooth. He sings some sort of folk song, like from a previous century; it's about colonialists, patriots, loyalists, a fair maiden, and a simple soldier boy, and it's filled with refrains of "Hey, nonny, nonny."

When Adam's finished, you can hear a pin drop.

"The part is yours!" Mr. Resnick says, wiping a tear from the corner of his eye.

Oh no! I practically scream out loud. Crazy, evil, only human some of the time, Adam has somehow wheedled his way further into our lives, charming everyone in Oceanville and the little make-believe town of Anatevka.

This totally can't be good.

18

Every night that week I toss restlessly in my bed. So many questions. So much confusion.

Admittedly, BL (before Luke), life was uninteresting, but manageable. All I had to do was get through my day: talk to my friends, stay awake in school, make the best of cheap, unfashionable clothes, and try to get through the night without feeling too discouraged.

Now nothing is making sense anymore. Either I am one of the few people in the world, other than Bible people, who is communicating with an angel and a demon or I am a psycho on the way to the psycho ward.

Plus, I don't understand why Luke didn't show up at the theater when he said he would. Was Adam right? Did he have other, more important responsibilities? Am I expecting too much from him? Do I like him more than he likes me?

I know I have to find him. But according to the latest *Teen Glamour* anti-stalking article, "Ten Reasons Not to Pursue That Guy," boys don't like to be chased down. Rule #3 of the article says: *If a guy makes himself unavailable, breaks dates, avoids you three times in a row, or threatens you even once with a restraining order, try playing it cool. Take a scented bubble bath or scrub away dead heel skin with a loofah sponge instead.*

And worst of all, tomorrow is Saturday. I can't even casually turn my whole school schedule upside down to pretend to coincidentally bump into Luke. What if Sheldon is right and Luke is afraid to sparkle or glow or lose control of his wings or something? What if he doesn't even show up on Monday?

But there is no way that I can keep David from martyring himself (now that he's made a mortal enemy of Adam), fight evil, study for my science test, *and* be a costume design assistant all by myself.

———————

By the time the sun rose, I knew it was time for me to rise as well. I had to confront Luke with all my questions, and I knew just the place to find him.

So there I was, standing on the crunchy-shell floor of Cowboy Clems, surrounded by lunch-special-eating patrons and hearing a cacophony of buzzing sounds from the timer clocks. If the clock buzzed before you got your food, you got to eat for free.

"Sorry, Luke doesn't work on Saturdays," the bartender says, a slim, toned guy, staring blankly at some action movie on the TV with a look on his face that seems to say, *Gee, I could be a famous TV star if only I wasn't stuck as a bartender at the crummy Cowboy Clems.*

From the corner of my eye, I spy a business guy with pieces of salsa stuck to his chin furtively tapping the timer-clock hand forward with his finger when he thinks no one is looking.

"Oh, so Luke's not here?" I ask the bartender as he makes circular swipes around the glasses with a not-too-clean-looking grayish-white rag.

I'm disappointed. *A little help here,* I say to the universe under my breath.

"Any chance he'll be in tonight?" I fish.

"I think he hangs out all day at that other place," the bartender says.

"Other place? Where's that?"

"Hang on a minute," the bartender says.

"Hey." He sprints across the length of the bar toward clock-cheater guy's table. "No playing with the buzzer."

"Jeez." The bartender strolls back, rolling his eyes. "Some people will totally compromise their integrity for a chimichanga."

"Yeah, well, societal moral decay and all that . . . So, um, where did you say Luke hangs out?" I ask.

"I didn't." The bartender grins. "It's not really information for public consumption, if you know what I mean."

"It's all right," I say. "We're really good friends."

The bartender shoots me a skeptical look.

"Seriously," I say.

"Well, okay. You look harmless enough." He moves closer. "I heard him saying that on his days off, he likes to go to the junkyard."

"The junkyard?" I repeat.

"Yeah, on Newbury Street." He shrugs, squeaking the rag all the way down into the bottom of a glass. "Don't ask me why. I don't ask questions. I just listen. You can grab the bus from the corner. It's only a few miles. You could probably walk it . . . if you were in shape."

His eyes flick across my waist.

Nice.

"Okay, thanks. The junkyard, then." I nod and turn toward the door, feeling as if no one could ever say anything totally surprising anymore, while I check my pocket for bus fare.

19

About twenty minutes later, I disembark at the old town junkyard. I'm happy to be off the bus with its gray dirty-window mood, sunken-eyed passengers, and smells like someone's garlic breath vibe. I inhale deeply, fish out a little vial of hand sanitizer, squeeze a few drops onto my hands, and cross the street to my destination.

Dark, ominous-looking clouds move in from behind a line of low, squat gray buildings not far in the distance. It's the kind of moody fall day you want to somehow gently wrap in tissue paper and put in your drawer, knowing that it won't last because the deep freeze of winter is creeping up autumn's behind.

I've never actually been to the junkyard before, although I've seen it from a car window my whole life and never given it more than a glance. It always looks lonely and deserted, piled high with stacks of tires, pieces of metal, and other steel-looking stuff all in a precariously balanced disarray.

I'm wondering if this is such a great place to be all by myself, when the bus is coming back (which I forgot to ask), and whether or not I do actually have the stamina to walk home if I have to. Not to mention how soaked I will get if those storm clouds decide to open up. I think I hear the low sound of cawing crows in the distance but decide to ignore it. I zip my jacket up higher against the slow-building chill churning around me.

There isn't a soul in sight. Crap. Suddenly I'm embarrassed. That bartender was probably pulling my chain. He thought I was too dorky to be Luke's friend so he sent me to the junkyard. The junkyard! Oh, the metaphorical injustice!

I mentally kick myself for being stupid and turn to start that long walk home, when something catches my eye. In the distance, standing on top of a heap of rubber and plastic, bending down, scavenging, examining, discarding . . . is Luke!

"Luke!" I call out.

He lifts up his head and looks around.

"Luke!" I wave and head toward him. "It's me!"

He smiles and starts climbing down his junk mountain. *What on earth,* I wonder, *is he doing scavenging through this crap?*

"Wow," he says happily, wiping his hands on his jeans. "There's a lot of junk here."

I take a moment to process that remark.

"But look what I found."

He fishes in his pocket and pulls out some pieces of wood painted red and a screwy-looking twisted piece of metal.

"Nice." I smile halfheartedly.

"I bet you're wondering what I'm doing here," he says.

"Well, I was, um, in the neighborhood."

Teen Glamour magazine anti-stalking article rule #5: *If you get caught stalking that hot boy around town, pretend you were just in the neighborhood.*

"You were in this neighborhood?" he asks. "Why?"

"I . . . um . . . I dunno . . ."

"Oh," he says, and shoves his hands down low into his pockets. He nods. One blondish hair dangles sexily over one of his hazel eyes.

We stand awkwardly like that for what seems like forever. A dog barks and a motorcycle engine revs somewhere in the distance. The sun winks behind the clouds blowing across it.

"You didn't come to rehearsal," I blurt out.

"I know," he says, pushing the hair out of his face and looking off to the side. His expression changes to a combination of far away and guilt.

"Had a little incident with Adam. Of the murderous kind. Thought you'd be there," I say.

Luke looks down and kicks a piece of junk with the toe of his shoe. The awkward silence continues. This isn't going well, and I suddenly lose my nerve.

"Okay, well then . . ." I retreat. "I guess I'll go wait for the bus. See you. Have fun with your . . . junk."

I turn to go.

"Jenna, wait," he says, gently grabbing my arm. "I know I said I'd come to the theater, and we could talk some more about my . . . well . . . situation. And I didn't. I'm sorry. I guess I owe you an explanation."

"No, you don't. You don't owe me anything," I lie, wondering, *What is it about elusive boys that's so appealing?*

"You're lying." He grins.

"Are you using your supernatural brain-waves thingie to read my mind again?" I ask.

"No," he says, with a mirthful expression. "It's just that you're a terrible liar."

Then another zillion awkward minutes pass, as he kicks around some pebbles with the toe of his sneaker and my eyes dart all over the place.

"So," I finally say, "if you want to hang out, now would be a good time, I guess, 'cause I'll have to go soon. I have homework and the communists are making lunch and I have this science project that's not due until Wednesday but I'd like to get a jump on it and—"

"Come on." He interrupts my rambling. "Let's sit down."

"Oookay." I look around. "Where?"

He leads me over to a bunch of tires, piles a few on top of one another and fashions me a little seat. He pats it and gestures for me to sit.

"Oh, nice," I say, trying to sound convincing.

"Mind if I keep scavenging while we talk?" Luke says, as he picks up something that looks half eaten and puts it in his backpack.

"There's so much here!" He spreads his arms wide. "It's hard to believe that people think this is junk!"

"Pfuaaah." I exhale, and nod my head in disbelief. "People. They have no sense!" I say, trying to be agreeable. "I know exactly what you mean."

"Do you really know what I mean?" Luke turns to me, excited.

"Well, yeah! I mean, just look at this place. It's, ah . . . ya know . . . There's all this pointy metal and dirty rubber, um . . ." I look at my palm, which is totally black from resting against the skeevy tire.

"No. I'm sorry." I sigh. "I have no idea what you mean."

Luke laughs.

"That's okay." He pulls up an old broken kitchen chair and sits down next to me.

"I just get excited about things. You've probably noticed . . ."

He looks off into the distance for a few moments.

"Do you ever feel like you don't fit in? Like anywhere . . ."

Is he kidding or what?

He looks back at me. His gaze is innocent. He's not joking.

Like, duh, always! says the voice in my head.

But I compose myself and say coolly,

"Occasionally."

A few cold drops of rain pelt my skin. I can only imagine how mucky the junkyard actually gets when water loosens up all the dirt and turns it into a thin muddy slosh.

"'Cause I feel like I don't belong anywhere," he says with great earnestness. "I mean, I had a life once but it didn't last. Then I was chosen for 'celestial being,'" he says with mock seriousness, making quotation marks in the air. "Now that I'm back in life, all I can think about is how much I missed. It's amazing being a human kid again, ya know? But it's kind of lonely too."

Luke feels like an outsider! His heartfelt admission excites me, like he's a kindred spirit. It never occurred to me that someone as perfect as Luke, someone supernatural even, could feel the way I do!

"You mean feeling you're different from everyone else?" I turn to him excitedly. "Like your family are strangers from another gene pool. And everyone in Oceanville, except for maybe a few people, seems conformist and robotic with no real dreams of being special, and you wonder, is it me that's weird or everyone else?"

"Mmm . . . no," he says. "I was thinking I feel different because I lived during the Revolutionary War, in Oceanville, died, became an angel, and now I'm a person again."

An embarrassed blush crawls up my cheeks.

"Oh. Well, that could be weird too, I guess."

I turn my ahead away from him and look down the deserted street. The wind picks up as does the light drizzle, and the sky darkens slightly to a bruised gray blue. I silently wish that the hole in the tire seat will suck me in. When it doesn't, I say, "We should go." I try to extricate my butt from the tire seat.

"Oh." He hesitates. "I didn't mean to make it seem like your troubles are insignificant or anything."

"No worries," I say, still trying to wiggle myself free. Damn this tire seat! It was like some kind of bottomless suction vortex.

"No really." He backpedals. "I can imagine that it's hard to feel sort of like an outsider in your own life."

"Seriously," I say. "Being supernatural and undead trumps being an unfulfilled middle school misanthrope."

"Well, yeah." He smiles.

I stop wiggling and sigh in despair. This tire is not letting me go.

"Listen, could you help me out of here?"

Luke's laugh is tender. He grabs my hand, and pulls until I pop out of the tire vortex with an embarrassing suction sound. I hop out, bumping into him.

We're standing close, and then he does an incredible thing. He reaches over, gently lifts a strand of my windblown hair, and tucks it behind my ear!

A few quiet seconds pass, then I sense his awkwardness. He pulls back, turns around, and starts scavenging through the junk again. He stops, picks up a colored piece of glass and holds it to the light like a prism. Colors flash as he turns it. His face lights up. He's like a boy who's found a treasure in a glinty garden rock, and he places the glass gently into his backpack.

"So you want to know why I didn't come by rehearsal the other day?" he asks, still digging for treasures in the grime.

"Um, yeah," I say. "Especially since David and I were left fending off Adam alone."

"I knew that Adam couldn't touch you with the pendant on," he says. "I didn't know David was gonna jump into the act, though. The thing is . . . You know that boss I was talking about the other day at the beach?"

"Yeah," I respond.

"Well, he kind of runs my life, or death, or celestial incarnation, or whatever you want to call it. I mean he's a nice guy and everything, but he's like a father. Like an authority figure. I kind of have to listen to him. You know, probably like your father."

I think of iPod Dad. Plugged in. Tuned out.

"Em, not really. But isn't he the one who sent you here to bring Adam back before the equinox door closes or something?"

"Well, yeah," Luke says, continuing to collect little pieces of glass, wire, and wood. "But there's always a bigger picture. He's got a make-love-not-war kind of philosophy. He thinks that whatever happens will happen eventually anyway. Sometimes I'm not sure I agree, but I don't want to irritate him, ya know." Luke says it uncertainly, as if he's trying to convince himself.

"But that's what teenagers kind of do," I say. "Irritate and embarrass their parents. Except in my case, where they kind of irritate and embarrass me."

"You see, I have to be the one to work this out with Adam because, as I've said, we have a history together. When we were human. Well, I was human.

"Anyway . . . long story." He switches to a cheery tone, as if he's trying to change the subject. "I bet you didn't know that I knew some of your ancestors too, in the 1700s. Your great-great-great-bunch-of-great ancestors were the original keepers of the pendant."

He picks up a broken hanger and points it at my chest.

"Plus, there are some other people in town now whose ancestors were here during that time."

"Really, like who?" Now I'm curious.

"Oh, like David Lipski for one," he says casually. "And,

um, Sarah Johnson," he half mumbles, his eyes darting away from mine.

"Sarah Johnson!" I exclaim. "No way . . . How do you know? You don't even know Sarah that well."

Suddenly I remember something that Adam said in the park. About a blonde that Luke used to hang with. About a cute blonde . . . Ugh! Could it be?

"Wait a minute. Did you date Sarah Johnson's ancestor?" I ask.

Luke shrugs.

"A few times," he admits. "But it was not a big deal. I eventually saw that she was just like Sarah. Self-centered. Kind of nasty. Especially to you?" he fishes gingerly.

"And just how do you know that?" I ask, suddenly feeling embarrassed and touchy about it. "More mind reading?" I snap harder than I intend to.

Luke turns and looks at me earnestly, as if he's reading my expression.

"More like being perceptive." He taps a finger against his head. "You wanna talk about it? Angels are better than therapists. And cheaper."

I hesitate. If I tell him, will he think I'm a loser? But I want to tell him, so I take a deep breath and I spill: the story of the fro-yo dis.

And true to his word, he really does listen, not only to my words but also to my feelings. When I'm done, he waits a few beats, spies a marble, picks it up, and holds it in front of us. The colors are foggy but swirly and the marble is chipped.

"Perfect," he says, and places it in his pocket.

"Listen, Jenna," he finally says. "You need to let all that hurt stuff go. Bad feelings, resentments, feeling cheated, living in the past, all that stuff. It poisons your life. At least that's what Deets says."

"Deets? Your boss at Cowboy Clems?"

He nods, and a few more minutes pass in silence, but they're not awkward anymore, they're comfortable. It feels like we're friends now, not having to fill up every second with chatter.

Then Luke stands tall and exuberantly spreads his arms out wide.

"God, I love the junkyard!" he exclaims. "But I bet you really want to know why I'm hoarding all these little pieces of junk."

"The question has crossed my mind," I say.

"Well, it's really because I love Outsider Art," he announces with passion. "You've heard of it, right? Tramp art, folk art? Mixed media, made from found objects? I use this stuff to make sculptures, pictures, and jewelry."

At that moment, the sky finally opens up. All those innocent tiny droplets morph into big, cold wet splats, quickly picking up speed and momentum. The wind swirls, causing the slanting rain to hit us like tiny bullets.

Along with the rain comes a dark V shape moving ominously across the sky. It's a formation of crows. Their caws fill the air.

"Come on!" Luke urges, and in one swift movement, he grabs his backpack, throws his arm around me, and practically lifts me off the junk mound and then rushes us toward the exit of the yard. With a look of concentration, he stares up the block and, within seconds, the Main Street bus wheezes its way around the corner.

"Did you just will the bus to come?" I ask.

"It was coming anyway. Maybe I just willed it to come a little faster," he says.

The bus squeals to a halt and the doors grind open.

Then Luke turns full toward me and looks down into my face. He smooths his shiny, wet hair over his head with the palm of his hand. He swipes the rain from his eyes and cheeks and smiles. But whereas he looks damp, romantic, and cute, I can only imagine what I look like to him: my hair plastered to my head and face, water dripping into my eyes, mascara running down my cheeks. I try to discreetly swipe at the clear snot that drips from my cold, red nose onto my lips. Ugh.

The crows overhead are cawing more loudly now, and Luke's face looks taut with concern. One fat blue-eyed, brown-eyed seagull screeches down out of the grayness and lands on the bus stop sign.

It looks at Luke.

Clickety, click, click, clickety . . . Screech!

Luke purses his lips and sighs. He pushes a loose strand of hair back behind his ear.

"I have to go." He turns to me.

I look at the bird. It's chewing on its toe.

"Seriously?" I say. "You're kidding, right?"

"I wish I was." Luke shrugs.

I glare into the bird's marble eyes. The bird glares back.

"Screech!" he announces, and then he dramatically whooshes back through the rain and fog.

"Kinda now," Luke says, almost apologetically.

I want to ask Luke for his cell phone number, if he even has a cell phone. But we are truly getting soaked to the bone. I glance at the idling bus and I can practically feel the impatient stares of the passengers boring into us through the smeared, mucky windows. The bus driver clears his throat impatiently.

"So, will I see you at the next *Fiddler* rehear—" I start to say.

But before I can even finish that sentence, Luke gently pushes back my wet hair from my face and leans in toward me. Then, before I can think *Holy mother of crap, he's gonna kiss me!* I feel his arm tighten around my waist and he pulls me toward him until I am squished against his hard chest. Then he leans over in what feels like slow-mo.

My mind races to remember a recent article I read in *Teen Glamour* magazine entitled "Ten Don'ts for the First Kiss":

1. Don't lick your lips.
2. Don't pucker.
3. Don't make a smacking sound.
4. Don't giggle . . . Gah, if only I could remember 5 through 10!

I make a snap decision to improvise, close my eyes, and tilt my head up. I feel the heat of his soft breath on my face. He plants one on me! Smack on the lips, no less! And the pressure of his mouth on mine feels a little tickly and his breath is sweet and then his lips are gently moving around mine (but not in a gross way!) and my mouth, which seems to have a mind of its own, is responding in turn. And it's like some perfectly synchronized mouth waltz.

Plus, my whole body feels kind of warm and swoony, like on the cover of one of those bodice-ripper drugstore romances where a woman dressed in an off-the-shoulder red velvet *Gone With the Wind* dress is arched against some guy with Edward's pale angular beauty and dark wavy hair and Jacob's remarkably muscular torso. And the guy's whole faux rapturous expression says, *I want you now!*

And the woman's expression and body language say, *No, yes, no, yes, no . . . well, okay . . .*

Then Luke softly pulls away. The rain has soaked us through, but I don't feel wet or cold. We smile shyly at each other and I'm kind of dazed.

Just then, some gangly teenager from inside the bus yells, "Hey, Romeo and Juliet, I'm in a hurry here!"

And then the bus driver says, "Let's go, kids. I've got a schedule to keep."

And before I know it, I'm turning around and stepping up onto the encrusted rubber-matted steps and chinkling some change into the coin-deposit slot.

"Jenna," Luke says. "I'm sorry."

"For what?" I ask, turning back to face him.

"For getting you so involved."

"Wait, but I want—"

The doors slam shut, the bus jerks, and I stumble into a seat. The driver steps on the gas, and we lurch forward. I glance out the smeared double-paned gray window to catch one more look at my supernatural beloved . . . but he is gone.

20

For the rest of the day, I feel floaty and tingly and I know that I'm probably wearing a dumb smile on my face. I try to remember that Luke is "under orders" and could disappear at any moment, but I still can't help thinking about our kiss.

At dinner, I see my family through a misty gaze of affection and they, in turn, seem mildly perplexed by me. Even Michael, with his Neanderthal instincts, seems to sense my elevated spirituality, which prompts him to tenderly inquire (while shoving copious amounts of food into his gullet), "What the hell's wrong with you?"

Communist Mom smiles. "Someone's in a good mood today."

"I bet I know why," teases Michael.

"Oh really, why?" asks Mom.

"'Cause she went to the beach with that cowpoke-waiter guy," he says.

I almost gag on my drink.

"What?" says Mom. "When was this?"

"It was sometime the other day," Michael says.

"Michael," I warn.

He grins, shrugs, and keeps eating.

"I was walking the track and I saw you making your way

toward the beach. What? It's boring here. Just adding a little conversation."

"Not during the school day, I hope," Mom says.

Presumably sensing a change in the atmosphere, iPod-Dad looks up to lip-read.

"I had a free period," I lie. "What's so terrible about that?"

"I don't know if I like you going to the beach with strange boys," Mom says. "I'm not sure that it's . . . safe."

"You're kidding, right?" I respond. "You and I have met, right? It's not like this is an everyday thing, me running off to the beach with boys."

"He's not from the neighborhood, and we don't know him. And I don't know that I care for him."

"You just said you don't know him," I counter.

"Well, I'm very intuitive about people. There's something . . . strange about him. I can't put my finger on it. Don't you agree, Daddy?"

I glare at Dad, who nods his head in a type of noncommittal circular motion, presumably hedging his bets.

"Besides, what would Jared say?" she asks.

"Um . . . so what," I say.

"Well, he's practically your boyfriend, that's so what," she says.

Michael barks a laugh.

"Excuse me, but no he isn't," I say.

Mom shrugs.

"Sometimes we don't see that what's right for us is right under our noses." She smiles, scolding me with her fork for emphasis.

We follow her glance over to Dad, who has resumed ignoring us and is busy picking food out of his teeth.

"Besides," Mom continues, "that waiter boy is too good-looking. It's suspicious."

"Thanks," I retort sarcastically.

"Oh I don't mean that you're not attractive. I just mean that it's not . . . normal. Last week I saw a movie on the women's channel about an extremely good-looking man who deceived this nice, regular girl by pretending to love her. Then he tried to kill her by stranding her in a deserted cabin with snakes and ran off with her money *and* her best friend. But he didn't know that she had been a Navy SEAL and knew Krav Maga, a type of martial arts used by Israeli defense experts, so she chased him down and kicked his behind."

"I don't have any money to steal," I say. "I'm fourteen."

"Well, it was a very good movie," she says conclusively. "Speaking of movies, why don't we all go this weekend? I haven't been out to a movie theater in months and . . ."

At this point, I sense a change in topic. I shoot Michael a very dirty look, and barely listen as they swap pedestrian stories about their lives: the triumphs and defeats of Michael's football practice, Dad's nod to questions about gossip at his office, and Mom's observations from her part-time job as front-desk woman for Dr. Blechman, Long Island's first holistic veterinarian practitioner.

"Holistic, shmolistic," Mom says. "Spending good money on acupuncture and vitamins for a dog so he can turn around and drink from the toilet bowl?"

For the rest of the evening, I try to concentrate on homework. (Does anyone really understand what a participle is and/or care that it's past?) But mostly I'm on the phone with Tess going over every little detail of my junkyard rendezvous and subsequent kiss, to which she responds with exclamations like:

"Oh my God, that is hot."

"What will you wear when you see him next?"

Plus:

"I bet Carlo is a really hot kisser too. He's puckering his lips into that tuba all day, after all."

Of course, I do not disclose the minor details of Luke's nonhuman, reincarnated, celestialness because I don't want to overload Tess with too much unbelievable information in one phone call.

By morning, once my head is clear, I decide that there might be a way to do some research into Luke's past and get a few questions answered on my own. Since I have yet another babysitting gig with David, I figure I'll kill two birds with one stone and just drag him along.

Bernice volunteers to drive us wherever we want to go, but true to form, we're not more than two miles from our block when she says:

"I'm going to drop you kids off at the corner. I have to be at the other end of town in ten minutes and all those downtown lights hold me up."

I can't help wondering why the lights would hold her up since she never stops for any of them, plus the fact that Oceanville is not exactly a bustling metropolis.

"I understand, Mrs. Lipski," I say. "But it looks like it's starting to rain and—"

However, before I can even finish my sentence, she's back on her cell phone and screeching over to the curb, or I should say, halfway *onto* the curb.

I hear the *click* of the automatic doors unlocking.

"Bye, kids. Have fun." She finger-wiggle waves into the rearview mirror.

We disembark and she zooms off.

On account of the rain, the town is pretty much empty, gray and desolate. I see our shadowy reflections in every dark store window we pass. There's that faint woodsy, musty scent of Adam in the air. I feel a tingle of foreboding, like somehow David and I are in danger, but I'm determined to get to the library to do some research on Oceanville and its residents before and during the 1700s.

"Okay, what gives?" asks David. "Where are we going anyway? I have a *Fiddler on the Roof* rehearsal later. It's a big day for Boy #3. I think Resnick is going to give me another line. Did I tell you that last week he added 'Oy' to my line *We're going to America*? So now it's *Oy, we're going to America*."

"That's thrilling, David," I respond, shuffling him along in front of me and quickening my pace.

"He didn't like the chicken joke, though. You know, hold the chicken and make it pee. He said it was vulgar. But I might just slip it in anyway. I mean what's he gonna do once the show starts? He can't stop me from improvising.

"Hmm . . ." He continues to ponder. "Maybe I could turn

Boy #3 into a real character. I could give him a song, character motivation, a love interest—"

"That's great, David," I say distractedly.

"That's great? Man, you really are in another world today, aren't you? And you're nervous too. Why do you keep looking all over the place?"

"I just wish that Bernice had actually dropped us off at the library instead of here on the deserted street," I say. "Where did she have to go in such a hurry anyway?"

"It's aerobics day," David says. "Could we slow down a little? I'm getting tired of jogging down Main Street."

"Hmm . . . ," I answer, looking around furtively. Every movement looks suspicious, every noise sounds like danger. I can't help but wonder what tactic Adam might come up with this time to try to get the pendant from me.

I hurry David across the road.

"Another aerobics class?" I say. "Shake Your Funky Groove?"

"No, Shake Your Funky Groove is on Mondays and Wednesdays," David says. "On Sundays, it's Shake That Funky Thang. STFT is way grosser than SYFG. A lot of butt work. It's especially disturbing for a kid sitting in the back of the room, if you get my drift."

"Hmm . . . butt work, yeah," I mutter.

A flock of large crows *caw* overhead, causing my heart to beat faster. Just another two blocks, I remind myself, and then we'll be at the library, inside the library, surrounded by the safety of other people.

"Really, what's the matter with you today, anyway?" David asks. "You're so jumpy."

He pokes me in the middle of my back and I jump twenty feet in the air.

"I'm not jumpy!!" I scream, turning on him with burning eyes. "And poke me again and I'll twist your finger off."

"Okay, okay, you're not jumpy," he says, backing away, palms up. "Sheesh."

That's when I feel a presence. I turn but no one is there. I keep walking, but then I hear the door to Crumbles Bake Shoppe bang closed and the little atonal doorbells jingle. Behind us, I hear footsteps. I grab the corner of David's windbreaker and pull him along.

"Let's go," I say.

The footsteps follow. The street is completely deserted now. A dreary bleakness covers everything, as if every drop of color has washed away with the rain. A strange sticky-sweet smell hangs in the air and wafts toward us. There's another loud *caw* as more crows dip and swerve overhead. And the footsteps behind us quicken.

"Come on," I whisper breathlessly to David.

He tries to turn around.

"You're not still afraid of that Adam guy, are you? 'Cause I've been working on my superpowers. Not only am I agile and spry but I think now I can add *crafty* to my list of abilities. I'm a pretty smart kid. I can outthink a bad guy." He nods knowingly.

"That's great, David," I whisper hoarsely, pulling him along.

"Jeez, Jenna, where are we—"

"Shhh!"

We turn the corner off Main Street onto a short block of creepy houses. Shutters are drawn for a rainy, lazy Sunday morning. Would anyone hear us if we screamed? The footsteps behind us break into a trot.

David and I break into a trot as well, as David informs me that, even for superheroes, sometimes the best action is retreat. Ahead, I see the library, also disturbingly desolate, the white panels glowing in the low, dense fog.

"Come on, David!" I urge. "We're almost there!"

"Jenna, Jenna," the voice behind us moans, but I don't stop.

The corner church bells chime for services, drowning out the repetitive call of the voice behind us. Meanwhile, sweat gathers under my arms and in the folds of my waist. Only 100 percent cotton really breathes, but communist Mom buys mostly polyester blends.

The sound of my beating heart matches the pounding of my faux fashion clogs hitting the sidewalk over and over in syncopated rhythm. Then we're full-out running, and David is grabbing at my jacket.

"Jenna! Jenna! Stop!"

I can't tell the difference between the pounding of my shoes and the pounding of my heart. I sprint past the rosebushes that line the slate path to the library and up the steps. I give the large door handles a serious yank, but they don't budge.

"Wha—" Panic washes over me.

"It's not open! It doesn't open until noon on Sundays," David says, pointing to the placard by the door.

The footsteps pound up the stairs behind us. I grab David and hug him to me.

"Don't look, little David. It will be better that way."

"Fmmmmmaraphff," David responds, his face buried in my jacket.

I hoist David into the rosebushes.

"Hey, wait! Ow!" he yells.

I turn to face my assailant!

21

"Stand back, unearthly beast! Don't try to harm us!" I shout.

"Er, wait. What?"

Before me is none other than Jared Needleman, casually eating a sticky bun.

"Jared! What are you doing?!" I exclaim.

"I . . ." Jared turns a deep shade of pink and lowers his head. "Please don't tell my mother."

"Tell your mother what?"

"About me going into Crumbles Bake Shoppe."

He leans toward me, spraying me with bits of food. "That our bakery, the Frosted Pig, doesn't really make the best sticky buns. Crumbles does."

"Sticky buns? What the hell are you talking about?"

"What are *you* talking about?" he asks. "You called me an unearthly beast. I thought you meant because I was eating a sticky bun from . . . them . . ."

He holds the bun aloft.

"I don't care if you eat sticky buns," I say.

"Well I don't want to 'harm' you." He makes quotation marks in the air with his fingers. "You're my girl . . . neighbor!"

I hear David snickering from the rosebushes.

"I thought you were mad at me because Crumbles Bake Shoppe is the Frosted Pig's main competitor. I'm not supposed to go to Crumbles, but I believe that a successful business owner should do research, don't you agree?" Jared says. He shrinks. "But you won't tell my mother, right?"

"I don't think Jenna cares that much about your buns, sticky or otherwise, dude," David says, climbing from the rosebushes, plucking thorns from his jacket.

Jared exhales a sigh of relief.

"Why were you chasing us like that anyway, Jared?" I ask. "You scared me half to death."

"I wasn't chasing you. Didn't you hear me calling?"

"She heard you. She's just a little jumpy is all," David says, slowly aiming his finger into my back.

I glower at him.

"I mean not jumpy. She's not jumpy. Not at all." David steps back, palms up defensively.

"So why were you running like that?" Jared asks, popping the last of his bun into his mouth.

"I wanted to get to the library," I say.

"Wow. I've never seen anyone so frantic to get to the library before," Jared says.

I check my watch. 10:55. The deserted street is still making me uncomfortable.

"I have to do research."

I brush past Jared and David and head back down the library steps.

Suddenly, and much to my relief, a line of cars turns

down the side street and into the corner church parking lot. Congregants start making their way into the church.

"Research? What kind of research?" Jared asks, trotting after me. "Maybe I could help."

"Well, if you must know," I say, realizing that there is no way I am going to get rid of him until I answer his question, "I'm doing research about the history of our town, the Revolutionary War period, to be exact. So unless you're an expert on that, Jared, I don't think you can help me. Come on, David, I'll get you a Crumbles donut while we're waiting for the library to open."

"Wait a second," Jared says, jumping into my path. "It just so happens that I know quite a bit about the history of our town."

"This is serious, Jared. I don't have time to play games," I say, maneuvering around him.

"No really. I swear. Down at the cable station—"

Both David and I groan loudly and keep walking.

"Give it up," David says. "You can't help us."

"As a matter of fact, Mr. Smarty-Pants," Jared says, "not only do I know about Oceanville during the American Revolution, but also, I happen to know something about Jenna's ancestors."

I stop in my tracks.

"Really? Because this is important to me," I say, trying to look as serious as I can.

Jared blushes and smiles and I realize that perhaps I'm just a tad too close and my serious face is somehow being interpreted as a flirting face. I take two steps back and frown.

"Well," says Jared, "we made copies of all the Oceanville records from the town hall. I'll tell you what . . ."

He takes two steps toward me and, in what I'm supposing is his suave voice, says, "Why don't we stop by the Pig."

David snorts.

Jared continues, "Pick up some fresh-from-the-oven popovers, then we can 'pop over' to the cable station, you can get the stuff you need, 'pop over' to David's house, drop him off, then you and I can 'pop over' to my place, get comfy, watch a video, talk, and, ya know, get to know each other . . ."

Jared winks.

David and I exchange looks. I open my mouth to object, when suddenly David steps between Jared and me.

"Let me handle this, Jenna," he says authoritatively. "How about the three of us"—David gestures a little circle with his finger—"go to the cable station so Jenna can get the stuff she needs. No pastry, no popovers, fresh from the oven or otherwise, no sticky buns or sticky fingers involved, got it, Jared?"

David pokes his finger into Jared's chest.

"Well . . . I . . ." Jared frowns and steps back. "We can do that, I suppose."

Jared turns and starts walking up the street.

I smile big at little David.

"Why, David," I say. "That was very chivalrous of you!"

And then, David, spawn of the devil himself, actually averts his eyes and looks, well, vulnerable and tender like a small boy who's proud of the lopsided clay bowl he's given his mother for Mother's Day.

I reach out and tousle his hair.

We walk in silence for a few moments as we make our way to the cable station, and I notice that the sky finally looks as if it's beginning to clear.

22

We weave through the streets of town for about another fifteen minutes. David is happy, not only because he's missing another one of those Shake That Funky Thang aerobics classes, but because he's also missing his mother's mani-pedi appointment, which he animatedly describes as a gaggy, ugly-feet, toenail-clipping nightmare.

Finally we reach the "cable station," which I see is really one of those shacks on the sprawling property of the Old Vic Theater. It's a small, brown-shingled one-room structure, almost like a detached garage. It's not much to look at, but the coat of white paint around the door and windows makes the place look a little cheery, plus there are potted mums and a scratchy brown welcome mat laid in front of the door.

"Half of these buildings are empty, so we decided to rent one out," says Jared, as he unlocks the door and we enter the shack. "My mom bought the mums to make it homey."

"Eeooii, what's that smell?" David exclaims. He pinches his nose.

"Sorry," Jared says and scurries over to the garbage, pulls out a big full green bag and carries it past us out the door. "Wasn't expecting company. A couple of nights ago, me and the cable crew had Chinese food."

I look around. The place is small inside too, and scattered with dirty paper cups and plates, cobwebs in the corners, plus a variety of computers, cables, cameras, and equipment.

"This is where the magic happens!" Jared exclaims. "I know it's a bit messy."

He opens a few garbage bags and starts shoveling crap into them.

"You mean it's a place for you guys to make cheap cable shows?" David says.

"David," I scold, feeling defensive of Jared. "Stop being such a brat."

"Yeah, you better cut it out." Jared slants his eyes at David.

"Or what?" David challenges.

Jared glares at David for a good ten seconds, then he takes out his cell phone and pretends to talk into it.

"What's that, Mrs. Lipski, you're having your mani-pedi appointment? And you want us to drop David by the nail salon? Oh . . . What, you're having a bikini wax too?"

David tries to snatch Jared's phone, but Jared pulls it out of reach.

"Will you two stop it," I say.

"All right, all right. I get it," David skulks.

"Could we get on with it, Jared? I'm not getting any younger," I say.

"Yeah, and I'm starving," says David.

"Are you hungry, Jenna?" Jared asks. "We have a fridge. I could make sandwiches." He walks over to a closed curtain.

"This is where we do celebrity interviews. Right in this area," he says, with a flourish of his hand, like a model introducing a game-show contestant to a prize that awaits.

Then he swishes the curtain open, revealing a kitchenette.

"What celebrities?" David asks.

"Local people of interest, restaurant owners, business people, hobbyists," Jared responds.

"Oh, *those* celebrities," David says, rolling his eyes.

"I know that some people think that small-town documentaries are just"—Jared makes quotation marks in the air with his fingers—"'boring,' but let me tell you, documentaries can be plenty interesting. Did I ever tell you that our last documentary won tenth runner-up in the best short amateur documentary award category? We even attended a ceremony at the Howard Johnson party room on Sunrise Highway in Massapequa. It was very fancy, with a light buffet and entertainment, namely that famous ventriloquist act, Maury Maurowitz and his dummy, Bobby Fink. Ever hear of them?"

Jared starts pulling down and examining papers, notebooks, and a few crammed accordion folders from a dusty shelf. Then he plops them onto a nearby desk.

"No, not really . . . I don't think so . . ." David and I mutter over each other.

"He was very good," says Jared. "Maury, that is. Although Bobby was funny too."

David and I exchange perplexed looks.

"How many documentaries were there in the competition?" David asks.

"Well, there were eleven," Jared mumbles. "But the competition was very stiff. The judges said we showed a great deal of promise."

"Uh-huh," snarks David. "And was Bobby Fink one of the judges?"

Jared stops and glares at David.

While they're bickering, I start shuffling through the papers.

"Is this everything you have on Oceanville during the Revolutionary War?" I ask.

"I think there's one more folder," Jared says. "And here are some newspaper clippings about the Bloody Harvest Dance of 1773. I think that was a big deal."

"What happened?" I ask, reaching for the material.

"You can read about it, but before you start, how about we have lunch first?" Jared asks.

Eating is not on my mind, but I can see that the boys are hungry and nothing is going to happen until they're fed. So we decide to make some peanut butter and Fluff sandwiches and grab some cans of soda.

After we eat, Jared turns on the desk light and pulls up a stool.

"You can sit here, Jenna." He happily pats the stool.

I sit down and he saunters over to the wall light switch and dims the overhead lights. Then he pulls a chair toward mine.

"Why don't we take a stroll through history together?" He winks.

David immediately jumps up and blocks Jared's stool with another stool that he's pulled over next to me, and then he sits down.

"Lights on, Romeo," David says to Jared.

Jared harumphs and reluctantly turns the lights back on.

"Look, how about you guys play a video game or something?" I say, suddenly feeling claustrophobic with them bothering me. "I'm guessing you have the latest in Wii and Xbox and all that other stuff here, Jared."

"Well, maybe not the latest." Jared puffs up. "But I'd like to think that we have some cutting-edge game technology. Come on, David, I'll show you."

"Yeah, yeah," David mumbles, as Jared makes his way to the video game area on the other side of the room and starts enthusiastically rooting through piles of DVDs. Once Jared is preoccupied, David leans in toward me.

"What are you really looking for? Does this have anything to do with angel boy and psycho-crow boy?"

"Why don't you let me look first, David," I say, taking the folder from him. "I'll call you over if I find anything. Go play with Jared."

We glance over to Jared, who has turned up the already-loud music and is going through some kind of bowing warrior-preparation movements. He swings an invisible sword wildly and poses like a samurai, crouching with his arms thrust out in front of him.

And that's the thing about video games: on the screen, you see some attractive, coordinated wiibot mirroring your movements, and everyone else sees someone who looks like a hallucinating, uncoordinated crazy person.

David opens an envelope and an old drawing floats to the table.

It's a faded black-and-white etching of Luke!

He looks stern and "ye olde" in some kind of Revolutionary War patriot's uniform. I turn the picture over. It reads: *Luke Arnold, fifteen years old, 1771.*

"Wow," David murmurs. "Now that's just weird."

Not really, I think. "Oh, and here's another etching," Jared says, pulling out another paper from a folder.

It's a small cameo. David takes it from him. "This one kind of looks like you," he says to me, squinting closely at the etching. "Except dorkier, with buck teeth and bad skin."

At this point, Jared wanders over and takes the picture from David.

"This must be one of your ancestors, Jenna," he says, turning the picture over. In small scratchy handwriting it says: *Miss Biddy Bloom.*

"See?" Jared puffs up proudly. "I told you there was some stuff here about your ancestors." He holds the picture up. "And it looks like she's wearing a necklace. Looks kinda like that big thing your parents gave you that you're always wearing lately, that they said was in your family. I guess it was an antique after all."

"Lemme see." I take the etching from Jared. "Where did this come from?"

"Oh this is the book that Mrs. Murzsky wrote just last

year," says Jared. "You know her, she's the town librarian and historian, the really old one."

"Let's see." David reads the cover: *Everyday Life During the Revolutionary War.* Wow, sounds riveting. A real bestseller, I bet." Then he pretends to snore.

"Mani-pedi," Jared threatens flatly, placing his hand on the pocket where he keeps his cell phone.

David glares at Jared, but says nothing.

I scan the table of contents until I come to:

The Bloody Harvest Dance of 1773.

"Ooh, the word *bloody.* Something exciting," David says, reading over my shoulder.

This is something important. I can feel it. I turn to the page and read aloud:

"March 3, 1773, is a date that will live in infamy in the annals of the history of Oceanville. On that ill-fated night, a fight broke out between patriots and loyalist soldiers, leaving many wounded or dead. However, the fight began not as a result of political conflict, but over matters of the heart.

"The brawl began between Luke Arnold, son of a prominent local family, and a strange young man townspeople of that time described as dark and mysterious— Adam Jones. He was, presumably, orphaned, and had come alone to town a few months previously. Local rumors and gossip took on a supernatural tone when it was suggested by many that Adam was unnatural and might have been a warlock. It was felt that he had

caused a spate of illnesses, fighting, bad crops, and failed business ventures.

"Witnesses report that the town schoolteacher, Mr. Deets, attempted to break up the fight, but before he could be stopped, Mr. Jones impaled Mr. Arnold with a knife.

"Witnesses also report that local young girl and unrequited love interest Miss Biddy Bloom, during an attempt to revive Mr. Arnold, gave him the disk-shaped pendant she wore around her neck. With his near-dying breath, Mr. Arnold hurled the pendant at Mr. Jones, piercing him through the heart. This violence sparked the rest of the fighting that night.

"Both young men died later from fatal injuries."

23

David and I are both silent for a moment. Then I whistle low. So Luke and Adam have a serious history together. Maybe that's why this Mr. Deets guy, who must have been disguised as a teacher back then, sent Luke through the equinox to fetch Adam.

Jared has wandered over to the fridge by this point and is picking at some snacks.

"Wow," David says. "Supernaturally intriguing."

Intriguing indeed! Even with all the crazy, for a second, I can't suppress the irrational feeling that the worst part of the whole story wasn't the double homicide of Luke and Adam or the battle between the patriots and loyalists, but that I had a dorky ancestor named Biddy during a time in history when beautifying products were not available.

"It kind of all makes sense though, if you think about it." David nods knowingly.

"What's supernaturally intriguing?" Jared asks, dragging a stool across the floor and parking it in front of David.

He then hops his stool over so he can squeeze in next to me. But as Jared pivots and leans back to sit, David pushes the stool away with the toe of his sneaker.

Then suddenly:

Jared hits the floor with a thud!

He rolls onto his back like a turtle, grabbing at the air with his stubby arms, trying to absorb the shock of falling while trying to right himself. He's stuck that way for a good five seconds.

David bursts out laughing.

"Are you okay, dude?" he asks, feigning innocence. "For God's sake, roll over."

Jared rolls over onto his feet. His face is beet red and he's clearly livid. He glares so hard at David that I think his eyeballs are going to pop from their sockets. He's about to lunge for his neck when I jump in front of him.

"He did that on purpose! He pushed the stool away so I'd fall!"

"David," I scold.

David leans around my side.

"Nyeh!!" He sticks out his tongue at Jared, sprints out from behind me, and heads for safety behind the couch. Jared takes off after David, who's way too fast for him. David then takes a sprinting detour around the camera equipment with Jared at his heels.

"Jared, stop it!" I yell. "You know he's just trying to goad you. Let it go. Try to be the bigger man!"

"*Try* to be the bigger man!" David taunts. "He doesn't have to try!"

Jared freezes, his face red, his body taut—rigid and frozen in place. His mouth opens and shuts, opens and shuts, like a fish flopping on the dock, but nothing comes out.

David stops laughing and looks quizzical.

"Jared?" I say, moving toward him cautiously.

"Armpit wax!" Jared jerks back to life and throws up his hands.

David and I exchange confused looks.

"Armpit wax! I'm calling the nail salon! I'm calling your mother! I'm telling her you want to be picked up in time to see all the ladies get bikini waxed. And . . . and . . . their armpits waxed!"

"I think he's totally lost his mind," says David.

"Hairy-toe wax!" Jared screams, waving the phone and chasing David around the furniture and around the cable equipment, lunging for him and missing.

Jared takes one last lunge at David, who wiggles from his grasp, runs to the door, throws it open, and sprints out.

Jared, winded, finally stops and leans over his knees, panting.

"Why on earth do you babysit that kid?" he asks. "You're not still trying to make money for clothes, are you?"

Jared plops onto a stool and heaves a heavy sigh.

"'Cause I think you look good," Jared says in a way that's heartbreakingly tender.

Gah. I needed this now like a hole in the head. Suddenly I feel sorry for Jared, and sad about his unrequited love for me.

"Ya know, Jared," I say hesitantly, "sometimes you end up liking someone who's not from your block or even your space-time continuum, dimension, or time frame. Sometimes you end up liking a person who's technically not even alive. Do you know what I mean?"

"No," Jared says. "Is this something I missed in Science?"

"Look, none of this really matters now. There are more important things to worry about here."

"Like what?" Jared asks.

"Like stopping an evil entity from being . . . well, evil," I say.

"I'm not following," Jared says. "You mean David?"

"Well, him too. But Jared," I say, pulling up a stool and looking him square in the eyes, "the thing is that there's something . . . supernatural going on here."

"Supernatural?" he says, flattening his tousled hair across his head. "I don't know what you mean. You mean like love is supernatural?" he asks hopefully.

"No!" I hold up my palms, hop up, and step back, putting at least two feet of distance between us. "No, no, no. Not at all. I mean . . . forget it."

"Well then what?" he asks.

"It's not important now." I sigh. "I gotta go get David."

"Well." Jared stands and looks out the door.

I collect my coat and backpack.

"You do realize though," Jared says, "that while we've been talking about neighbors, love, and space-time continuums, David has disappeared into the fog."

"He wha—?"

"David!" Jared yells out the door into what has now become thick white vapor.

Silence.

"See?" Jared shrugs. "He's gone."

24

Oh great, I think. *Where did the little urchin go now?*

I walk out into the swirling mass.

"David!" I shout over and over, but there's nothing but white, eerie quiet.

This doesn't feel right. I know that if he gets into trouble again, Bernice might actually get annoyed. But even worse than that, what if Adam is lurking somewhere? David finally pissed off the wrong person when he pissed off Adam. What if Adam hurts him, or worse? Didn't the history book say that Adam was accused of creating chaos, trouble, and strife? Isn't that what he wants to stay here to do? And what if he tries to use David as bait again to coerce me into giving him the pendant? With David all alone in the fog, this would be a perfect opportunity.

Is that a crow's *caw* I hear, muted, through the fog? And how do I get in touch with Luke? Until this equinox thing-ie closes, Luke and the pendant seem to be the only things standing in the way of Adam.

Jared follows me out the door.

"Where do you think he went?" he asks.

"If I knew that, Jared"—I sigh—"he wouldn't be lost."

"Well, I just hope he didn't—" Jared starts. "Mmm . . . never mind."

"What?" I turn on him. "You hope he didn't what?"

"I . . . nothing . . . I just . . . nothing."

"Say it, for God's sake, Jared. You hope he didn't what?"

"Well, I was thinking of the pond. And the fog. Ya know, him tumbling into the pond by accident. But he can swim, right?"

"Oh my God, Jared! You think David drowned in the pond?"

"I didn't say drown. Did I say drown? Who said drown?" Jared backpedals.

"Don't help anymore." I groan, turning away.

I start through the silent mist, stumbling, squinting, arms outstretched.

"David! David, when I find you, I'm so gonna kill you!"

Jared stumbles after me.

"Maybe he went back into town?" he suggests.

"Ya think?" I ask hopefully.

"Yeah, maybe he went to Crumbles." Jared brightens. "That's where I'd go."

"Oh my God, I just remembered," I say, glancing at my watch. "Bernice is picking us up in town in twenty-five minutes. What am I gonna tell her? That I lost her son, David?!"

"Now, it's not your fault, Jenna." Jared holds up his palm in a comforting way. "You said it yourself. Something supernatural is afoot. Not that I know what that means, but David is the spawn of the devil."

"That's true." I nod. "Maybe he's just hiding."

Then I turn and look at Jared, really look at him. He's so

big and colorful against the background of all that gray-white mist. And it's as if I'm seeing him for the very first time, like I'm seeing the essence of Jared Needleman. The inner Jared, the caring, helpful Jared, beneath the often unkempt and know-it-all exterior.

"You have a little . . . um . . . Fluff," I say, tapping my finger at the corner of my mouth.

"Oh." He wipes the corner of his own mouth. "Thanks. Sometimes I get it everywhere and then hardly even feel it. It's so light."

"Well, it is called Fluff after all," I say.

"Hmm," Jared says. "And a good name for it too."

"Seriously." I nod.

And then we both stand there awkwardly for a few moments. Jared pushes his hands down into his pockets, looks away, and gnaws at his bottom lip.

"Why don't you go look for David in town?" he says. "And I'll go look around the pond."

"That would be great, Jared," I say, as I turn toward what I hope is the street back to Main Street.

Then:

I hesitate and turn back to him.

"Listen, I know David can be hard to take sometimes, and he likes getting a rise out of people. But he's not a bad kid really. I bet you didn't know this, but he kind of dreams of being a hero."

"Whatever." Jared shrugs.

We stand for a few more awkward seconds.

"Okay, well, thanks," I say. "I've got my phone, so call me if you find him."

"Will do," Jared declares.

I turn to go but then pivot back one more time.

"Oh, and Jared? Be careful."

Jared grins, steps into the deep fog, and is gone.

25

Somehow I stumble back to town, chanting quietly to myself and trying to send a telepathic message to Bernice:

Please stay longer at your mani-pedi appointment . . . please, please, plea—

Omph!

I bump straight into Luke.

"Luke!" I exclaim. "Boy, am I glad to see you."

Something about the mist gives his skin an almost luminescent quality, causing his eyes to pop. Or maybe that's just an angel thing.

"Likewise," he says, and takes a step toward me, sending that tingling electric jolt all the way up my spine. "Sorry I've been out of touch. Meetings with the big guy . . . responsibilities, duties, lectures, blah, blah, blah."

He breaks eye contact and looks off into the distance. Something like frustration or dissatisfaction crosses his face. I want to ask him what's wrong, but I have to find David first.

"Listen," I say. "I have to find David. I have no idea where he is and Bernice is going to be waiting at the corner for us in like ten minutes."

"Bernice?" Luke says. "Don't worry about her. She'll be late."

"Seriously?"

He throws his arm around my shoulder and we start walking up the street.

In public. Up the street!

"Right now she's at the plant nursery shopping for garden gnomes. Then she's going to stop at the market to cheat on her diet with their free cheese-sample buffet. I'd say we have at least an hour, depending on whether or not they have Jarlsberg."

He steers me to a stop in front of Crumbles.

"Besides," he says. "There's the little superhero now."

I look in the window, and sure enough, David is sitting at a little table, looking content, eating a donut and flipping through a comic book.

I sigh deeply and smile. I'm about to open the door when Luke says, "He looks happy. Why don't you leave him in there for a while, so we can hang out."

"Okay," I say as we continue up the street.

"Hey, I was thinking," he continues. "Maybe tonight you and I can go to the movies. Forget everything. See something in 3-D. You know, with the special plastic glasses? I haven't done that yet. I hear it can get you nauseous, but if we sit in the back and don't get too much butter on our popcorn we should be okay."

"That sounds awesome," I say.

But before I can say anything else, Sarah Johnson and her cronies burst from Maude's Chic Fashion Boutique amid a flurry of sweet chinkling doorbells, practically knocking us over. I can't help thinking about the awful buzzing sound you hear when walking in and out of the automatic doors at the Bulk, or even worse, that sharp embarrassing noise when a cashier accidentally forgets to remove one of those pierced-plastic security thingies.

Sarah immediately catches Luke on her radar.

"Hi." She approaches. "It's Luke, right?"

At the sight of Sarah moving closer, Luke startles and moves away from me, which Sarah seems to take as admiration of her beauty. She smiles in an obnoxious, self-satisfied way.

Then, with a quizzical expression, her eyes dart sharply from Luke to me and back.

"Hi. Sarah, remember?" She tilts her head, glistens, and smiles, which to me looks more like she's baring her teeth. "From Chorus?"

"Hi, Sarah," Luke says. "Sure, now I remember you."

"In a good way, I hope?" Sarah flirts.

Luke just grins and doesn't answer. Awkward silence ensues, until Sarah makes an uncomfortable throat-clearing sound. Her fan girls are planted about a foot away, pretending to chat and text while I can see their ears practically vibrating in our direction.

"So you're new in town, right?" Sarah asks.

"Um, newish," Luke responds.

"Oh." Sarah sounds perplexed.

More awkward silence follows as Sarah waits for a counter-flirt that doesn't come. She shoots me a withering look, expecting I'll just apologize for being in the same space as all of them. I stare straight back at her.

"Well, in case you need directions," she says, "me and my friends are heading toward East Street. Ya know, if you want to come along."

"Thanks," Luke says, putting his arm around me again. "But Jenna and I have something to do."

"Something to do," I echo with a smile.

For a moment a look of pure astonishment crosses Sarah's face. Her fan girls go slack jawed in disbelief. Amanda actually drops her phone.

"Okay." Sarah recovers quickly and smiles again. "Sure. Maybe next time."

Then she turns, flipping her hair in the process.

"Bye, Luke." Her voice tinkles warmly, like Maude's stylish doorbells. "Bye, Jenna," she honks flatly, the words sounding like the afterthought they were meant to be.

The group then whips around and their stylish boots click in unison on the sidewalk, like fine horses trotting up a cobblestone lane.

"Luke," I say. "Before you say anything else, I have to tell you something."

"Okay." He stops. "I'm listening."

"I found out about the whole Revolutionary War double-homicide at the barn-dance thing," I say.

"Oh."

Luke then takes a step back, shoves his hands into his pockets, and hangs his head slightly. A stray hair dislodges from his ponytail and I'm tempted to reach up and tuck it back, but I hesitate. I still can't get my brain around the memory of him kissing me and that that meant we were maybe dating or something, and that I could actually touch him without the pretense of spilling something or bumping into him by accident.

After many minutes, he finally says, "Pretty weird, huh?"

"It's all weird," I say.

Then he just starts walking away from me, up Main Street, looking pained and lost in his own thoughts.

"Damn it, Jenna."

Oh no, now what do I do? I sort of have a boyfriend and I screw it up by snooping.

"You're pissed," I say, trotting after him, painfully aware that trotting is not my best look. "I'm sorry. I shouldn't have snooped. I should have just asked you about your undead past."

Luke stops and turns.

"I'm not mad at you." He sighs and pushes his fingers through his ponytail.

"Okay," I pant. "So can we stop trotting now?"

"I'm mad at myself. I was stupid and cocky and impulsive and a lot of people got hurt that night. And not just the ones who got killed, if you know what I mean."

He starts race-walking up the street again.

"Oh yeah, of course. I know what you mean—"

"You're a terrible liar, Jenna," he reminds me.

"All right, no," I say. "I don't know what you mean."

"I mean the survivors—my family for one. The families of the others who died in that fight. After I died, my mother almost died of a broken heart, and my father was never the same."

"How were you supposed to know that Adam was going to try to kill you?" I say.

"But then I killed him. I actually killed a person, Jenna. And that's not the worst," he says in an anguished whisper. "I'll tell you what happened. The truth. If you want to know."

He looks so fiery and intense. We are having our first confessional moment. I rack my brain for any helpful articles from the True Confessions section of *Teen Glamour* to help me through this moment. But all that flashes through my mind are stories about embarrassing accidental farting, unknowingly tracking dog poo from your shoe into your boyfriend's car, or handling awkward menstrual leaks when wearing white. But there was nothing about past-life murder confessions, demons, angels, and/or fighting between patriots and loyalists during the Revolutionary War. I was already on supernatural overload.

"Well, I really don't need to know the *whole* truth," I say nervously.

I suddenly remember the article "Ten Reasons to Keep Mystique in a Relationship": *After all, a little mystery in a relationship is often a good thing and everyone has an idiosyncrasy or two . . .*

"All right, I'll tell you," Luke says, clearly so caught up in his own angst he didn't even hear me.

"Er . . . okay," I croak.

"I'm a murderer," he says.

"Well, now, *murderer* is a really strong word. You killed in self-defense," I try. "Besides, technically, Adam's really not a person. He's more like an animorph."

"No, that's not what happened!" he says way too loudly.

A passerby gives us a strange look.

I take Luke by the arm and lead him around the corner under the awning of a closed store.

"We really don't have to talk about this," I say.

"Please, Jenna, I want you to know," he implores. "Adam shoved me first and we were fighting and I got cocky and pulled a knife. I just meant to scare him, but I slipped and cut him. I thought he was dead but he was alive. And then he stabbed me, but before I lost consciousness, I remember your ancestor, Biddy, rushing toward me and placing your pendant in the palm of my hand. She whispered for me to fling it at Adam. So I did. It lodged in his chest and then he was dead. And then . . . I must have been dead too because it all went black. But don't you see—technically, I killed him first. I'm the murderer."

He hangs his head and looks as though he's collecting his emotions.

"So many times, I've asked myself, Why do I deserve to be an angel? That's why I'm such a 'good soldier,'" he says sadly, making quotation marks in the air. "Because I don't deserve to be a soldier at all. I don't deserve to have another chance, and life, or to have you. Even though I want both more than anything."

He takes me by the shoulders. "I don't want to stay here if I'll somehow risk being the cause of another catastrophic tragedy where innocent people are hurt and killed and sucked into the vortex of the epic supernatural conflicts of heaven and hell!"

"So does this mean we're not going to the movies?" I ask meekly.

"Do you think I'm a freak?" Luke asks softly.

"For the record," I say, "you're one of the most sensitive, creative, and interesting guys I've ever known. And I mean 'interesting' in a good way."

What I don't get, I think, *is why, out of all the girls in Ocean-ville, you picked me.*

"And I picked you," Luke says, "because, among other things, you, Jenna Bloom, have a kind heart."

I am stunned. Not so much about the weird mind-reading thing, although it *was* kind of disturbing, but I never thought about having a kind heart. I mean, we all want to be nice, of course. But Luke said it like it was something important, like it was something that really mattered. And suddenly I want it to matter. I rack my brain for all the kindhearted things I have ever said or done.

"Well," I say, "I do try to put a dollar in the Johnny Fund jar at the Bulk Emporium when that charity guy comes around. Although between you and me, I've never gotten a straight answer about who Johnny is, and I've often suspected that he's really the charity guy, who doesn't seem to have a job and is always lurking around the store leering at the moms.

"See there?" Luke squeezes my hand.

"I'm also inspired by Helen Keller," I say. "I felt bad for Mrs. Golowski when her husband yawned almost all the way through her entire performance as Annie Sullivan in *The Miracle Worker,* and was fast asleep by curtain call."

"That's what I said." He smiles. "A kind heart."

"Thanks." I blush. "But one request."

"Name it." He steps in toward me and pushes a hair from my cheek.

"Could you not do that mind-reading thing anymore? It's kind of intrusive and freaky."

"Oh sorry," he says. "No worries."

And then he leans in and our lips are about to lock when, suddenly, I hear:

He rocks in the tree tops all day long . . .

Luke hesitates. Curse that phone.

Luke steps back. "You better get that."

"Hello!" I flip open my phone and snap.

"Hello, Jenna. It's me, Jared Needleman."

"Yes I know, Jared." I sigh. "Kinda busy here."

"I found David."

"What do you mean you found David?"

"I mean I know where he is," he sputters.

"Well, I know where he is too," I say, looking at Luke, who's making a what's-up? face. "He's in Crumbles."

"Ah . . . no, he was just here," Jared says. "But don't worry. I think he's alive."

"What?!"

I bolt around the corner and down the block with Luke at my heels. When I get to Crumbles I look in the window and it's empty. I swing open the door.

"Hey," I say to the bored-looking counter help. "There was a little kid in here about fifteen minutes ago. Shaggy hair, about yay high, nine years old—"

"He left," the guy says.

"When?"

"Dunno, about ten minutes ago, I guess." He shrugs.

"Did he say where he was going?" I ask.

"Not to me, lady."

I step back out into the street.

"Okay, where are you Jared?" I say into the phone. "And where's David, and what do you mean, you think he's alive?"

A not-good feeling is rolling over in my stomach.

"You better come quick—" Jared starts, and then the connection dies.

Overhead is the screaming *caw* of crows, heading straight for the Old Vic Theater up ahead.

So not good.

I grab Luke's hand.

"Let's go!" I say.

26

As we close in on the Old Vic Theater, Jared comes into focus. He's bouncing up and down in the doorway, waving his arms like a kid in class who knows the answer to a question and is desperate to share it. I can practically hear him making those monkey noises.

"Ooh, ooh, ooh!"

Finally, huffing and puffing (me, not Luke), we reach the front door.

"Holy mother of crap!" Jared shrieks. "That weird guy grabbed David!"

"Who grabbed David?" Luke's tone is even but deadly serious.

"The guy! The guy I saw at the playground! Light skin, dark hair! I thought he was a dog, but then he turned into a guy! I don't know! And now he's inside the theater!"

Luke rushes through the lobby into the theater with me wheezing behind him.

It's dark, shadowy, and gray.

"David?" I ask apprehensively, squinting into the shadows.

A spotlight flicks on and there's Adam, center stage.

"Where's David?" I shout at him.

"What's it worth to you to know?" he asks.

Luke leaps up onto the stage in a totally sexy athletic way and strides toward Adam.

"Give him back. He has nothing to do with this," he says.

Adam ignores him. Sighs, bites his nails. Picks up a few props and tosses them aside as if bored.

"I'm not going to ask you again," Luke says, as he moves toward him threateningly.

Is there going to be another fight? Jared and I hold our collective breath.

"Oh come on," Adam says. "What are you gonna do? Kill me twice? Technically I'm not really alive anymore and neither are you."

"Are you holding David ransom for the pendant?" I ask.

"Nah. I've got David because I don't like him. But this is a good game, don't you think?

"And I'll get the pendant from you somehow, plain girl." He turns to me, his manner casual, his vibe deadly.

"What is it about this ugly pendant? How can having it give you the power to stay here?" I ask.

"The explanation of how the shape, weight, and design of it interact with cosmic, mystical, and celestial elements is way beyond your understanding," Adam sneers. "Let's just say that it's like a mystical key for me. That, and I happen to think it goes well with my look.

"But if you don't comply freely, maybe I'll pick off everyone you know and love until you have no choice but to give it to me."

He gestures to Jared.

"Maybe I'll take this big one next."

"Wha—" Jared stumbles back in fear.

Surprising even myself, I step in front of Jared. "You stay away from him! He has more worth in his little pinkie than you have in your whole taut, sexy, muscular body!"

Somehow, that didn't come out right.

Adam laughs, low and sexy.

"I really do like it here, don't you Luke?" he says. "Much better than that smelly, muddy, pre-antibiotic colonial time. This twenty-first-century teenage world"—Adam opens his arms wide—"where everyone wears their pajama pants and drinks fancy coffees and watches reality television shows, and is plugged into iPods and iPhones and iTunes, where it's just I, I, I. It's truly . . . What's the word? It's *epic*!

"Yeah." Adam sighs and slicks his hair back across his head. "I think I'll stay and be your worst nightmare. I think I'll blend in and be a good Oceanville teenager for as long as I can." He walks downstage and crouches so he's practically in my face. "Then it won't be long before the whole town begins to disintegrate into an ash heap of fighting, chaos, infection, whatever. That is, unless . . . Well, you know."

"If I give you the pendant, then you'll never leave," I say.

"Well, never is a long time. I'll stay awhile, probably a few generations, but if you give me the pendant freely, I'll spare you and your loved ones."

He stands up and looks out into the audience, growling solemnly, practically glowing with dramatic presence.

"You can go down hard, or you can go down easy, but with hell as my witness, I'll get what I want!"

A few terrible silent moments pass until, suddenly, there's thunderous clapping coming from the back of the theater.

"*Bravo!*" a voice bellows with great emotion.

All heads turn in unison. Mr. Resnick trots up the aisle, an enraptured expression on his face.

"Bravo!" he yells again.

With a dramatic flourish, he wipes an invisible tear from his cheek.

"That was marvelous, marvelous! Very moving," he gushes. "Come down into the pit, boys.

"What good fortune that I just happened to stop by the theater to pick up some sheet music," Mr. Resnick continues.

Luke glowers at Adam, who smirks and jumps down from the stage. Luke follows.

"Tell me, first, what was that gripping scene you were working on? I'm not familiar with the work."

"Em, it's from a play called *Where's David?*," I say, and then shoot Adam what I hope is a very dirty look.

"*Where's David?* Hmm. Never heard of it." Mr. Resnick ponders.

"We wrote it ourselves," Adam offers.

"Ah, very good. And I'm so glad to see that Adam, our new Motel, is getting familiar with our stage."

"Wha-wha-what?" I stammer. "He's Motel now? But he doesn't even live in Oceanville."

"I just moved back to town," Adam says.

"And isn't that just our marvelous, divinely inspired good fortune?" Mr. Resnick smiles broadly.

"No, not really," Jared mumbles.

Adam shoots him an icy, amused look.

I elbow Jared in his ribs.

"Well, we should probably go." I maneuver around Mr. Resnick. "Have to rehearse *Where's David?*," I say through gritted teeth. "And there's that other play I'm working on, *If I Can't Find Him, Bernice and Lenny Will Kill Me.*"

Luke and I start briskly up the aisle toward the door, until Mr. Resnick steps into our path.

"Not so fast, mister," he says, wagging his finger at him. "You know I was expecting you to show up for auditions."

"I'm sorry, sir," Luke says. "I had responsibilities I had to attend to."

"Well, no matter, because I have some delightful news for you."

"Ooh, I wonder what the delightful news could be, Luke," Adam says with a tinge of sarcasm.

"I just found out that Waldo, the boy we borrowed from the wrestling team, who was cast as Tevye—"

"You mean Walter," I interrupt.

"That's right. Well, it seems that he dislocated his shoulder at a wrestling match, but that's not the good news, of course. The good news is that now the part of Tevye is available! Mr. Resnick takes a step back, squints his eyes, and observes Luke and Adam.

"Hmm . . . wait," he says, tapping his index finger against

his cheek. "I actually think that you, Adam, would make a better Tevye and that Luke would be a perfect Motel."

Adam shrugs his consent.

"Luke, what do you say?" Mr. Resnick continues. "The part is yours if you want it."

"Em, well, I . . ."

"Come on, son," Mr. Resnick says. "Do the part. Save us and our little community-theater production from damnation or at the very least, bad reviews."

"Yes, do save us." Adam smiles.

"Em, well, okay." Luke submits.

"Fabulous!" Mr. Resnick claps his hands. "Now the show is only a short time away, but I think you boys have the talent to pull it off. You're fighters. I can feel it in my bones."

"Fighters," Adam agrees, "to the death."

"We'll start working right now. Are you boys free?"

"Well, there is something I need to . . ." Luke says.

"Wonderful!" Mr. Resnick ignores him.

Luke shoots me an apprehensive look.

"I'll find David," I whisper to Luke as Mr. Resnick takes them each by the arm and leads them to the piano.

"Oh what a relief! Where are all these talented boys suddenly coming from?"

"You don't want to know," I mumble.

"What's that, Jebba?"

"Never mind."

"By the way, Jebba, would you and Jerry go outside and pull that awful old rowboat out of the middle of the pond?

I don't care if it is historical. It's such an eyesore. We must hide it somewhere before our show opens."

"The rowboat . . . on the lake?" I gulp.

I'm rocking that bad feeling again.

"I noticed it on my way in through that blasted fog," Mr. Resnick continues. "I think there's some kind of animal curled up in there too."

"An animal," I say.

Luke and I exchange panicked looks.

"I'm hoping that the wretched thing just sinks," Mr. Resnick says.

27

Jared and I rush back up the aisle and out of the theater, toward the pond and the rickety peeling old rowboat sinking slowly into the murky water. There's an animal in it all right. It's David, lying at the bottom of the boat, asleep, unconscious, I can't tell. At any rate, he isn't moving and I can only hope that he isn't dead.

"Is that really David in there? What's he doing lying so still? Is he dead?" Jared says, as if reading my mind.

As if on cue, David moans low, but is still unconscious from what I can see.

"David!" I shout. "Wake up! David!"

No response.

"Well, it's obvious that somebody has to go get him," I say.

"Yeah, somebody." Jared's eyes dart away from my face.

"Somebody." I nod. "Yeah, somebody strong."

"Has to be strong," Jared agrees.

"Somebody soon . . . who's strong," I say.

"Yeah." Jared nods. "Better be soon."

Many seconds tick by.

"I know!" Jared finally exclaims.

"Oh my God, you're awesome, Jared." I sigh with relief. "I'm sure the water isn't as cold and gross as it looks. You better hurry. I'll wait right here for you on the shore."

"Wait. What?" Jared backs away. "No, not me! I was gonna say we should call the paramedics or fire department or police or something. Just call 911. Those guys are super-strong. I see them at Crumbles all the time."

Gah!

"We don't have time for 911, Jared. Besides, they'd make this big, noisy deal about rescuing David, with sirens and fire engines. The whole town would be gathered here in like five minutes. They'd take him to the hospital, then they'd call Bernice and Lenny. Then the story would probably show up in the *Oceanville Gazette* police blotter. I'd never work in this town again!"

"Well, when you put it that way . . ." Jared ponders. "But who then?"

"You! What about you, Jared! You're, ya know, kinda . . . watchamacallit . . . strong."

Jared beams and stands erect.

"Well, I do work out with light weights three times a week."

"You do?" I ask incredulously.

"Well, not every week. But anyway, we're getting off track. The fact is, I can't swim."

"You can't swim? I never knew that. We live so close to the beach and you can't swim?"

"Didn't you ever wonder why I never went in the pool at all those neighborhood barbecues? Or why I only waded in the ocean at all those cabana parties?"

"I just thought you didn't want to put on a bathing suit," I say.

"No," Jared protests. "I'm perfectly comfortable with my physique. I just can't swim. You'll have to do it, Jenna."

Jared turns to me and places his hands on my shoulders.

"No matter how gross, how smelly, how murky, how dirty, how inhabited with potentially stinging creatures this festering cesspool of a pond is, you've got to swim in and get David . . . You've had a tetanus shot within the last ten years, right?"

"Fine." I pull away from Jared, exasperated.

I move closer to the shoreline and peer in at the brown-green sludgy water, and suddenly I'm having shameful low, *not* kindhearted thoughts like: Would it really be that terrible if David actually sank in the boat? Do I really want to completely ruin one of my only decent pairs of jeans, my new canvas sneakers, and the somewhat cute shirt that communist Mom bought from the Bulk Emporium designer-knockoff sale just last month?

I lean in even closer to the brown murk. Little tiny fish snippets zip back and forth at lightning speed and the water reeks like garbage.

What am I thinking? I can't do this. I need to get Luke. Then:

I hear the loud cawing of crows and a great flapping of wings, sweeping down, practically brushing the tops of our heads.

"Whooaa!" I hear Jared yell behind me. "Those are big birds."

Then:

At the other side of the lake, through the vibrant autumn

leaves, I see the golden eyes of a monstrous wolf. It pulls back its lips into a snarl. Within moments, the whole of its giant girth is lumbering out from behind the trees.

It's Adam, part of his game. It's a warning.

"Dog! Stray dog!" Jared yells. "Don't touch it!"

Jared pulls me back by the sleeve.

"When we did our documentary *Mangy Mongrels at the Mall*," he continues, "I learned all about how stray dogs run amok in suburbia, carrying rabies, and how it turns them into frothing, biting machines. And that one looks mighty mean."

Jared pulls his cell phone from his pocket.

"Darn. No reception. I'm going to call animal control. There's reception by the theater. I'll be right back."

The minute he leaves, the wolf retreats into the trees and disappears.

I peer down into the gunky water again. Still smelly. Foamy brown gunk is collecting on the shore. There has to be another way.

And then, at that very second, the rowboat exudes a big, loud *glug* and starts to sink right down into the watery sludge.

28

"David!" I scream. No answer.

Clearly, there's no choice and I know what I have to do. Maybe I am brave after all, or maybe I am even more cowardly than anyone I know. Too cowardly to go down in the history of Oceanville as the girl who was too grossed out by pond scum to save the life of the kid she babysits. And of course I could see the headline in the *Oceanville Gazette*. Posthumously, David would be remembered as a "charming genius" whose light was snuffed out way too early, instead of the kid nobody could stand.

I'm going in. I take a deep breath, reach down to pull off my designer-knockoff sneakers, feel the sludge squishing between my toes, and decide to keep them on as I take my first steps into the mud and keep walking.

Gross! Cold! Slimy!

I make my way up to my waist, and start doggy paddling toward the boat.

"David!" I shout. "I'm coming for you. If you can hear me, wake up! David, if you're just pretending to be asleep, I'm gonna drown you!"

For some reason, the boat suddenly bobs back up, and relief washes over me.

"Thank God," I say, as I make my way to it.

Overhead, a swarm of crows is circling. Suddenly something grabs at my legs and pulls me down! I lunge for the side of the boat, yelling and sputtering. I'm pulled underwater, where I struggle to open my eyes.

Adam stares fiercely at me. His face is a grotesque morphed mask of a boy, a crow, and a wolf. His brutal eyes pierce me like lasers through the murky water. For a moment, he lets go and I frantically eject myself to the surface. He bobs to the surface as well.

"Scared yet?" he asks.

"Leave me alone!" I croak, splashing water in his face.

He smirks and lunges for me, but I quickly scramble around the side of the boat.

Holy crap! He's gonna drown me! My mind races. I have to give him the pendant if I want to live. But then again, how can I? For some reason I have been entrusted with the responsibility of keeping Adam away from this space-time continuum. But am I brave enough to risk my own life to save Oceanville from evil? And where is Luke?

Adam glides toward me with long athletic strokes.

"Help!" I shout out into the void.

Adam reaches me, grabs me, and pulls me under again. I struggle. The pendant floats in front of me like some big weird cheap-looking fish. Adam grabs for it, but even underwater, it rejects his touch and shocks him, momentarily stunning him into unconsciousness. I look on in horror and relief to see him sink, motionless, to the bottom of the pond. Can a person who's technically not really alive still drown?

I'm not waiting to find out. Frantically, I sputter back to the surface and start knocking on the side of the boat.

"David!" I scream. "Wake the hell up!"

I feel the water undulate beneath me. A dark form is heading to the surface.

Desperately, I try to climb into the boat, scratching and pulling and grunting, cursing myself for all those times in Gym when I didn't try harder to climb the ropes or do sit-ups or crunches or pull-ups or . . .

When a hand reaches down from the boat and grabs for my shirt.

"David!" I scream, and scramble for his hand. "You're alive!"

"Of course I'm alive, you tool. Here, grab my hand."

Somehow, between both of us pulling and pushing, I manage to pull up and flop into the boat.

"Jeez," says David. "What the hell have you been eating? You weigh, like, a ton."

"Thanks, David," I say.

"Seriously, you're Moby-freakin'-Dick." He rubs his scrawny arms.

All is quiet for a few glorious seconds. The sun feels cool on my wet skin. The sky has cleared. I close my eyes and sigh.

When, suddenly, Adam leaps up from the water, his face contorted in grotesque rage.

"Ahhhh!" he yells.

"Ahhhh!" David and I yell together, pulling back in startled fear.

We watch in horror as, magically, Adam rises from the water and hovers over the boat.

"Give it to me!" His voice is low and murderous and he looks crazy.

He holds out his hand. "Or mark my words, you'll pay!"

In that moment, something comes over me. I'm wet and smelly. I have pond scum on my teeth. I've had enough and I'm pissed.

From the corner of my eye, I spot an oar lying on the floor of the boat. Before it occurs to me that it's probably too heavy for me to wield, I heave it up. With one great motion, I lift it over my head and spin around like a player in Jared's clumsy ninja Wii game. I hear the wood slice the air with a great *whoosh* and then slam it straight across.

"*Yeah well, mark this!*" I scream.

But just as the oar is about to make contact with Adam's head, he floats to the right.

"You missed," he says.

"She might have missed, but I won't!"

Luke is suddenly behind me. He grabs the oar from my hands, spins it around, and slams it straight across Adam's head. Score!

Adam looks stunned, then bounces backward into the water with a great splash and sinks below the surface. Beaten only for the moment, however, he reemerges as a big black crow, caws up angrily toward the sky, and disappears.

"Boy, am I glad to see you." I smile up at Luke.

Luke smiles back and places his hand on my shoulder.

"Are you two all right?" he asks, using the oar to row us back to shore.

Just then a fat white-and-blue seagull lands on the side of the boat. It screeches angrily.

Luke sighs and places the oar back in the boat.

"Gotta go. Later?" he says.

I nod.

Faster than a hummingbird moves, Luke's enormous, beautiful white wings sprout from his sides. In less than a blink, we hear an enormous *swiiiiissshh* and he's gone.

I see Jared jogging up and around the hill toward us.

"I couldn't get reception anywhere," he huffs. "So I figured I'd come back. Is the dog gone? Are you all right?"

"Whooaa! That was slammin'!" David exclaims.

Now shivering uncontrollably from both adrenaline and cold, David and I manage to climb from the boat.

"We're all right, Jared," I say. "But right now, I'm freezing. We need some dry clothes."

"I bet we can get some from the theater dressing room," David says.

So we all trudge to the theater.

"Let's go in through the back," I say. "I don't want Mr. Resnick to yell at us for dripping pond water all over the theater."

We slip in and make our way backstage unnoticed, and park in front of a long rack of costumes.

"What are the choices here, Jared?" I ask.

"Well," he says, "the costumes are based on the shows.

There was *High School Musical* 1, 2, and 3, but there weren't really any costumes for those. They just did *The Miracle Worker* and, according to some of the backstage guys, before that was *Sweet Charity*. A few months back, they did *Oliver!*"

"Okay." David shrugs. "But I'm not sure how we're gonna explain to Bernice why I'm dressed like the Artful Dodger and you're dressed like a hooker with a heart of gold. And she's totally gonna notice the smell."

"Listen, guys," Jared says. "It's getting late and I have to go. I promised my parents I would help out at the Pig this afternoon. But you have my cell phone if you need me."

He pats his pocket and winks.

"Okay, that's great, Jared. Thanks," I say.

He turns to go, leaving David and me to search for dry clothes.

I find an Artful Dodger costume for David (three-quarter-length tattered black pants, a white shirt with tattered three-quarter sleeves, and a black jacket). Because I refuse to put on a corset, garter belt, and black stockings from *Sweet Charity*, I'm left with either another outfit from one of Fagin's boys or Annie Sullivan's floor-length gray dress that I'm way too short for.

"I say go for the Artful Dodger outfit. That Annie Sullivan moo moo is gonna make you look like a squat freak," says David.

"Just say what you mean, David," I say. "Don't worry about my feelings or anything."

"What?" he says. "I'm just trying to help you."

"Don't help me."

"I didn't say that you *are* a squat freak. I said the dress—"

"Let's go," I interrupt, ducking behind a tall, wide chest of drawers to peel off my wet, smelly clothes and put on the badly fitting little black suit.

"You decent?" I ask as I pop my head around the bureau.

"Yeah, come on out," David says.

He admires himself in a floor-length mirror. Whereas he looks kind of cute, my own reflection is appallingly gruesome.

"I can't walk down the street like this. We look like organgrinder monkey twins."

"*Ha!*" he barks. "Organ-grinder monkey twins! That's a good one. Ha!"

"I'm glad you're amused," I reply stonily.

"Maybe there's an old coat in here somewhere."

I riffle through the clothing rack.

"We don't have time for shopping, Jenna," David says.

He turns my wrist over and glances at my watch.

"Bernice will be there in a few minutes. Come on, let's go. She hates to wait."

He starts to sprint away, but I grab his sleeve.

"David, how did you get in that boat anyway?"

"Well, I got tired of waiting for you at Crumbles. I had left my phone at Jared's cable shack though, so I figured I'd go to the theater for a while. Borrow someone's cell and call you there. But on the way I ran into Adam and . . . I don't remember the rest. I guess I'm pretty much one of his archenemies now, aside from you and Luke of course."

He opens the stage door and sprints out into the light, glancing over his shoulder as he goes.

"I still could take him though," he says. "One day when, ya know, my powers develop."

"Yeah." I smile. "One day."

But then I think of Adam's departing threat. He could do a lot of damage even in the short time before the equinox ends and he's pulled back to wherever he goes.

And something else pops into my mind: When the equinox ends, what happens to Luke?

29

Just as David predicted, Bernice is pulling up to the corner as we arrive at the designated spot. We scramble into the car and she smiles at us in the rearview mirror, never hesitating in her cell phone conversation. She squeals away from the curb. David fishes a little camera from the side-door pocket.

"Say cheese!" He snaps my picture.

What seems like a thousand pin lights dance around my eyes.

David admires his handiwork.

"Another good one for Facebook," he says, holding up the picture for me to see.

"Thanks, David. I look like a little pilgrim boy in a shrunken suit having a bad-hair day."

"Pilgrim boy with a bad-hair day! Ha! Good one. That's just what I'll tag it. You know, you're getting funny in your old age."

"I'm hilarious," I reply flatly.

Within minutes, Bernice is already whizzing up my street and has two wheelied into the driveway so fast that it's like she's broken the sound barrier. So when I arrive home ten minutes later, I'm sure I'm at least two weeks younger.

"Bye David," I say, stepping out of the time-warp mobile.

"Mmm," he says, already dismissing me. He pulls his

iPod out of the backseat pocket, plugs himself in, and turns the music up.

"Here's for today." Bernice whirs down the window, reaches across the seat, and hands me an envelope of cash. "And I've included a little extra."

"Thanks, Mrs. Lipski," I say, taking the envelope.

"And I hope you haven't forgotten our bar mitzvah in New Jersey, Jenna," she says. "It's coming up soon, and you're our number-one babysitter."

Of course there is no number two, but I don't say that.

"No I haven't forgotten, Mrs. Lipski," I say instead. "It's the opening night of *Fiddler on the Roof.*"

And the closing of the equinox, I think to myself.

"So, I'll be with David during the show and then afterward I'll take him with me to the cast party."

Mrs. Lipski turns to David and shouts, "Don't worry, snuggles, your dad and I will be there for the Sunday matinee!"

David smiles and gives her a thumbs-up, but when she turns back around the thumb gets switched up for another finger and he turns his iPod louder.

I open the envelope and see that Mrs. Lipski has given me way more than what I usually get.

"Wait, Mrs. Lipski," I say, gesturing to the money. "I think you made a mistake."

"You don't have to thank me, honey." She pats my arm. "You deserve the money. Besides, I know that"—she lowers her voice—"David can be a bit of a handful sometimes."

"I heard that," David pipes up from the backseat.

"But you know"—she glances back at him and whispers the words—"that he really loves you."

"I heard that too," David says. "And no I don't."

Mrs. Lipski rolls her eyes and nods yes at me.

"I'll see you later, honey."

She pats my arm again.

Then before I can say another word, she's back on the phone, has hit the accelerator, and has left me in a cloud of gas fumes.

"Yeah . . ." I sigh. "I guess I kinda love him too."

30

Later that evening, I hear a pelting of pebbles against my window. I look down and Luke is standing in communist Mom's Bulk Emporium flower garden.

"Can I come up?" he whispers loudly.

"Ah . . . sure, of course." I give him an eyes-bugged-out smile. "Gimme a sec?"

Gah!

The first romantic boy-underneath-my-window moment of my life and all I can do is panic about my disgustingly messy bedroom: strewn with dirty laundry, half-eaten Keebler cookies, half-full glasses of milk that are starting to thicken into cream, dust bunnies, an unmade bed, papers and crap on every desk and bureau surface. Plus a terrarium in a Bulk-size caffeine-free soda bottle that I made in third grade and that has surely morphed into some kind of dystopian man-eating vegetation by now.

Mom, me, and Michael have a deal. As long as we don't spread out garbage all throughout the house, we can keep our rooms any way we please. And even though my room is bad, Michael's room could easily be in an episode of some hoarder reality show, where people are totally buried under their own disgusting filth.

"Give me a minute to straighten up," I squeak out the window.

"I don't care if your room's messy, Jenna," Luke says.

And then before I can blink, he's no longer in the Bulk garden, but standing in the middle of my messy room. I start zipping around like a Tasmanian devil, picking up dirty laundry and assorted crap and shoving it into an already jammed-to-capacity closet.

The truth is, Luke is the first real boy, or in his case, not-totally-real boy, who's been in my room, other than Jared Needleman, who used to come upstairs to play Candy Land.

"Sorry," I say to Luke. "It's a little messy."

"Well," he says, picking up the dystopian biosphere, looking for a place to sit, and then giving up. "It is sort of casual."

He picks up a huge dog-fur dust ball and examines it. I grab it from his hands.

"That's from Beaver. The goldendoodle," I say, grabbing it away and, upon noticing that the trash can is overflowing, shoving the hairy ball into my pocket.

"Isn't he the neighbors' dog?" Luke asks.

"Yeah, that's right," I say.

"Then why is his fur . . . Never mind." He shakes his head.

"I pet-sat him one time a few months—"

"Jenna." Luke moves in close and stumbles over my sneaker. "Omph!"

"Ooh, sorry, I got that," I say, picking up the sneaker.

"Jenna," he repeats, placing a steadying hand on my

shoulder. He takes the sneaker from me and chucks it onto the bed. "I wanted to give you something."

"Give me something? What is it?"

He reaches into his pocket and pulls out a brown leather cord. Dangling from the end is a heart, very handmade looking, a tiny bit lopsided, made of red wood inlaid with a design of shiny pieces of twisted metal. It's odd and beautiful and not like any heart I've ever seen before. He hands it to me.

"Is this made from your finds from the junkyard?" I ask, gingerly turning it over in my hands.

"I love it," I say. "It's perfectly imperfect. Kind of like me."

"Here, let me put it on you," he says, gently fastening it around my neck. "There." He looks satisfied. "You can wear it with the pendant. Extra protection."

So then we're standing there in the middle of all my crap and there's this awkward pause. He sighs and hooks his dangling hair back into his ponytail.

"Jenna, there's something else, something I need to tell you—"

Then, without warning, Michael opens the door and sticks his big Neanderthal head in.

"Hey, Jenna, Mom says dinner—"

Michael spots Luke.

"Oh whoa."

"Hello. Knock, knock," I snap.

Michael turns and raps his knuckles on the door.

"Anybody home?" he sings sarcastically.

"Luke, you remember Michael." I sigh heavily.

"Hi Michael," Luke says, reaching out to shake his hand. Michael gives him an oafish stare.

"Shake his hand, Michael," I instruct.

"Hey, I know you. You're that waiter from Cowboy Clems and the guy Jenna cut class to go to the beach with," Michael says.

"No," I say, climbing over my stuff, shoving Michael back out the door, and then trying to push the door shut against him. "He isn't."

"Sure he is. Sure you are."

"Get out, Michael." I put my hand against his skull and try to jam him out.

"Hey, I've always wanted to know something," Michael says. "What exactly is the difference between the chimichanga supreme and the chimichanga extreme? It's the extra chipotles, isn't it?"

"Goodbye, Michael." I successfully push him back through the door, close it, and lock it.

"Sorry," I say to Luke. "You were saying?"

"Jenna's not coming down!" I hear Michael screaming through the hallway. "I dunno. She's got that waiter in there! I dunno, they're talking or something! I *dunno!!!!*"

"Oh God," I mutter.

We listen as he clumps down the hall and down the stairs.

Luke turns to me, but suddenly he isn't looking me in the eyes.

"I wanted you to have this necklace as . . . a keepsake," he says.

An alarm goes off in my head, and I'm reminded of a recent *Teen Glamour* magazine article entitled "Ten Sure Signs That He's Breaking It Off:"

1. He gives you a keepsake!!!!

I'm so frantic I don't even remember signs 2 through 10.

"What?" I say, trying to keep my voice from sounding shrill.

"Mr. Deets, my 'boss' "—Luke makes quotation marks in the air with his fingers—"is thinking that maybe I should go, ya know, back."

"Back?!" I gulp.

"He thinks I'm getting too involved in this time period and . . . with you." He sighs.

"But you're helping protect Oceanville from Adam," I protest.

"There are always Adams," Luke says. "Throughout time. Everywhere. They slip into society when they can, but in the end it's really people and free will that give Adam and his kind power. Mr. Deets is a fatalist. He thinks these situations have to play out in order for people to learn and develop. He thinks I might be interfering too much. Besides, you have the pendant. Adam can't get it from you. You're smart and brave enough not to give it to him. The equinox will be closed soon and he'll be gone."

"But . . ." I panic. "I thought you liked it here."

"I do," he says. "I dunno. It's still under discussion, but the thing is, I wanted you to know that . . ." He looks down shyly. "That I . . ." Then he takes a deep breath, lifts my chin up, and leans toward me.

"I—" he whispers.

When suddenly:

Rat-a-tat-tat.

"Jenna!"

Oh. My. God.

It's communist Mom. Rapping at the door.

"Jenna, honey," Mom sings through the door. "Why don't you invite your little cowpoke friend to dinner? We always have plenty."

"Shhh. Pretend you're dead," I whisper to Luke. "I mean, um, you know what I mean."

"Jenna?" Mom's voice is urgently insistent now.

"Aren't you going to answer her?" Luke whispers to me.

"I'm hoping she'll go away."

"Jenna? I don't want to invade your privacy, but you know that Daddy and I don't really approve of boys in your room," Mom says.

"Jared's in here all the time," I answer.

A pause.

"That's different. I mean *strange* boys," she says, emphasizing the word *strange*. "Boys not from the neighborhood, who I don't really know anything about."

She rattles the locked doorknob.

"You really should let her in," Luke says.

"I'm fine, Mom," I say loudly.

"I dunno, Daddy!" we hear her yelling. "She won't come out! I told you! I *dunno!!*"

Just kill me, I think.

"Don't worry, Mrs. Bloom," Luke says. "I was just leaving."

"Er, okay, well, now?" Mom asks.

"Mom!"

"Okay, well, um." Mom hesitates at the door. "Trust you . . . love you."

Then we hear her clomping back down the stairs.

Luke leans over and whispers in my ear:

"Me too."

Then he turns and in a flash is out the window and gone.

31

Over the next week, I'm consumed with feelings, some good and some confused. On the one hand, I feel dreamy, swoony, and moony. I replay Luke's words over and over in my mind. Does he really love me? Do angels ever lie?

On the other hand, I'm worried about the chance that he might leave. Aside from my feelings for him, the cold hard facts indicate that I will never again for the rest of my life have a boyfriend as awesome as Luke. I can only hope that he doesn't do anything, or agree to be sent anywhere until we get a chance to talk again.

In Miss Manley's gym class, I actually forget to crab kick the medicine ball when it's lobbed my way, and then the stitching gets stuck on my earring and it takes Miss Manley, the Grimm's–fairy tale nurse, and Custodian Tim to dislodge my head from the ball.

In Science, I'm too preoccupied to be grossed out about slicing into the pig fetus, even when Jared completely deserts me, opting to go into the other room with the animal activists, vegetarians, and the anemic-looking kids who are prone to vomiting.

Between classes, when the hallways are more crowded than a subway during rush hour, I see Luke. He reaches across the crush of people and touches my arm.

"Later." He winks.

This sends Tess into an apoplectic fit of "Oh my God," and "He so likes you," and "Did he ask you out?" And leads me to promise to fill her in later as the crowd divides us onto separate paths at the stairwell.

That afternoon, when I get to the Old Vic, I'm jolted out of my Luke preoccupation because everyone is abuzz with rehearsal frenzy. Chorus members and dancers are rehearsing, backstage elves are sawing and painting and, unfortunately, bending over. Mr. Resnick is preparing his actors onstage.

And I'm starting to worry about when fashion guru Lisa Golowski is planning on getting us started on costumes. No sooner does that thought pop into my head when a backstage elf galumphs toward me, wipes his drippy nose with his hand, and then uses said hand to give me a note. It's from none other than Lisa Golowski, and it says:

Hey Jenna,

Superbusy with school this semester, even though my mom insists I help with costumes. I suppose I can only be thankful that the show is not Sweet Charity, and my mom isn't prancing around stage in a garter, black stockings, and a corset again. You cannot possibly imagine the crap that I took from the other kids at school after that fiasco. As far as Fiddler goes, the costumes are pretty straightforward.

Everyone is a peasant, so we're talking about

244

black trousers and light shirts for the boys, gray skirts and blouses for the girls, and kerchiefs for the girls' hair. Everyone wears scruffy black boots. Remember, there's no budget so I would say make do with what's backstage and alter whatever you can. Can you sew? It's not hard. Pin, tape, and hot glue if you have to. Just worry about the main characters and make the chorus people pull together some old crap from their own closets.

Call me if you're really stuck, but don't be insulted if I'm hard to reach.

Good luck.

Lisa 😊

So now I am officially main costume elf?! How am I going to manage that all by myself, and now with so much human and celestial drama afoot!

Just then Tess catches my eye and excitedly waves me over from her piano bench.

"So Luke was actually in your room? Did you make out? Now, wait, first question, did you clean your room? Oh my God, at least please tell me you got rid of that funky-hamper smell. Were you studying for a test? Did you make out?"

"Well, it's complicated," I say, and then fill her in with an abbreviated version of the events. I was going to mention Luke's possible impending departure, but before I can get that far, she's like:

"Oh, wait . . . I want the rest of the dirt, but here comes Carlo. He's so cute, right?"

Just then Carlo comes squeezing up the theater aisle, carrying his tuba around his neck. It shifts back and forth as he walks, and it looks as though he's trying not to knock anyone unconscious with it.

"*Scusi, scusi,*" he chants as people duck and bob from his path.

"Hi Carlo. Glad you could make it to rehearsal!" Tess says, trying to steady the excited quiver from her voice.

He removes the tuba from his neck and carefully places it on a chair near her piano.

"*Cha!*" he exclaims happily.

"Em, this is my friend Jenna." Tess introduces me.

"Hi," I say.

"*Bwe.*" He reaches over and shakes my hand.

Tess and I exchange perplexed looks as he sets up his music stand. Then he comes back and stands in front of Tess.

"You!" he says.

"Me?"

"You, you!" He points happily.

Then he holds up his hand and points to his backpack.

"You!" He holds up his hand again.

"I think he has something for you in his backpack," I whisper to Tess.

Then he walks in a circle and pretends to be plucking something from the auditorium floor.

"Pluck?" Tess fishes.

"Pluck!" he exclaims. "You!"

"He wants to pluck me?" she whispers to me, as he pantomimes plucking the air over and over.

"Wait," I say. "I think he plucked a flower. You plucked a flower?"

"*Si!*" He nods enthusiastically.

Then he slaps his hands together.

"You slapped a flower?" Tess asks.

He rushes back to his backpack and pulls out a book.

"Oh, I think he pressed a flower," I say.

Carefully, he opens a music book and gingerly picks up a dead-looking flat daisy and proudly hands it to Tess.

"Oh thank you." She glows, and then, not sure where to put it, places it gently on top of the piano. "I love it."

And just then, thankfully, Miss Manley heads over to organize the musicians for their rehearsal.

"Hey," Tess says. "You didn't get to finish telling me about you and Luke."

"Have to be later, I guess." I shrug.

"Okay, but I want details," Tess says. I make my way over to Sheldon, Kayla, and Bea.

"So is it true?" Kayla leans across Sheldon and Bea and beams at me with wide-eyed amazement. "Are you really going out with . . . him?" She lowers her voice to a whisper and gestures toward the stage, where Luke stands next to Sarah, who is tugging on her too-revealing (if you ask me) cami top.

"Well, yeah, sort of." I blush.

"Amazing." Kayla sighs in disbelief.

"You're kidding!" Bea exclaims.

"Shhh!" a few rehearsing kids snap at her.

"You're kidding." She lowers the volume. "I thought that was a cruel rumor someone started just to humiliate you!"

"No, believe it or not, it's actually true," I say.

"Oh, no offense," Bea says.

"No offense," Kayla echoes.

"You know we love you," Bea says.

"Love you." Kayla nods with feeling.

"It's just that, well, Luke's so hot and you're so . . ."

"Cold?" I offer.

"Not cold, just so . . ." Bea struggles. "Not . . . hot."

"And besides," Kayla says, "Sarah Johnson wants him."

"Well, obviously, but did someone actually tell you that?" I ask.

"It's all over the school." Kayla is all breathy and excited.

"Well"—I rally—"just because she's gorgeous and sexy and hot and available and irresistible . . . and, ya know, hot?"

My resolve peters out.

"Well, yeah," Bea says, and Kayla nods.

Then, from the stage:

"Is this where we kiss?" Sarah asks Mr. Resnick, sidling up to Luke.

"No, you don't kiss, Sheila," Mr. Resnick says, sliding between them. "No kissing. In the little Russian village of Anatevka, no one kisses before marriage."

"But we're, like, betrothed or something," she says.

"You're not betrothed yet, Sheila." Mr. Resnick sighs. "How many times must I tell you? Your father has promised you to Lazar Wolf, the portly, unattractive butcher. An upstanding and familiar member of the community."

Sarah glances over at Ashton Hill, the boy who is playing the part of Lazar Wolf. He sits on the edge of the stage, blows his nose into a tissue, and then examines it.

"Ewww," Sarah says.

"That's right. Ewww, Sheila," Mr. Resnick says excitedly. "That emotion you're feeling, your revulsion, that's called actor's motivation. You don't want Alan over there. You are repulsed and revolted by Alan."

"Hey!" Ashton frowns. "I heard that."

Jared, who is in the corner of the stage barking directions at stage elves, notices me and waves.

"You want Luke!" Mr. Resnick exclaims.

"Well, that's a no-brainer." Sarah sniffs.

Mr. Resnick places his arm around Luke's shoulder.

"So now, Luke," Mr. Resnick continues. "This is the scene where you discover that the girl you love loves you back and where you secretly, behind her father's back, promise yourselves to each other."

Luke looks up and his eyes find me in the seats. He grins and I feel my face burn all shades of pink and red.

"And," Mr. Resnick continues, "that leads into the rousing song in which you talk to God and ask for courage and thank him for giving you this opportunity. You are like one of the biblical heroes of old and God has given you the strength to know what you want, and to go and grab it! So, let's sing that song!"

Mr. Resnick reaches an emotional crescendo and shakes his fists with great feeling!

At the piano, Tess hits the opening chords. Carlo hits a note on the tuba. Luke nods and hums to the music as if he's catching up with the words.

Hmm, hmm, hmm lion's den . . .

"Now that's hot," Sarah suddenly coos in a slithery voice.

"Yes, Sheila." Mr. Resnick wipes his eyes and trembles with emotion. "Great musical theater is hot. Very hot, indeed."

Out of a worthless lump of clay,
God has made a man today . . .

But the rest of us sense that Sarah is not responding to Mr. Resnick's passion for theater, or to Luke's passionate song. Her expression has taken on a predatory quality, and is focused on something, or someone, heading up the aisle.

Reflexively, Sheldon, Kayla, Bea, Tess, and I turn to see what she's really referring to.

Striding up the aisle, dressed in black jeans, a black T-shirt, and sleek black boots, with a sexy malevolent smirk on his alluring face, is none other than Adam.

"Hope I didn't keep you waiting," he says, and then, ever so quickly, his eyes dart over to me.

A hush falls over the theater.

"Oh," Sheldon exclaims softly. "Is he in the show now too? Who knew that *Fiddler* could be so fabulous!"

Adam smiles but his eyes are cruel and stony. He glances over at Luke and then his gaze settles on Sarah. Even from the cheap seats, I practically see the electricity *zzzzing* between them.

"Ooh, now here's an interesting dramatic twist." Sheldon sits up with delight. "Looks like our little missy Sarah not only likes your man, and by the way, you so need to get on that, but now she's after new hot boy as well!"

"And," Bea sings, as softly as she can manage, "don't forget her boyfriend!"

"Oh my God, that's right!" Sheldon pulls in a breath. "I forgot about Dean. Although I don't know how I could forget about Mr. Adorableness, of the well-defined pecs. What a hunk fest Oceanville is turning out to be! I mean, what's next? Is Robert Pattinson moving to town?"

This sends Kayla and Bea rocking with giggles.

"Oh and I just know that Adam is talented," Sheldon says. "Someone that perfect-looking just has to be good at everything."

"Sheldon, just because people look good doesn't mean they *are* good," I say churlishly. "There are a lot of homely people who have good hearts."

"Who cares about homely people!" Sheldon says. "Homely people should stay home! Everyone loves the good lookin.' That's why models should run for president. We would totally rule the world, and just think how cute our stamps would be."

I catch Luke's eye and he shoots me a worried look from the stage. It is officially official: Adam is here for a while and the worst is yet to come.

32

The next few days pass by uneventfully, if you don't count the bad feeling in the pit of my stomach and the fact that I think flocks of black, ominous crows are following me everywhere I go.

And although Luke hasn't mentioned leaving again, and I haven't pressed the topic, I can't help but worry that one day he'll just be gone.

What's more, David is suddenly acting more suspicious than normal. When I saw him in front of his house after school the other day and called out, "Hi," he averted his eyes and rushed up the path to his front door, past the new golfing gnome, practically knocking it onto its clay butt.

"David?" I called out. "Are you okay?"

"Gotta go," David answered brusquely. Then he scurried into his house and slammed the door.

Plus, not only do I have to deal with David and all the supernatural weirdness, there's the tiny problem of having only a few days left to turn twenty-first-century Oceanville teenagers into turn-of-the-century peasants. How am I going to cut and paste about fifty costumes so that they don't fall apart right onstage?

"I can see it in my head," I complain to Tess as we make our way down the hall to lunch. "The whole chorus raising their arms for the opening song, 'Tradition!' and every-body's pants falling down."

"That would suck," she agrees.

"I ordered the book *Sewing for Ninnies*, though," I say, "and I've been reading it in my spare time. Kayla knows a lot about sewing too, so she's going to help me."

As we enter the lunchroom, Tess smiles widely and gently pokes me in the ribs. Luke is already sitting at our table, finishing up his first salad plate. He spots us, waves, and heads to the salad bar for more.

"I just can't get used to seeing him at our table," Tess whispers. "It's so awesome. I wish Carlo had the same lunch period as us though."

The only good news in all of this is that my relationship with Luke is going very well. It's been about two weeks since he's been here, and he now eats lunch at my table every day!

The first time Luke sat down with us was kind of awkward and even Sheldon and Bea were pretty quiet and guarded, but it didn't take long for everyone to warm to his gentle ways and his quiet but sincere exuberance for school. Not to mention his extreme hotness to the max.

Not unexpectedly, though, our romance has created a swirl of disbelief around the school that a guy like him could be going out with a girl like me. Sarah, of course, even while continuing to date Dean, has a big cactus tree up her butt about it and has started circulating rumors such as:

- I give Luke money to sit with me and pretend that he likes me. This rumor is especially clever because everyone knows that he has an after-school job at Cowboy Clems, which implies that he could use the extra cash.

- Luke is secretly a hermaphrodite (a person with a set of both male and female sexual organs) and therefore likes no one and everyone at the same time.
- He's gay.
- He's gay and has a thing for Sheldon.
- He's my cousin (and I pay him to sit with me).
- He really has a crush on Sarah but is too shy to tell her and our table is close enough to hers so he can crush on her from afar.

Jared has suddenly begun sitting with us too, presumably subscribing to the idea that you should keep your friends close and your enemies closer.

Of course, Adam registered for school about a week ago, and he's already charmed the cool kids and is fast becoming one of them.

"I can't believe that our little lunch table has become the social hub of Oceanville!" Sheldon remarks. "And I also can't believe how much Sarah is chatting up Luke at the salad bar."

"And isn't that that weird, scary kid from the other day who's in *Fiddler* now?" Jared looks over, watching the three of them pile chickpeas onto their plates. "He just came out of nowhere and snagged the lead role in *Fiddler*, but I personally don't see the big deal about him."

"Let's see," Tess says, ticking off her fingers: "Gorgeous, sexy, hot, talented, charismatic. Did I leave anything out?"

"Evil," I say.

All eyes at the table turn to stare at me.

"I mean, evil hot."

"Mmm . . . I hear that!" Bea sings.

Sarah playfully slaps both Adam and Luke on their arms and bursts into laughter.

"OMG, you guys are just so funny!"

"Will you look at Sarah flirting with both of them," Tess remarks with disgust. "Doesn't she ever get her fill of hot guys? She looks at Adam as if he's . . . I don't know, something to eat."

"Well, then maybe she'll get full on him and stop looking at your man like he's dessert with a cherry on top." Sheldon points a carrot stick at me for emphasis.

"Why don't you sit with us, Adam?" Sarah coaxes. "How about you, Luke? Bored much?"

She swings her eyeballs over to our odd little group.

"No, I'm good. See ya," Luke says.

He returns to our table, swings his legs over the seat next to me, places his tray down next to my PB&J sandwich, and flashes his famous crinkly eyed smile.

"Mmmhmm, take that, nasty beyatch," Sheldon says under his breath, but loud enough to hear. He glares at Sarah.

Sarah frowns for a moment and then quickly recovers by slipping her arm through Adam's and leading him to her table, where her boyfriend, Dean Gold, looking supernaturally handsome himself, as well as a few of his cute team-mates, immediately start chatting Adam up about some kind of sports. Generally, once Dean likes a guy he's automatically considered to be one of the cool kids. I can only presume that he either isn't threatened by Sarah's flirting with Luke and Adam, or it doesn't cross his mind that some other guy could possibly be competition for his awesomeness.

Wow! I think, allowing myself to put worries aside and feel joy for the moment. How did I get so lucky as to have a boyfriend who, although not quite human, is so wonderful in every other way!

I feel triumphant. I feel invincible. I feel happy.

That is until I feel Adam's eyes boring into me. Ignoring him, I pick up my Bulk PB&J sandwich.

"Wha—!"

I startle and jump back, spilling my drink all over Luke's lap.

My Bulk white bread is filled with worms!

"Oh!" Luke jumps up.

"Oh no! Here!" Tess, Kayla, and Bea frantically exclaim. They hand Luke bunches of napkins.

"S'all right. I got it," he says, wiping his drenched lap. "No big deal."

"Jenna." Luke places his hand on my arm. "Are you okay?"

I look back down and my sandwich is normal again.

Should I tell Luke that my crunchy peanut butter was just crawling across the bread or will it make him upset? He is so happy here in Oceanville. No, my kind heart just can't let me ruin his day.

"I'm fine. It's nothing," I say. "I just thought I saw a spider."

I glance up. Adam grins at me in a menacing way.

"I'll go get some more napkins." Luke sprints back to the hot-food counter.

"Ooh, I hate spiders," Kayla says. "Too many legs. Why does something need so many legs? A thing can only go in one direction at a time."

Jared straightens in his chair. "Well, when we shot our documentary *Don't Be Creeped Out by Crawlies: Spiders Are Our Friends* we found out quite a bit about their biological makeup and ecological purpose. For example . . ."

Then the conversation is a blur of noise and blah, blah, blah buzzing in the back of my ears.

I feel something in one of my hands. I look down. Out of nowhere, a folded note has appeared in my palm. In old-fashioned curlicued penmanship, it reads: *It's not over.*

Then the note disintegrates into dust right through my fingers and onto the floor.

Adam sneers at me, then smoothly turns his attention back to his new group of friends.

33

There's another *Fiddler* rehearsal today after school. The pace has picked up as everyone prepares for opening night, and Bernice drops David off at the theater every afternoon. He still seems a bit quiet, and I can't help wonder if all this supernatural danger has frightened him. Despite his cocky personality and dream to be a superhero, he is just a little kid after all. However, he's still been pulling a few pranks (such as gluing Miss Manley's coffee cup to the cup holder) and he's also flipped me the bird and told me to bite myself, a few times, so I figure that he's generally okay.

In the dressing room, I take instruction from my new sewing bible, *Sewing for Ninnies*, chapter 2, "Cheapskate Designers: Use What You Got," and lay all the costumes from every show ever done across the dressing room floor.

Much to my surprise, my mind starts making sense of it all. I can actually envision *Fiddler* costumes pieced together from all this old stuff. Could it be that I will pull this off? Could this be something that I am good at?

There isn't anything from *High School Musical* 1, 2, or 3, of course, but I can definitely use the little black pants from *Oliver!* for the town boys in *Fiddler*. I can extend the hems with scraps from a very large Mary Poppins skirt.

Then there are many long skirts from *The Miracle Worker* and *Carousel*, which I can use for the girls of Anatevka, following instructions from chapter 7 of SFN, "Couldn't You Just Dye?!," by dyeing them darker colors.

Then there is the wedding dress from *The Sound of Music*, which I can use for Tzeitel's (Sarah's) wedding dress and a nightshirt for Tevye's dream sequence.

I can even trick out pieces of corsets from *Sweet Charity* for added signature style. And I can make the shroud for the angry ghost of Fruma Sarah from the dressing room curtains!

I feel just like some kind of freaky Maria Von Trapp. Climb every mountain, indeed!

"Jerry! Backstage elves!" I hear Mr. Resnick shouting from onstage.

Curious, I make my way into the wings to watch the rehearsal unfold.

"Let's get the stage prepared for the graveyard dream sequence. I need Adam, our new Tevye, Tevye's wife, and the ghost of Fruma Sarah," says Mr. Resnick.

Suddenly I feel hands on my waist, which makes me jump back.

"Hi." Luke leans in toward me. "I'm waiting for my cue."

Jared appears, squeezing between us, waving his clipboard around like the guy on the airport tarmac who guides the planes onto the runway. "Outta the way! Coming through!" he announces. "All right, get the bed center stage!"

The butt-crack elves practically knock us over with the rolling bed.

"Tom, Matt, get ready with the high wire," Jared instructs into his headphone mouthpiece.

He waves his hands around at a few of the elves perched on the catwalk as they lower some kind of harness down toward the stage.

Sarah appears and struts over to the bed, then sits down and gently bounces up and down, like she's testing it for softness. This causes snickers and low wolf whistles from the crowd.

"No, dear," Mr. Resnick says. "This is a scene between Tevye and his wife."

He takes her gently by the shoulders and moves her downstage.

Then he turns and addresses the house seats.

"Elves, let's scatter a few of the tombstones around the bed so the ghosts can hide . . . I need chorus and townspeople for the ghosts and ghouls!"

"David!" I prompt from behind the curtain.

He lifts his eyes from his comic book, spots me, and then ignores me.

"Get up! You're a townsperson!" I wave my palm up and down.

David rolls his eyes, but then hops onto the stage along with Sheldon, Kayla, Bea, and all the other chorus extras. Tess makes her way to the piano, looking ready for her cue.

"Come on! Townspeople and ghosts and *neighbors*!" Jared shouts, shooting Luke a dirty look. "Chop! Chop! Onstage!"

At this point, everyone is onstage already, just staring at him.

"Shake a tail feather! We don't have all day! Get a move on! No time to dillydally!"

"I think they get it, Jared," I offer.

"Humph," he replies grumpily, his glance passing from me to Luke and back again.

"Golda! Tevye's wife! We need you in bed with Tevye!" Jared stomps across the stage.

Now it's Adam's turn on the bed. He ambles over and sits down. Then he throws up his legs, crosses them at the ankles, folds his arms behind his head, and slowly leans back onto the propped pillows. His well-defined biceps pulse through his tight, short-sleeved T-shirt. I can almost hear every girl in the room go silent from near fainting.

"Bring down the harness!" Jared orders the stage elves.

The harness is lowered from the rafters, looking like a big kid's swing with straps.

"Golda! Golda!" Jared yells into the empty auditorium. "Tevye's wife, Golda!"

"I don't think anyone's out there," Adam remarks casually from the bed.

We hear a crackling coming from Jared's headphone.

"Wait, what?" he responds. "She's where?

"Mr. Resnick," Jared continues, "one of the elves says that Golda can't be here until later. She's at the orthodontist getting her braces tightened."

"Gah!" Mr. Resnick exclaims, and throws up his hands. "Can't she wait until after opening night to have straight teeth?!"

He glares at all the kids onstage.

"Anyone know her lines? Well, has anyone been paying attention?"

"Oh, I've been paying attention." Sarah aims a dead-on flirtatious glare at Adam. Then she slithers toward the bed and crawls in next to him in a way that's rated at least PG-13.

"Well, all right." Mr. Resnick sighs. "Fine. Let's get the ghost of Fruma Sarah into the harness."

"Ghost of Fruma Sarah!" Jared marches around and pushes everyone out of the way. "Ghost of Fruma Sarah! . . . *Ghost!*"

Silence in the auditorium.

Another buzzing noise comes from Jared's headset.

"Wait . . . what?" Jared says into his mouthpiece.

"Margaret Lipshitz thinks she got a bee sting and went home for her EpiPen," Jared announces.

"Oh good lord!" Mr. Resnick bellows. "Where are we going to find another girl who doesn't mind shrieking like a ghost while being hoisted around through the air by a bunch of backstage elves?"

"I'll do it." Kayla steps forward meekly.

All eyes turn toward her in disbelief.

"What? It might be fun," she says, and then shrinks back.

"You're too small, Kayla," Adam says. "Isn't that right, Mr. Resnick?"

He gets out of the bed and walks over to the harness, looking as if he's assessing its size.

"You need a shorter girl with a thicker waist."

Then he swings his eyes around until they land directly

on me. Forty other pairs of eyes swing around and glare directly at me too.

"Me?" I squeak.

"No," says Luke, stepping out in front of me. "Too dangerous."

"Pish posh," says Mr. Resnick, grabbing my hand and pulling me toward the harness. He passes me to Adam, who starts strapping me in.

"It's perfectly safe," Adam croons, prompting me to place my feet through the holes of the swing. "Back in my hometown, my parents were in the circus—"

"Mr. Resnick," Luke tries to intercede. "I don't think this is a good idea. She has no experience in a harness and," he speaks low, "she's kind of clumsy."

"I heard that," I say.

Adam continues to strap me in.

"Don't be nervous, Luke," Mr. Resnick says, pushing him back. "It's perfectly safe. We used it on Sunny Banerjee for every performance of *Mary Poppins* and she's much heftier than Jebba here."

"But—" Luke looks at me helplessly.

Mr. Resnick starts a flurry of activity and Luke gets shoved aside.

"Townspeople, places behind the tombstones," Mr. Resnick instructs. "Let's start from Fruma Sarah's ghost's entrance. Okay, boys! Hoist her up!"

"Whaaaaaaaaa!!!!"

Suddenly, I'm yanked up by the crotch, thirty feet above the stage.

"Start her swinging!" yells Mr. Resnick.

"Whoooooaaaa!"

Then I'm swinging!

"Now, Tevye," Mr. Resnick instructs Adam, who's climbed back into the bed, "you're telling your wife about the nightmare where you're being haunted by Lazar Wolf's dead wife, the ghost of Fruma Sarah. Remember, she's a very angry spirit and wants to kill you for trying to marry off your daughter, Tzeitel, to her husband . . ."

He then turns to the backstage elves.

"Cue music!" he shouts, and hops down into the orchestra pit.

Tess plays, but I can barely hear the music for fear.

"Haaaaeeeellpp!!" I'm yanked around even higher.

"Good, Jebba!" says Mr. Resnick. "But instead of yelling 'help!' try screeching 'boo!' or 'eee!' And don't look so frightened. *You're* supposed to be scaring *us*."

"Cue lights!" Mr. Resnick shouts.

The stage goes black and wonky, except for the white spotlights, which have taken on a ghostly glow, like many haze-encircled moons. I look down, and suddenly everyone is frozen, including the elves who are supposed to be controlling this contraption. Somehow, I'm swinging harder now and then I'm outside the theater and it's nighttime and I'm in the park, swinging high, out of control, through the dark, shadowy trees.

And the faint music from *Fiddler* has turned into Michael Jackson's "Thriller."

"Luke!" I shriek.

"Jenna!" I hear him call back, but I can't see him and I can't release myself from the harness. I look up. Adam is above me, large and sinister and seemingly suspended in midair himself. Like a giant puppeteer, he's controlling me, swinging me into near misses with tree trunks and rooftops. I struggle to free myself, but I can't.

"Adam, let me down!" I scream into the night.

Then Adam is before me, sitting in a tree, looking like one of the wicked witch's flying monkeys from *The Wizard of Oz*.

"Had enough?" he asks casually, leaning against the tree trunk.

And suddenly I have had enough, but not like he thinks.

"I'm not giving you the pendant, Adam," I say, fighting back light-headedness, fighting the urge to barf, feeling my PB&J sandwich crawling back up my esophagus.

"You sure?"

Then I'm yanked up higher and swung around more wildly, until I make my way back to him. Can I take this? Can he do this forever? What am I made of after all? *Why not give him the pendant?* I wonder for just a second, as my hand reaches up and closes around the hideous thing.

Vincent Price is laughing again:

Aha-ha-ha-ha-ha-ha . . . Aha-ha-ha-ha-ha . . .

Adam leans forward, exultant expectation on his face.

Will it matter if he stays? How much worse can Oceanville, or the world, get anyway? But . . . What if Mr. Deets was right? What if it isn't the Adams who make life bad, but the people giving in to the Adams who caused the problem in the first place?

"Just do it," Adam goads in a low voice. "This is your last chance to give it to me freely because I'm not leaving. Give it to me and I won't hurt you. Don't make me find a way to take it."

"No," I say, feeling suddenly good about myself. "Just . . . no."

Adam stands in the tree, his face a mask of rage, and then I hear a great flutter of wings. Luke?!

I'm yanked upward once more, and instantly, I'm back in the theater, flying out of control across the stage. There's a great commotion under me and I'm dropping. Fast. Then it's as if time slows for a few moments. Luke has me in his arms and is lowering me onto Golda and Tevye's bed.

Then:

Bam.

Back in real time. Crazy turmoil all around me. I'm surrounded by Tess and my friends. David is there too. He looks up, then looks at me, his face piqued. It's as if he saw exactly what happened.

A frightened-looking Jared unhooks me from the harness, and I hear a chorus of:

"Are you all right?"

"Holy crap!"

"That was radical."

And:

"I thought she was dead."

"Stand back, everyone." Mr. Resnick parts the crowd like Moses. "Jebba, are you all right?"

"I'm okay," I croak, and climb off the bed.

"Wow, that harness got out of control and you just kept flying and spinning around!" Jared says.

"Are you sure?" Mr. Resnick asks, placing his hand on my shoulder.

"Yeah, I'm good," I say.

"Sorry, Mr. Resnick." The butt-crack elves race toward him. "The cables just went crazy. We don't know what happened."

"Well, fix them and test them out before we use them again. Carefully. On a boy. Someone bigger. Jerry, maybe you can volunteer," Mr. Resnick says.

I spot Luke, standing apart, his face quiet. Sad. I feel for the heart necklace around my neck. Then the crowd closes in around me. I blink and Luke disappears.

34

The remainder of rehearsal flies by in a blur. Mr. Resnick insists that I rest in the auditorium for a while to make sure I feel okay and then I spend the next half hour avoiding Adam and trying to track down Luke. I can only imagine that one of Mr. Deets's seagull recruits called him away for some reason, but I can't help shaking the bad feeling that something's up.

Later that afternoon, I enter my house and am about to walk past the kitchen when I hear Michael's voice. "Hey, that cowpoke guy was here looking for you."

"What? Luke was here? When? What did he say? Where is he now?!"

"I dunno." Michael shrugs and then turns his whole body into the fridge, as if it's the secret wardrobe and he's trying to gain entrance to Narnia.

"Whaddaya mean, you don't know?!" I say frantically, grabbing his arm and swinging him around. "What did he say?"

"He said, um, something about going . . . I think. Or maybe it was coming . . ."

"Did he say he was coming over?" I enunciate slowly as if talking to a child.

Michael shoves a piece of leftover meat loaf into his mouth.

"Dunno. But I don't think Mom or Dad will be too happy to see him."

"Gah! Thanks, Michael," I say sarcastically.

Luke still doesn't have a phone or computer and I still have no way of getting in touch with him. I am just going to have to wait for him to show up or call.

Exasperated, I head down the hall, past my parents sitting on the couch in the den. Dad is plugged into his iPod as usual and I can hear faint operatic singing coming from his head. Mom is multitasking: watching TV while leafing through a *People* magazine.

"Jenna," she calls out. "Don't start anything new. We're going out to dinner. We thought we'd try something different tonight."

I screech to a halt and throw my body around the corner.

"Something new?" I ask.

Michael rounds the corner, wiping whipped cream off his mouth with his sleeve. He farts.

"Excuse me," I say, offering him a prompt.

"You're excused," he says.

"Stop eating, Michael. We're going out," Mom says.

"Where we goin'?" Michael asks.

"Well, kids"—Mom beams; she puts the magazine down in her lap—"lately, your father and I have been feeling . . . What's the word, Daddy?"

Dad opens his mouth to speak.

"Restless." Mom speaks instead. "Everything is so familiar. So . . . What am I trying to say, Daddy? It's all so—"

He tries to speak again.

"Predictable," she interrupts. "It's . . ."

Her eyes dart around the room as if a synonym for *boring* is written somewhere on the walls.

"So . . ."

"Facile," Dad says, and all eyes swing around to stare at him.

"Easy," he clarifies.

"That's right. Too easy." Mom grins. "So that's why we're gonna do something different tonight."

"Hey, maybe we could go to Manchu Gardens," I offer excitedly. "It's a warm night. We could sit in that pretty garden by the koi pond—"

"I never get enough to eat there," Michael complains. "Too much rice, and small portions."

"We thought"—Mom builds to a crescendo—"we'd go to . . ."

Michael and I lean forward.

"Cowboy Clems!"

"Cowboy Clems?!" I groan. "What's so different about that?!"

"Wait." Mom holds up her hand. "In . . . Brooklyn!"

"Whooaa, Brooklyn," Michael repeats. "I'm stoked. Can we take the train?"

"We drive," Dad says.

"Brooklyn?!" I wail. "But that's not different. Cowboy Clems is a chain and Brooklyn is, well, Brooklyn."

"Whaddaya think?" Mom beams, ignoring me. "Brooklyn is very chic with all those tall brick houses."

"You mean brownstones?" I say.

"And I heard from the Salingers that the Brooklyn Cowboy Clems is very upscale. Totally different menu." Mom waves her hand around as if erasing a large, old imaginary menu.

"And friendly service. And afterward maybe we can walk around the Brooklyn promenade and people watch," Mom says. "Won't it be nice to see the water?"

"Mom, we live in Oceanville," I say. "We're a few blocks from the water."

The communist Blooms continue to ignore me and chatter excitedly among themselves. I sigh heavily and head up the stairs to my room.

"Oh, and Jenna!" Mom shouts out. "I left a shopping bag on your bed. I bought you some cute things at the Bulk. They were having an end-of-season fire sale. Why don't you put on something new for our hoedown at Cowboy Clems? Get it? Hoedown at the cowboy restaurant?"

I leave them to their giggles and guffaws and shut my door behind me. All the way to Brooklyn. In a Bulk outfit. Woo-hoo, I can barely contain my enthusiasm. I slam onto the bed and look out the window. It's turning into a beautiful, clear, pinkish-and-blue dusky late afternoon. The feathery finger clouds remind me of angel wings.

Where the hell is Luke?

35

Once at the Brooklyn Cowboy Clems, I'm astonished (not) by how remarkably similar (exactly the same) it is to the Oceanville Cowboy Clems.

At communist Mom's prompting, I'm wearing my new Bulk outfit: faux-denim jeans and a hideous pastel-pink sweater with the words *Ain't She Cute* written across the front in rhinestones. Not to mention a sparkly new pair of slip-on shoes that keep slipping off because they're made out of cardboard, glue, and staples.

And as I sit there, I close my eyes and just start wishing: wishing that Luke was with me, wishing I knew how to call him, wishing there was someone who could help me without thinking that I was certifiably crazy. Sigh. Wishing.

When:

"Howdy. I'm Cowpoke Deets. Can I take your order?" a voice says flatly.

My eyes fly open.

There in front of me, real as day, is Mr. Deets. Can it be, I wonder, *the* Mr. Deets? The head angel guy, Luke's boss, in charge of angels and an army of seagulls?

I give him the once-over, and realize that he's not what I expected. I somehow thought that he'd be an older, more elegant version of Luke. But this guy is somewhat paunchy, bald, dressed in worn jeans, the standard cowpoke shirt (except with a stain) and the ugly brown shoes that I've seen Mom eyeballing for Dad at the Bulk Emporium.

His name tag reads: *Manager.*

Is that supposed to be ironic? Is "manager" just a colloquial expression for "head guardian angel"? Am I finally going to get some divinely inspired answers?

"Mr. Deets?" I ask, hesitantly.

He taps his name tag with his pencil and nods.

"That's me."

"*The* Mr. Deets?" I lean forward and whisper. "The Mr. Deets who knows Luke?" I interject a wink here. "Are you *that* Mr. Deets?"

"For God's sake, Jenna, what's wrong with you?" Mom asks, looking abashed. "His name tag says Mr. Deets. Let it go."

"You need more time?" Mr. Deets taps his pencil on his waiter pad and sighs impatiently.

And even though I'm staring at him hard, he makes no indication that he knows me.

"Let's see." Mom studies the menu as if she's taking her SATs.

"May I recommend the special family nacho platter?" Mr. Deets says as if he really wants to recommend that she hurry the hell up.

"Hmm," Mom ponders. "What makes it so special?"

"It's the secret sauce," Mr. Deets leans in and whispers.

"See, kids?" Mom beams with great satisfaction. "I told you this Cowboy Clems was different."

"What's the secret?" Michael asks.

"If I told you"—Mr. Deets lifts an eyebrow at Michael—"it wouldn't be a secret."

On the word *secret*, Mr. Deets's eyes shoot over to me for just a second. But it's a pregnant second. Is he trying to tell me something?

"Yeah, duh, no kidding it wouldn't be a secret," Michael snarks. "But isn't that, like, not legal, refusing to tell us the ingredients?"

"Michael," Mom scolds, looking embarrassed. "Mind your manners. We're in Brooklyn now."

"Sorry," Michael says.

"No, that's not illegal. And just for the record, there are a lot of secrets in life, kid," Mr. Deets says. "If you ask too many questions, you might get answers that you're not ready for."

Another glance in my direction! Is Mr. Deets speaking in some kind of code for my benefit?"

"Are we still talking about food?" Michael asks, perplexed.

"Sure." Mr. Deets shrugs, angles his pencil against his pad, and looks at us expectantly.

"Oh . . . okay." Michael gazes back down at his menu as Mom goes ahead and orders the special family nacho platter as well as an assortment of burritos, chimichangas, tacos, and sodas, making sure that refills are free.

Mr. Deets scribbles down the orders, takes the menus, and ambles away.

"Er, I forgot to order something," I say, getting up. "I'll tell Mr. Deets, I mean, the waiter."

"You are such a pig!" Michael scoffs.

I let that remark pass.

"You don't have to get up, Jenna," Mom says, raising her arm. "I'll just call him over."

"No, no, that's all right! I, um . . . have to go to the ladies' room anyway."

And before she can offer to join me, I'm up and scrunching over the peanut-shell-covered floor toward the bar.

"Can I speak to the manager, Mr. Deets?" I ask the bartender.

"I think he's in the kitchen," she says, signaling with her thumb to the swinging doors behind her.

"Well, could you get him for me? It's really important."

She gives me a glowering look, like, "What am I, the hired help or something?" Then her eyes slip down to the *Ain't She Cute* emblem on my sweater. Her mouth curls up at the corners in a tiny snicker. I cross my arms over my chest and stand my ground.

"Tell me what you need, and I'll send him over when he comes out," she says, like she's doing me some big favor.

This is going to be harder than I thought.

"No, I really need to see him 'cause he's the manager and, um, my dad's really annoyed," I lie.

The bartender glances around me at my dad, who's happily swaying to his iPod music and eating chips.

"He doesn't look annoyed," she says, squinting her eyes at me.

"That's just the calm before the storm. Trust me." I lean toward her and speak low. "He can get violent."

Just then my whole family bursts into gales of laughter.

"Fine," the bartender snaps, slapping her cleaning rag onto the bar.

She disappears behind the swinging doors and is back five seconds later.

"Mr. Dects left for the night," she says. "But I told Jacques to come out. He's our night manager."

From out of the swinging doors emerges some middle-aged guy who I assume is Jacques.

"Can I help you?" Jacques asks.

Now his eyes swing down to the *Ain't She Cute* emblem across my chest. He frowns slightly and I can almost hear him mentally answering my sweater with *No, she really ain't*. I make a mental note to myself to burn the sweater when I get home.

"I need to talk to Mr. Deets," I say, tightening my arms across my chest.

He glances out the large storefront window.

"There he is, on the corner, waiting for his bus," Jacques says.

And sure enough, Mr. Deets, who, if he is who I think he is, probably could have conjured up a sporty car for himself, is standing at the bus stop, pulling his jacket in close against the chill, just like a normal guy.

I glance over at my family. The waitress is maneuvering their special family nacho platter, the size of an air mattress, onto the table and they're all delirious with anticipation. I figure that it will keep them thoroughly occupied for at least ten minutes.

"Can I help—" Jacques begins to say.

"No, I'm good," I interrupt, and sprint across the crunchy floor, out the front door, and onto the dark, busy sidewalk. I'm just about to cross the street when a big bus pulls up to the bus stop and Mr. Deets steps forward to board.

36

"Wait! Wait! Mr. Deets!" I shout, rushing across the street. "Please stop! I need to talk to you!"

Mr. Deets glances my way, but the bus blocks him from my view. I hear the doors close with a loud *whoosh*. After a few seconds, the gears grind thunderously, the bus coughs up a great billow of smoke, and then it pulls away.

"Oh no," I groan, and I'm about to turn back when there he is, still standing on the corner. A large white seagull sits atop the bus stop sign.

"Mr. Deets!" I spring toward him breathlessly. "Thank you for waiting. I need to talk to you."

I shiver in the cool night air and curse my thin sweater for the third time that night.

Mr. Deets shoos the seagull away and it angrily squawks off into flight.

"What is there to talk about?" Mr. Deets glances at his watch.

"Well, first of all, I know this may sound crazy . . . But are you Luke's . . . supervising angel?"

Mr. Deets looks at me like I'm insane for what seems like the longest five seconds of my life.

"Okay, sorry." I feel my cheeks flush bright crimson. "My

bad. Reading too many supernatural books I guess. Well, bye."

I turn to go.

"What exactly is it that you want to talk about?" he says matter-of-factly.

I turn back.

"So it's true?" I ask. "You're an angel?"

"Sure." He shrugs.

Then suddenly I feel suspicious, like what if he's a psycho who likes to talk to teenage girls and I just gave him a whole lot of information to string me along. Like that phony psychic at the Camp Ronkonkama Renaissance Faire who asked me about myself and then told me stuff that, in hindsight, was just a spin on what I had told her.

"Then why do you work at Cowboy Clems?" I slant my eyes at him.

"It's an undercover gig. I like to stay close to the masses. Be immersed in the culture of the time. You know. Word."

He makes a rapper sign.

"Used to be everyone respected teachers. That was my old gig. Now no one respects anyone, but everyone wants to go out to eat."

"Okay. Whatever," I say. "But how do I know for sure that you're really who I think you are?" I say.

"I guess you don't," he answers.

"So you're telling me I should just trust you," I say.

"I'm not telling you anything. Except that if you want some answers you better ask the questions faster because my bus is coming."

"Okay, first question: Why does an angel need to take the bus?"

"I just told you. The masses. Besides, I like the bus. Next question."

"You're not gonna make this easy, are you?"

"Life is rarely easy."

"That's it. Life is rarely easy. I could have read that in a fortune cookie."

"Plus, you would have gotten a cookie," he says.

"Fine." I turn to go. "You're either an incredibly infuriating angel or you're a psycho who's messing with me. But I'm hungry and I'm cold and I'm going back inside."

"That's because communist Mom didn't buy you a thick-enough sweater," he says.

I stop dead in my tracks and turn back once again.

He rustles through the bag at his feet.

"Here." He hands me a hoodie, deep blue with velvet trim. I turn it over and there's delicately embroidered writing on the back. It says:

I ♥ Angels.

"That's really funny," I say, kind of astonished.

"I know you typically don't like clothes with messages written on them," he says. "But this one seemed appropriate."

I hesitate, putting the hoodie back into his hands.

"You're afraid to take it," he says. "That's good. You shouldn't take gifts from strangers, but since the cat is out of the bag, I'll fess up. Yes, I'm who you think I am."

He holds out the hoodie again. Gingerly, I take it from him.

"Thanks. It's great," I say, pulling it on. "It's just the right size. And it's warm too. So is this from . . . heaven?"

"Heaven? No, it's from the Bulk Emporium," he says. "It's very hit or miss there. You have to know how to look."

"Hmm," I say, zipping the hoodie closed. "I'll keep that in mind."

"So what do you want to know?" he asks, then glances up the road again.

I take a deep breath. There are so many things I want to know, but I know that he isn't going to hang around long so I get right to the point.

"I want to know if Luke can stay here for a while as a human or maybe as a human-angel hybrid or something. This way he can finish growing up. You know he really didn't get to do that before."

"That's true," Mr. Deets says. "But his destiny took him on another path. He's only supposed to be here temporarily on assignment, you know. To help banish Adam back to where he should be, before the equinox closes."

"Isn't there another way to get rid of Adam?" I ask.

His eyes travel down to the pendant around my neck.

"What? This?" I hold the pendant up. "I know that as long as I keep this from Adam, he can't stay."

"That's not all it does," Mr. Deets singsongs.

"You mean, like how the pendant was used to kill Adam at the Bloody Harvest Dance? You want me to *use* the pendant . . . as in, *kill* Adam with it?" I whisper.

"I'm just sayin' . . ."

He glances up the road again.

"You are the keeper of the pendant, after all," he says, matter-of-factly.

"Yeah the *keeper*. Not the *killer*."

"But what if Adam somehow manages to kill *me* to get the pendant?" I ask.

"Well, he could, I suppose . . ." Mr. Deets says, pulling a pair of gloves from his pockets and putting them on. "But I don't think he will. He knows there would be tremendous spiritual consequences for that kind of behavior. Worse than you can imagine. I don't think he'd risk it just to be a twenty-first-century kid at Arthur P. Rutherford Middle School. He'd have to be crazy."

Mr. Deets stops talking and glances up the road.

"That's it. You're gonna leave it up to us to figure out?" I ask.

"Whaddaya want me to say?" He shrugs. "You have free will and, by the way, Luke does too, now that he's half human again. But he has a job to do. He was chosen, out of many souls, to do it. Sometimes there's a bigger picture than what a single person can see. As for Adam, his type slips through the void all the time. It's not what he tries to do, it's how you people handle him that's important. Bad things happen when good people do nothing—"

"Didn't I read that once on a graphic tee at the Bulk Emporium?" I say.

"You know all the little annoying decisions that you have to make every day?" Mr. Deets responds, ignoring my remark. "What to eat, what to wear, what courses to take in school? Well, life is like that, only on a bigger scale. And more annoying."

Within seconds, the bus turns the corner and grinds up the block. The doors whoosh open.

"I want you to help us," I say. "Or at least give me some practical advice."

"You'd better get back inside Cowboy Clems now. Your family is just beginning to wonder where you are. Oh and your mother will think she bought you that sweatshirt."

He ascends the steps and swipes his bus card through the automatic-pay slot.

"But—"

"You're a smart, resourceful kid, Jenna. Keep being true to yourself!"

I roll my eyes.

"I know. Another fortune cookie platitude." He grins and tightens his scarf.

"That reminds me. One more thing," he says.

He pulls a fortune cookie out of his pocket and tosses it to me.

Then the doors slam shut.

I unwrap the cookie, crush it, and pull out the fortune.

It says:

Be careful.

Then the bus pulls away from the curb and is gone.

37

I slip back into Cowboy Clems and arrive at the Bloom table just in time to see the special family nacho platter licked clean, although Mom did save me a few nachos and put them in the little plastic Tupperware that she brought with her to lock-and-seal any leftovers for the ride home. Then Mom kicks up a conversation with the lady at the next table about her earrings and is thrilled when the lady informs her that she has at least forty similar pairs at home.

"Oh my God, Daddy," Mom exclaims, "there's a Bulk Emporium outlet located in Brooklyn!"

Dad nods pleasantly with the other husband while the conversation turns into a communist shopping lovefest.

I feel Michael's eyes boring into me from across the table. "What?" I snap.

He leans forward.

"I know the secret," he whispers.

"What?" I'm suddenly alarmed.

"The secret. Come on. How stupid do you think I am?"

"Uh . . . pretty stupid?"

"Wrong answer." Michael leans back and grins at me. Then he glances out the window to the exact spot where I was talking to Mr. Deets.

Could Michael possibly know? I wonder. And how much

could he know? Could he know about Luke and Adam? Would he tell Mom and Dad? Would they have me committed?

"But . . . How did you figure it out?" I ask.

Michael taps his head with his finger and winks.

"Well, okay," I say, reluctantly. "So now you know. What are you gonna do?"

"Oh, I don't know yet," he teases.

"You could keep your mouth shut," I offer.

"Nah, what's the fun in that?" he counters.

"You're bluffing," I say, leaning toward him. "You don't know anything."

"I'll tell you what," Michael says. "I'd keep my mouth shut for"—he looks around furtively and leans in closer to me—"money."

"Money?!" I exclaim. "I don't have any money! You want the angels to pay you money?"

"What angels?"

"Mr. Deets, Luke—I thought you said you knew," I hiss.

"Who's Mr. Deets? You mean our waiter? What the hell are you talking about?"

"What are *you* talking about?" I say. "Who's supposed to give you money?"

"Cowboy Clems, of course," he says.

"Cowboy Clems? Why would Cowboy Clems give you money?"

Michael sighs loudly, slapping his body back into the plastic-upholstered seat, which exhales a big *whoooo*.

"For discovering the secret. The special secret, dummy. Duh, Jenna. Isn't that what we're talking about?"

Then he leans in real close again, all the way into my face.

"It's the chipotles," he whispers. "The little ones. Lots of 'em. They mush them up and mix them with sour cream and salsa and I think some hot sauce and stick 'em right between the black-bean stuff and the chips. Sneaky, huh?"

I break out in a light sweat. Chipotles. That's what he was talking about.

"A person has to get up pretty early in the morning to fool you, Michael," I say, slumping with relief back into my seat, which also makes a *whoooo*.

"You got that right." He pretend-shoots me with his thumb and forefinger.

After dessert, and a lot of bean belches and discreet farting from *some* family members, Mom suggests we go for a walk across the Brooklyn promenade (so Michael can finish farting before the car ride home) and enjoy the lights of the New York City skyline in the process.

"Isn't this wonderful, Daddy?" Mom takes a deep breath and loops her arm through Dad's as we make our way up the promenade. "Oh, and kids, there's the Empire State Building."

She leads Dad and Michael over to the railing and points across the water.

"Which one is it?" Michael squints.

"Which one is it?! The tall spiky one with the lights!" Mom shrieks impatiently. "Aren't you getting an education in school?"

"They're all tall with lights," Michael says.

I wander away and leave them to their pointing and bickering.

The evening air does feel wonderful and the walk gives me a good opportunity to clear my head. The promenade looks romantic, dotted with old-fashioned streetlights and slatted wooden benches, and the view of the New York skyline is majestic. If only Luke were here, it would be perfect. I lean against the railing and gaze across the water, which glistens with an inky, wavy reflection of the city lights.

I absentmindedly fiddle with the heart necklace hanging around my neck.

Then:

I feel someone's eyes on me. A few yards away, Luke stands in the shadows, by a park bench, between the lampposts, looking so beautiful in his dark-wash jeans, black turtleneck and awesome brown leather jacket. He smiles.

I glance back at my parents, who have veered over to the bicycle ice cream truck parked by the side of the promenade.

Michael Jackson's "Wanna Be Startin' Somethin'" plays in ice cream bells.

Another Michael Jackson song. They always seem to play when something supernatural is going on. This time it must be a good sign.

I rush toward Luke.

"Luke," I gush. "Where were you?! I was looking for you! Why haven't you called? I thought maybe you weren't coming back!"

I laugh nervously but he doesn't. He pushes his hands into

the pockets of his jeans and looks across the water to the skyline.

I recall a recent *Teen Glamour* magazine article: "Ten Don'ts: How Not to Scare a Guy Away":

1. Don't run toward him with a crazy look on your face.
2. Don't gush and pant.
3. Don't demand to know where he's been and why he hasn't called.

Oh God, I already broke the first three rules. I need to calm down.

"I mean, it's good to see you," I say.

"Didn't you get my note?" he asks.

"What note?"

"When I stopped by your house the other day. I gave it to Michael. He was busy fixing a sandwich, but I said don't forget . . . Never mind." He shakes his head.

I feel my stomach slip to my feet. Everything about his body language is wrong. He's standing too far away. His hands are jammed into his pockets. He's not looking me in the eye. He's pulling in and away. He's leaving. I can feel it.

"I spoke to Mr. Deets," I say. "We talked about you and Adam."

"Mmm, and I bet he said something about free will, what good people should do, and be careful . . . right?"

"Well, maybe something like that." My eyes slide away from his.

"Look, Jenna." Luke hesitates for a few seconds, looking off toward the water, as if he's collecting his thoughts.

Then he looks sadly into my face. "Mr. Deets wants me on another assignment. He says the equinox is closing soon—"

"Opening night of *Fiddler*, actually," I interrupt.

"He says Adam will never get the pendant from you and he'll have to go back to his realm. He says I'm needed other places." He kicks at a pebble with the toe of his shoe. "He thinks I'm getting too attached here."

In a bold move, breaking rule #4 Don't cling, and rule #5 Don't beg, I move toward him and grab the lapels of his jacket. I take some comfort in the fact that I'm at least way too proud to break rule #6 Don't cry.

"Please stay."

Luke gently takes my hands and unclenches them from his jacket. He takes another step back.

"I can't stay," he says. "I don't make the rules. Bye, Jenna. It's been a . . . wonderful life."

He leans in and kisses my cheek. His sweet pine smell makes my knees buckle. He tenderly touches the heart around my neck with his fingertips.

"I love you," I blurt out.

Luke's smile crinkles sadly.

He turns to go. Two girls pass by.

"Smooth," one says, as she and her friend burst into giggles.

For a moment, I feel like I *am* going to break rule #6 and cry . . . and maybe puke and then maybe even fart from all those damn black beans. But then, suddenly, I surprise even myself and I start to feel really, well, pissed.

I sprint after him. The hell with *Teen Glamour* rule #1 (*Don't run toward him with a crazy look on your face*). What does that magazine know anyway?

I grab Luke's arm and turn him around.

"I cannot believe you're giving up so easily. What kind of an angel are you anyway? So you had a brief life and a tragic death, and then an angelic rebirth and now you're trying to corral a demon back to wherever he goes back to. Boo hoo! It's always you, you, you!"

I turn and stare out at the lights—so bright, so unreachably far away, and then down at the water, lapping hypnotically against the pillars of the bridge, the ripples giving the illusion that all the little lights are sailing toward us.

"What about Motel the tailor?" I demand. "He took a chance. He dared to love Tzeitel even though it was against the rules. He walked into the lion's den . . . or something like that."

Luke stares at me in astonishment.

"Choose life! Take a chance! Have the courage of your convictions! Be that guy!"

"You don't understand, Jenna," Luke says, with strain in his voice. "I'm not a regular guy. I can't just hang around here and go to school and be in plays and go to proms. I wish I could, but I have responsibilities. Don't you think I want to stay? I was chosen to be an . . . angel." He says the word low.

"Well, you're a person too. Sort of. You have free will," I say.

"No, not so free." He looks away, his expression tight.

"Wait," I say. "Are you angry? 'Cause that's a good thing."

"No," he protests angrily. "I mean, yeah. I mean, you're pissing me off, okay! You don't get it and you're making this hard."

"Well, duh, life is hard. Flying around with seagulls and being an angel is easy! Making choices for yourself is hard!" I say.

And the voice in my head is finally like, *Holy crap, shut up already. What are you doing?*

"What *are* you doing?" Luke responds stonily.

"And stop reading my mind!" I say a bit too loudly, as people turn to stare.

Luke gazes out at the water for a number of long, awkward moments. Then he turns to me, reaches out, and touches my chin to turn it up toward him.

"Jenna, try to understand . . ."

I bat his hand away and then it's my turn to glare at the water. I can feel rule #6 breaking as hot tears well up in the corners of my eyes.

"Then just go," I snap.

I catch a glimpse of Luke's face, shadowed in the lamplight.

For a moment, I'm glad that I hurt him, like he was hurting me, but within seconds, my anger dissolves into shame. Then before I can say *I don't mean it*, he takes another step back into darkness and is gone.

38

To say I feel emotionally demolished would be an understatement. It feels like all the color has been sucked up from the world. Not only was Luke the most awesome, hottest kindred-spirit boyfriend in the world, he was also probably the only one I would ever have.

After our breakup, I have a vague recollection of finding the nearest park bench and curling up on it in the fetal position in a complete state of despair and abandonment. Even though it was probably minutes, it seemed to me as if hours, or even eternity, had rolled past me. Then Michael is standing over me saying, "Jeez, what the hell are you doing? People are staring. Get up before Mom and Dad see you."

And I feel little plops of ice cream drip from his cone onto my head.

I sit up and he thrusts a suspiciously licked-looking cone at my face.

"Here, Mom got you a cookies and cream," he says.

———

The next few days are also a blur. I receive another letter from Lisa Golowski, the phantom costume design supervisor, mostly telling me about her woes as a college student, the backstabbing, the deceit and ruthlessness of the other design students. She also writes about how much she loves the program and how it is preparing her for a glamorous life in Broadway theater. She never wants to come home to Oceanville for as long as she lives (except maybe for a couple of homemade meals and to do her laundry). She closes the letter by saying that she is sure I have everything under control, wishes me luck, and tells me to e-mail if I need her. Again, however, she reminds me not to be insulted if she doesn't respond because she is superbusy.

School is practically unbearable. Somehow I make it through my classes but in Gym, I manage to get hit in the nose with the badminton racket and have to spend the rest of the period with the nurse's smelly ice pack right up against my nostrils.

Lunchtime is also positively grim. I have to break the news to everyone that Luke is gone. I decide to embellish a story I saw on an old *Oprah* rerun, Mom's favorite show, about this man who had to rush his family out of town because some crazy mafia guy was after him and he didn't want to get whacked.

This leads Tess, Sheldon, Kayla, and Bea into a whole sympathy conversation about me, as if I'm not even there or am dead, or both.

"OMG, that's so awful!" Bea leans across the table singing low. "Jenna must be so brokenhearted, like totally annihilated."

"I know," Kayla gasps breathlessly. "She'll never find anyone as hot as that again."

"I'll say," Sheldon adds. "It was a miracle a guy like that

liked her in the first place. No offense, Jenna. You know we love you."

Kayla and Bea nod vigorously.

"Now that's not right," Tess defends me, absentmindedly patting my shoulder. "There's no reason why Jenna should be, all, like, oh I'm gonna die now. I mean Luke was totally hot, of course, anyone with eyes could see that and it was a little weird that out of all the popular, pretty, hot, athletic, rich girls at school, he was dating Jenna . . ."

She turns to me.

"No offense, Jenna. But you will totally find someone else. Ya know, one day . . . probably."

Tess clears her throat and averts her eyes.

Then everyone turns to stare at me as if I'm some pathetic dog that was dropped off at the pound and will never get back home.

Sheldon kicks Kayla under the table and they all break into a halfhearted chorus of:

"Don't worry, Jenna, it's his loss . . . absolutely . . . totally . . . seriously."

Then there's this really awkward silence.

"And you'll always have us," Tess says.

"Always have us . . . totally . . . absolutely . . . seriously."

Then there're some sympathetic sighs, another depressed silence, and then awkward small talk about the cafeteria's apple brown Betty and how, lately, it's been particularly cinnamony and nutty.

I'm feeling way too low to tell them that, while I'm not particularly desirable to the naked eye, Luke saw the beauty in me and loved me for the perspective I gave on his short, undead life. Plus, I made him laugh and I have an extremely good heart. I fiddle with my little folk art necklace and stare out the picture window, hoping that Luke will come gliding around the corner like he did the first day I saw him at school.

By the time the day ends, I desperately need to be alone, so I decide to skip the bus and walk the two miles home, which doesn't sound like much when you're reading *Little House on the Prairie*, but in actuality is a very long-ass distance.

I'm just rounding the corner at David's house when I hear his bus pulling up to the curb. At the same time, a big white truck, beeping and honking, with the words *Gnancy's Gnomes* on the side backs into the driveway. The rolling metal back door yawns open and two workmen start hauling stuff out of the truck.

"I didn't see you get off the bus at the corner. How come you walked home all by yourself?" David approaches me.

"How do you know I was by myself?" I ask.

David lifts one eyebrow and gives me a skeptical look.

"Okay, fine. So I was by myself. I wanted to be alone, okay?"

"Whatever." David shrugs.

"So, why have you been acting a little weird lately? I mean, weirder than usual," I ask. "Is all this supernatural stuff starting to get to you?"

"I dunno. I wonder if I'm such a great superhero after all."

He shrugs again. "I mean I haven't been that good at protecting Oceanville from Adam."

"Oh, you've been great, David," I say. "Really brave. Seriously."

"Mmm . . ." He seems indifferent but I can see a smirk tugging at the corners of his mouth. "I guess I've been okay. I need to keep working on it."

"Where do you want these?" the big burly gnome-delivery guy interrupts, carrying a gnome under each arm.

"Just spread them around, I guess." David waves his hand.

"Bernice likes it when they look lively," David says, turning to me. "I'm like, Ma, they're plastic gnomes, how can they look lively? But ya know, she's not that bright."

"Yeah," I agree. "Anyway, I just wanted to tell you that things will be back to normal soon. The good news, I guess, is that we'll all be safer."

"Really? Safer?" He turns to me, his interest piqued. "Whaddaya mean?"

I take a deep, shaky, sad breath.

"Luke is gone."

David looks puzzled, then surprised.

"Luke is gone?" he repeats.

"Yes," I say.

"How could he do that?!" he exclaims. "Where did he go? When did he leave?"

"It's a long story," I say, placing my arm around his scrawny shoulders, "but he did it because it was his duty. And also because he's afraid to stand up to authority to get what he wants, but according to *Teen Glamour's* article 'Ten Traits of That Perfect Guy,' even perfect guys have flaws."

"This is nuts!" he says. "I can't believe he just up and left!"

"I know. We'll all miss him," I say. "His almost-perfect hotness, that one dangling hair always coming out of his ponytail, his crazy hazel eyes, his gentle warm personality and good sense, his cool thrown-together look, his—"

David hoists himself onto a gnome's mushroom, so that he's my height. He turns to me with dread and fear on his face. He grabs my shoulders.

"Jenna, I don't give a rat's ass about Luke's"—he makes quotation marks—"'little endearing ways,' and neither should you. This isn't about missing him."

He hops off the gnome and pulls me out of earshot of the delivery man.

"That sappy puss head was the only thing keeping Adam from finding a way to stay here, to kill you, and to maybe turn me into his . . . well . . ."

He drops his voice.

"His wingman."

"But Adam needs the pendant to stay, and I'm not giving it to him," I say, clutching the pendant around my neck in my palm.

"Don't you see?" David says. "Adam isn't done trying to get that pendant from you. He's very cunning. He's the most clever arch villain I've ever encountered."

"Uh, you mean the only arch villain." I roll my eyes.

"Yeah, whatever," David says, "but the thing is, he won't

give up until the equinox is actually sucking him away. Don't you realize that almost every single time Adam has tried to attack you, Luke has been there too?"

"I hadn't thought of it that way," I say, feeling a sudden tingle of anxiety up my spine.

"I've been told that, in the end, he won't actually risk killing me to get the pendant?" I croak. "There'll be consequences."

I gesture skyward with my eyes.

"Yeah? Says who? Adam is having too much fun here in the twenty-first century. This time period was made for someone like him. He can sow the seeds of evil and chaos and no one will even realize it until it's too late! I've seen this before, Jenna," David says solemnly. He reaches up and places his hand on my shoulder. "This is the stuff that classic comic book plots are made of."

He ticks them off on his fingers: "Supernatural: The Anime Series, Batman, Spider-Man, vintage Green Hornet, issues 8, 10, and 104. All your boyfriend did by leaving was leave us vulnerable."

"But . . ." I squeak meekly. "Bad things only happen when good people do nothing, right?"

David sighs in exasperation and hits his palm to his head.

"What is that? A saying written on a graphic tee from the Bulk Emporium?"

Oh no, I think. David is actually making sense. I slump into a gnome hammock and my butt hits the ground with a *thud*.

Just then, Bernice and her book group ladies come ambling out of the house, teary and sniffling, dabbing their eyes with tissues. I work myself back up to my feet.

"Oh, and there's my little Broadway guy now," Bernice gushes to her friends. "Did I tell you that David has a starring role in this weekend's teen production of *Fiddler on the Roof*!"

"Ooh, the star!" the ladies gush.

"Ma, how many times do I have to tell you?" David rolls his eyes. "I'm Boy #3."

And then it hits me: holy crud!

The show!

Aside from murder and mayhem and other wordly evil, how am I going to tell Mr. Resnick that, just a little more than a week until the show, he has lost one of his leading men?!

39

The next day, I try to sneak into rehearsal unnoticed. My plan: get backstage, put the final stitches and glue on the costumes, and slip back out before getting caught up in any Luke-is-gone hysteria. It's bad enough that I've been trying to cope with my own sadness.

I'm in the process of tiptoeing up the side steps to the stage, when suddenly Jared Needleman rushes up the aisle toward me.

"Jenna! Jenna! Luke is gone!" he shouts breathlessly, with a little too much glee and enthusiasm for my comfort zone.

"I know, Jared," I say.

"He's just . . . gone!" he repeats.

"I know, Jared."

"Did you know?!" He gapes at me incredulously.

I sigh heavily.

"I gotta get backstage, Jared."

"Mr. Resnick doesn't know. And I didn't have the nerve to tell him," Jared whispers, scurrying after me up the side stage steps.

"So I sent Barry, that nerdy sixth grader from stage crew, to do it.

"Come here." Jared beckons me over to where we can spy

from the sidelines behind the curtains. A nervous Barry tugs his pants over his butt crack and approaches a flustered Mr. Resnick, who's busy shouting directions at everyone.

"Um, Mr. Resnick?" Barry's voice quivers.

"Yes?" Mr. Resnick huffs impatiently.

"Um . . ."

"Well, what is it? Spit it out, Larry. I don't have all day."

"Um . . ." Barry looks around nervously. He crooks his finger and motions for Mr. Resnick to lean in closer to him as he, presumably, whispers the news.

Jared counts down:

"Five, four, three . . ."

We watch as all the blood drains from Mr. Resnick's face.

"Two . . ."

"One!"

"*What!!!!*" Mr. Resnick bellows so loud that all the birds fly wildly from the rafters. A flustered Tess accidentally hits a loud atonal chord on the piano, and Carlo makes a flat *honk* on his tuba. Everyone freezes.

"*He's what?!?!?!?!*" Mr. Resnick yells.

"He's gone, sir." Barry trembles.

"Out of my way, Larry!"

Mr. Resnick pushes to the front of the stage.

"Does anyone know anything about Luke?" he bellows.

"Wasn't he dating someone here?" a chorus member pipes up.

"Yeah, I heard that," someone else adds. "He was hanging with this girl. I heard he really liked her too."

I can't help but blush crimson and fiddle with the heart around my neck. I feel a strange sense of pride. *Yes, I was Luke's girlfriend.* I had never really said it to myself before.

"I heard they were, like, serious," another person adds.

I spot Tess motioning to me from the piano.

"Go on," she mouths, and gestures toward Mr. Resnick. "Tell him."

I can practically feel the heat of Jared's jealous glare burning up the side of my head. *I was Luke's girlfriend,* I think again proudly. I can say it. I can be it. And like the latest *Teen Glamour* article, "Ten Ways to Girl Power," rule #8: *I can own it.*

I straighten up, suck in my waist, and hold my head high.

"Mr. Resnick." I start out from behind the curtain. "I was Luke's—"

"It was me," a voice interrupts me, a foreign voice that isn't coming out of my mouth.

"I was Luke's girlfriend," Sarah Johnson announces, confidently sashaying up onto the stage.

"It was me, Mr. Resnick," she repeats loudly.

"Oh no she didn't," I hear Tess exclaim from the orchestra pit. "Oh no you didn't!"

Sarah ignores her.

"Well, where is he, Sheila?" Mr. Resnick pleads. "Call his cell phone. Tell him he can't do this to me . . . to us!"

"She's not his girlfriend." Tess marches up the stage steps, puts her hands on her hips, and glares at me, now partly hiding behind the curtain.

"I . . . I'm his girlfriend . . ." I step meekly onto the stage. One of the butt-crack elves blinds me with a spotlight.

There's this wave of whispering disbelief, like:

"Her?"

"Is she kidding?"

"Is she crazy?"

"Is she off her meds?"

"This is no time for jokes, Jebba," Mr. Resnick says, turning his back to me. "Sheila, you must call him."

Sarah shoots me an evil look.

"Of course, Mr. Resnick," she lies. "We're like this."

She crosses her fingers to demonstrate. Then she steps to the front of the stage, motions for a spotlight, and clears her throat.

"Luke wanted me to tell you all that he had a family emergency. His cousin was in an accident. A little cousin. A bad one. Not the cousin. The accident. It was totally fatal and he almost died. Luke, being the angel that he is, discovered that he was a match for his cousin's blood type and also for his organs, so he volunteered to give him . . . a bladder—"

"A kidney!" someone yells from the audience.

"Kidney." Sarah doesn't miss a beat. "Because everyone has three, you know."

"Two!" the voice prompts.

"Two. I meant that. Two kidneys. So he's giving his little cousin one of his kidneys."

She pauses dramatically for effect.

"And he also told me to tell you how grateful he was for this extraordinary opportunity." She spreads her arms out wide. "About how much he loves the theater. About how much he cares for each and every one of you. And especially you, Mr. Resnick. You were like a father to him, except a little bit older and a lot grayer. Anyway, he's truly, deeply sorry to leave you in the lurch. But it couldn't be helped . . . he just"—a sob catches in Sarah's throat—"had to go."

She wipes a tear from her cheek.

People break into a smattering of applause, including Mr. Resnick, who also wipes a tear from his cheek.

"But . . ." I step forward. "Wait a minute! That's not true, Mr. Resnick. None of it! I was Luke's girlfriend! I was the one he loved! I was the one he gave a lopsided folk art heart necklace to! I swear! See?!" I hold up my necklace.

"That looks like something a kid would make in art class." Sarah rolls her eyes.

"It's primitive folk art! It's supposed to look like crap!" I say. "Luke doesn't have a dying little cousin. He left this heart to show his love for me! To help me feel safe when in the presence of"—my voice drops to a whisper—"an evil danger."

A pregnant pause fills the room.

Then:

"Yeah, right." A chorus member snorts.

"Not now, Jebba." Mr. Resnick pushes me aside. "We don't have time for theatrics. We've got a show to put on . . . All right, everyone. It seems that we've lost our Motel the tailor, but as always . . . The show must go on."

A butt-crack elf swings a spotlight on a familiar figure as he strides up the aisle toward the stage.

40

"Adam, my dear boy, you're here," Mr. Resnick says, looking relieved. "I thought maybe you'd deserted us too."

The spotlight follows Adam as he hops up onto the stage.

"I wouldn't have missed this"—he casts a brooding gaze at me—"for anything on earth."

"All right, well." Mr. Resnick sighs. "I'll just have to put in a call to the wrestling coach and see if we can find Waldo again." He flaps his hands around. "I'll figure something out. I always do. But for now, let's rehearse your part of the song, Sheila, 'Miracle of Miracles,' where you and Motel the tailor commit yourselves to one another. We'll just muddle through without Luke for now. You can run your lines with Jerry. I'm going backstage for my cell phone and some tissues."

"I know the part," Adam offers, stepping in front of Jared. "So where are we . . . Motel professes his love for Sarah, yada, yada, yada . . . and then isn't this the part where he takes Tzeitel in his arms, like this?"

Adam turns to Sarah, sweeps her into his arms, and kisses her. At first, she's startled, as is everyone else, but then she relaxes into his embrace and kisses him back. And then they're, like, really kissing. A lot. And everyone is staring. A lot. Just standing, slack jawed, gawking at them.

"Oh my God." I hear Kayla gasp.

"Get a room," I hear Sheldon say.

"Get away from her!" a voice bellows from the front of the theater and before anyone can say or do anything, Dean Gold is sprinting up the aisle. In a matter of seconds, he's on the stage, pulling Adam away from Sarah.

He draws his fist back and punches him right in the nose! Then they're scuffling and fighting and grunting and rolling around on the floor. With a swiftness that is barely discernible to the naked eye, Adam pins Dean down and has his hands around his neck. Dean chokes for breath. Everyone is screaming. David jumps onto the stage and leaps onto Adam's back. Then Jared and I try to pull David off Adam and Adam off Dean.

Mr. Resnick rushes from backstage.

"Stop it! Stop it now!" he demands.

Adam gets off Dean and steps back. Dean works to catch his breath and glares fiercely at Adam.

"What are you doing?!" Sarah screams at Dean. "Are you crazy?!"

"I knew there was something going on here!" Dean growls. "It's all over school. But they said you were having a thing with Luke. But I didn't know you were having a thing with Adam too."

Deans wipes the blood off his lip with the sleeve of his jacket.

"What is going on here?!" Mr. Resnick huffs. "Is everyone all right?"

Dean looks daggers at Adam. Adam hangs back, smirking.

"Well?!" Mr. Resnick demands.

They both nod reluctantly.

"Who are you?" Mr. Resnick snaps at Dean.

"He's my *ex*-boyfriend," Sarah says. "Who's *crazy*."

"You're her boyfriend?" Mr. Resnick asks, handing him a tissue. "Her other boyfriend, I presume."

"*Ex!*" Sarah reiterates.

Mr. Resnick looks him up and down. "I've seen you around school. What's your name, son?"

"Dean Gold."

"Well." Mr. Resnick lifts his eyebrow. "Are you a fast learner?"

"He's on the honor roll," Sarah says. "I don't date stupid boys."

"Can you sing?" Mr. Resnick asks.

"No. Why?"

"Not at all?" Mr. Resnick pushes.

"No. I'm tone-deaf."

Mr. Resnick considers this, then places his arm around Dean's shoulder.

"You seem like a brave, outgoing young man. How would you like to save not only your girlfriend's virtue . . ."

"*Ex*-girlfriend," Sarah harrumphs.

"But save the day, as well," Mr. Resnick continues.

"Whaddaya mean?" Dean asks.

"How would you like to be Motel the tailor in our teen production of *Fiddler on the Roof*, hmm? What do you think? You'd be one of the stars," Mr. Resnick coaxes.

"I have team practice after school," Dean says.

"No worries. We'll work around that and the show goes up this weekend anyway."

"But I . . ." Dean throws a look over his shoulder at Sarah. "I've never been in a show."

"Pish posh," Mr. Resnick says. "We'll all help you. And Sheila will be here the whole time, under your vigilant, watchful eyes," Mr. Resnick whispers.

"I heard that," Sarah says. "*Not* under his . . . whatever eyes."

"Well, maybe, but . . ." Dean says, as if he's seriously considering the proposal.

"No need to thank me, Don," Mr. Resnick says. "I know you'll have to work hard, but it's a tremendous opportunity and I'm sure Sheila can coach you on the part. I think you've got a lot of charisma. I can tell about these things."

Mr. Resnick leads him to the piano.

"Tess, will you help Don learn his musical part *tout de suite*? And then you and Sheila can sew up your differences . . . hmmm?"

"Who's Sheila?" Dean asks.

"Humph." Sarah relents.

"Ah! You see?! It's all in the hands of the fates!" Mr. Resnick exclaims. "What did I tell you, children! Life in the theater is always fabulous and dramatic and very romantic!"

Jared sidles up next to me. He places his arm around my shoulder.

"Don't even think about it, Needleman," I warn.

He drops his arm and steps to the side.

Adam sashays by me.

"Yes, the theater is very romantic," he whispers in my ear. "And the drama hasn't even begun."

41

The next few days pass without incident, other than that I'm sad, restless, and inconsolable. Even my friends can't cheer me up. I just don't feel like socializing and I can only find solace in two things:

1. Making costumes for the show.
2. Thinking about Luke.

Rehearsals move along. Dean isn't half bad in his role as Motel the tailor. He is, indeed, totally tone-deaf, but he speaks his songs with feeling and it doesn't hurt that he's supremely incredible to look at. When not onstage, he mostly hangs around, texts people, flirts, and keeps his eye on Sarah, who, true to her nature, still finds ways to flirt with Adam right under our noses.

I can only surmise that the cool kids have some flirting code of conduct that, like, even if you're in a relationship, you're allowed to flirt with other people if you stay within certain boundaries and don't passionately make out with them onstage in front of a room full of your peers.

And speaking of Adam, if you didn't know he was some kind of unnatural spawn of the devil, you would think he was just an average teenage kid.

Except for a few things:

Over the last few days, the whole mood at the Old Vic has begun to change and deteriorate. Everyone is becoming edgy, and the air is getting thick with arguing and strife.

The backstage elves are bickering with one another over stupid things like props, and the placement and handling of plastic chickens, mules, and Tevye's big cardboard cow. Chorus members are accusing one another of stepping on one another's toes and/or meager lines. Mr. Resnick actually barked at Miss Manley and called her choreography stiff, to which she responded with a muttered obscenity that would make athletes in the locker room blush.

A few of Sarah's wannabes report that some of their personal items have gone missing, like iPhones and jewelry, and are accusing everyone in sight of stealing. I even hear some bickering among my friends. For example, Bea was crankily demanding that everyone else "Shhh," and Tess's affectionate exasperation with Sheldon is developing into snappish impatience.

Even the Old Vic itself is becoming darker. Colder. Damper. Crows are nudging out the sparrows for nesting rights in the rafters and making a superbig racket. There are rats scuttling around backstage and on the catwalks, and some kids even claim to see dark, moving shadows in the high places, which of course they assume are bats. Even the weather is different around the theater and its grounds: gloomy, misty, overcast, and damp.

But the strangest thing of all is how Adam is changing. It almost looks as if he's deteriorating too. He looks thinner, almost sickly. Whereas before, his cool, tight jeans and T-shirts perfectly accentuated his slim muscular frame, his body suddenly seems sunken, his clothes hanging just a little too loose. His face looks drawn and gaunt, and his brown sun-kissed skin looks sallow.

But it's his personality change that's the most jarring. His nasty but somehow sexy smirk seems edgier. More and more, he's forgetting his lines and his lyrics and missing his musical cues. He often stops and stares off and looks kind of crazy, distracted, and lost.

I even notice a lot of concerned glances passing between Mr. Resnick and Miss Manley, and a few times Mr. Resnick suggests that Adam see the school nurse.

"Hellooo, Adam, are you still with us in little Anatevka?" Mr. Resnick has to comment more than a few times.

"Sure," Adam responds, looking less sure each time he says it.

Around me, Adam seems completely unglued. He stares at me, stalks around me, and many times I feel him standing too close, staring at my chest. When I catch his eye, he snaps, "S'cuse me." Then he lowers his eyes and skulks back, looking like a beaten dog who's gotten too close to the master's steak.

Of course, this stalking, chest-staring activity leads to a few unkind rumors, giggles, and assumptions that he must be hot for me. Not to mention killer glares from Sarah Johnson, who just cannot, presumably, get over feeling guilty/competitive with me.

"What the hell's wrong with demon boy now?" David

whispered to me the other day. "He's like disintegrating and having a nervous breakdown at the same time."

"I wish I knew," I replied.

"Well, the good news is that maybe you were right. Maybe Adam is being called back to the 'mother ship,'" David shrugs, making quotation marks in the air, "and will just be sucked away at midnight after the opening show, when the equinox closes."

If only it were that simple. But that doesn't feel right to me. In my bones, I feel like Adam isn't ready to give up.

42

Finally.

It's opening night!

It's a few hours before showtime and the theater is abuzz with electricity, nerves, excitement, and a flurry of activity. Tempers are still short and everyone is tense but holding it together, busy with last-minute things and hopeful that the show will be successful.

Tess practices with the orchestra, essentially a flute, drums, a guitar, and a tuba. Carlo continues to flirt with Tess and, even though his English has barely improved, they seem good together and to be communicating well enough in the language of the heart.

Sheldon, Kayla, and Bea are in a corner of the stage, rehearsing their choreography for the chorus members. Sarah is in the dressing room, playing prima donna while her fan girls, Melanie, Emma, and Amanda, help her with her hair and makeup.

I'm preoccupied with last-minute costume malfunctions. I feel so important, a tape measure around my neck, pins in my mouth, armed with my hot-glue gun for superfast fixes. It's all "Jenna, this hem is falling down," and "Jenna, I popped a button," and "Jenna, if you drip hot glue on me one more time I'll glue your glue gun to your butt."

I've never heard my name so much in my life!

And, most important, everyone seems happy with what I now call my pieced-together Franken-costumes, or at least no one is complaining. Even Mr. Resnick is full of high praise: "You did a bang-up job, Jebba," he says, patting me on the shoulder. "Especially with no money, training, or skill. Kudos to you!"

I'm rushing backstage to fix one more "costume malfunction" before the curtain rises when I bump smack into Sarah Johnson. She's preening in front of the full-length dressing room mirror.

"Ah . . . s'cuse me," she says sarcastically, and then turns back to the mirror to fix her hair.

"What do you think?" She engages her fan girls. "Up or down?"

"Up! Down! Any way is awesome!" they gush, talking over one another.

It was just as I had seen her so many days ago, admiring her reflection at Maude's Chic Fashion Boutique. She catches my eye watching her, but suddenly for me everything is different. Sarah seems to sense it too, and it's as if we're having a moment, almost like a psychic connection, the kind you can sometimes have with someone with whom you're very close. Or in our case, had been very close.

Her thoughts seem to connect from her mind to mine. I feel like I hear her saying that she's just as insecure as I am. That she feels guilty about the way she treated me, but wants popularity more than she wants to be a good person. That, deep down, she's feeling the same as she did before. That she doesn't even know if those other girls are really her friends, and although it kind of pisses her off to see me have a boy-friend and do cool stuff, she's kind of proud of me and glad for me too.

I abruptly turn away and back to a costume fix. Am I imagining this, or has my relationship with Luke made me more aware of other people's thoughts and feelings? It doesn't matter. As a matter of fact, none of this drama with Sarah matters anymore. It hits me that her life is hers to work out, and I have better things to do and think about.

Will I always feel a little hurt by the big fro-yo dis? Probably. But now, not so much, and these thoughts feel light and freeing, like taking a deep cleansing breath by the ocean.

My eyes spring back to Sarah for just a millisecond. Our eyes connect again, and she smiles gently. A real smile this time, ever so fleeting. And it's like she's mentally saying to me: *Hey, Jenna, I'm glad we had this talk.*

Then her eyes slide away and up again to her hair.

"I think up looks better," I say spontaneously.

The wannabes stop talking, look astonished, and turn to glare at me.

"Mmm," Sarah says. "I think you're right, Jenna. Maybe up is good."

And that is that.

Ten minutes later, I'm still rushing around handling last-minute details, and I'm so excited that I don't even realize that David has not shown up.

Until my cell phone rings:

He rocks in the tree tops all day long . . .

"Jenna," says an urgent whisper on the other end. "It's me, David Lipski."

"David, where are you? I thought Bernice and Lenny were dropping you off on the way to their bar mitzvah in New Jersey. Curtain goes up in less than an hour. I made you a special Boy #3 costume. It's got this cool tattered effect that I learned from *Sewing for Ninnies*, and—"

"Jenna," he interrupts. "Listen, I'm in trouble."

"Whaddaya mean, you're in trouble? David?"

"It's Adam. He's . . . oh no . . . can't talk . . ."

"David! David! Where are you?!"

"Cable shack! Hurry!"

"David! Use your superpowers of . . . um . . . spry and clever! Spry and clever! . . . David!"

The phone goes dead.

43

Holy mother of crap!

I have to get to David and fast! I grab my jacket and stumble to the backstage door. Jared Needleman steps out of the shadows, blocking my way.

"Hey, Jenna. Where ya going?"

"I . . . I . . . I gotta go, Jared." I try to maneuver around him without actually brushing against him, but it's just not happening in that small space.

"Could you move?" I say.

"Where are you going? The show's starting in fifty minutes. Do you really think this is a good time to leave? Mr. Resnick is all set to give his opening-night pep talk. Where are you going?"

"David is in the cable shack." I lower my voice and lean in confidentially. "Look, he's in trouble, okay? I have to go get him."

"David? In *my* cable shack? What the heck is he doing there? Drat!"

Jared slams his fist into his palm.

"He'd better not be touching anything!"

"Jared, did you not hear the word *trouble*? David is in trouble!"

"Humph. Well, I'm sure it's something he's brought on

himself. Did I tell you that my dad and I are planning a new documentary. *Too Late for Adoption*, a moving psychological exploration of troubled children, their families, and the neighbors who have to put up with them. Guess who inspired the idea?"

"Jared! Get out of my way!" I shout.

Jared startles and squeezes to the side.

"You don't have to shout," he says, flushing pink as a few people turn to stare. "Okay." Jared waves his arms around authoritatively. "Nothing to see here. Move along. Mr. Resnick wants you onstage for his motivational pep speech, yada, yada. Curtain's in fifty! Full house out there, so don't screw up!"

I push open the theater door and race across the lawn to the cable shack.

44

It's cold but I run, lose my breath, racewalk, trot, walk, jog (what am I thinking?), and then walk as fast as I can across the grassy expanse to the cable shack.

So many thoughts are crowding my mind:

- What's going to happen to David?
- What's going to happen to me?
- Am I really the hero type?
- Would I sacrifice my life for someone I love?
- Will my kind heart triumph over evil?
- Will my funeral be well attended, or will it be a pathetic embarrassment of no-shows? Will they hire grief counselors at the school or just, like, have a moment of silence that people whisper and snicker through?

And:

- Why did I let communist Mom talk me into buying these cheap-ass sneakers that don't give me any traction or arch support?

Plus:

- Was the cable shack always this far away or does it just seem that way because I'm so out of shape? If I live, I'm so signing up for one of Bernice's Shake That Funky Thang classes.

Finally I arrive at my destination.

I'm scared, that's for sure.

Instinctively, I feel for the little lopsided heart around my neck. It's gone! Oh no! It must have dropped off with all that jog-trotting across the lawn, not to mention me pulling my hair back a few times while I was running. I panic and start making frantic circles, my head down, my eyes glued to the ground like a dog looking for a good place to lie down. No! I have to get to David. But where's the necklace? Did it fall into my shirt? I pull my shirt out and look down.

Oh no!

The pendant is gone too! I start looking even more frantically for that, when I see a pair of very expensive black boots in my path. My eyes travel up the black-jeans pants legs, to the black T-shirt, and straight into the face of the devil himself.

"Admiring my slick boots, or did you lose something?"

45

"Where's David?" My voice shakes.

We're alone in a big expanse. No one to hear me scream, no one to save my life. I am totally, royally screwed. Adam saunters past me and pushes open the squeaky cable shack door.

"After you," he says.

"That's okay, I'm good."

My body stiffens to the spot.

"I insist." He smiles.

Slowly I walk past him, very careful not to touch him even by accident. It's shadowy inside. Gray light filters in from the smudged windows. The place still smells like Chinese food and garbage. Adam closes the door behind us. I spin around.

"I'm serious. Where's David?" I challenge.

Adam shrugs.

"He ran off, I suppose. I'm not interested in David," he says, casually leaning his butt against a table. "The important thing is you're not wearing the pendant. Which means"—he steps toward me—"you're now vulnerable to me."

"Well, I might not have the pendant, but you don't have it either," I say defiantly.

"I'll find it," he says. "I'm sure it's somewhere on the path you jiggled down to get here. I have my ways of finding lost things. I'm part retriever you know. *Woof.*"

"Yeah . . . well," I stall, "if I don't get back to the theater, they'll look for me . . ."

Adam raises a doubtful eyebrow.

"Well, maybe not me, but they'll totally come looking for you," I say.

He stretches out his arms happily.

"Oh now I can be in a lot of shows if I want to. Maybe I'll suggest starring in *Damn Yankees!* next, as the devil of course. Or what about a supermodern musical version of *Faust*. You know, the story where the man is tempted by the devil."

Adam moves slowly toward me until he's got me backed against the counter. I reach behind me and feel around desperately for anything I can use as a weapon.

"But enough about me," he says. "Let's talk about you, or what's left of you for a few seconds anyway."

"What do you want with me now?" I tremble. "I don't even have the pendant."

"Nothing really," he says. "But I don't like you."

"Why don't you just let me go? I haven't told anybody about you yet, so why would I now? Besides, no one would believe me and I'd just look crazy."

"Hmm, interesting proposition." Adam appears to be thinking. He reaches around me, grabs a handful of nuts from a bowl.

I try to read his expression and for a second, I'm hopeful. Will he really let me go?

"Um . . . I'm thinking . . . Nah," he says, and suddenly his hand is up around my neck.

"But Mr. Deets says that if you kill me, there will be terrible cosmic consequences for you," I sputter.

"Well, they'll have to catch me first," he says. "I have a few tricks up my sleeve."

"But why kill me? Mr. Deets says you'd have to be crazy," I plead.

We both stop for a moment to process that remark, and suddenly I know I'm dead meat.

"I told you! I . . . don't . . . like . . . you . . ." Adam enunciates darkly, like the buckets of crazy that he's become.

"And by the way"—his tone changes to casual—"I'll totally be back at the theater before the curtain goes up. What makes you think I won't?"

His terrible black eyes pierce mine, invading my comfort zone and chilling my blood.

"But why?" I croak.

"Because I'm bad." He grins. *"Bad, bad, bad."* He singsongs the Michael Jackson song. "Besides, Luke likes you so much. He might even break the rules and come back, and I don't want him back."

"You really think so?" I babble happily, smiling through the little pre-faint dots swimming before my eyes. "Because I really do like him, like, a lot. Oh, who am I kidding? I really love him. I larve him. I luuuuve him. I—"

"Stop!" Adam screams, like the deranged maniac he is. "I've had enough of this."

He squeezes my neck tighter.

"Well, okay," I wheeze, barely conscious. "But have you had enough of *this*?!"

My hands tighten around the handle of something I'm praying is a big knife. I lift it, swing, and hit him square in the face with . . . a bacon-splatter screen. It bounces off his head. He doesn't flinch, but his grip loosens long enough for me to catch a breath.

"You're going to have to do better than that!" Adam tightens his grip again and I struggle backward over the counter.

"How about this!"

I grab a Chore Boy and scratch it down along his cheek.

"Ow!" He screams. He releases me.

That buys me the seconds I need. Sputtering and coughing for air, I grab the nonstick cooking spray and spray it into his eyes.

"*Guh!*" He grabs his eyes. "*Ow, ow, ow!*"

He flails his hands, his mouth wide with pain, grasping the air, presumably searching for the sink.

I'm grabbing wildly now around the counter, in the drawers and in the refrigerator, for anything I can, throwing objects at him: a milk carton, cheese, a tuna casserole, a variety of cold cuts. I pelt him with pieces of fruit salad, watermelon balls, cantaloupe chunks, and kiwi. I whack at him with one of those Pillsbury Doughboy cookie rolls.

"Take *that*! And *that* and *that*!" I screech.

Still blinded, he stumbles toward me. I shove a whole stick of I Can't Believe It's Not Butter! into his open mouth.

"*Ggchh!*" He gags and scratches at his lips, spitting butter all over the floor.

"*And this!*" I yell.

I grab an ice cube tray from the freezer and start piling ice cubes down the back of his shirt and pants.

"*Ah-ah-ah-ah!*" he screams in staccato as he hops around the room.

"*And this!*"

Finally I find a large, sharp butcher's knife. I plan to plunge it deep into his chest.

"*And this!*" I shout again.

I raise the knife high. The knife high . . . I raise the knife . . . I raise . . .

I drop the knife. I can't do it. Adam rushes to the sink to wash out his eyes.

I rush for the door, but just as I'm grabbing the handle, Adam yanks my hair.

"*Ahh!*" I shriek, as my head jerks back.

"You should have plunged this into me when you had the chance," he says, picking up the knife. "As if you could kill me anyway. That's what comes from having a good heart, eh? Nothing. You'll bleed and feel pain and die like anyone else, because now I'll kill you slowly."

I grope across the counter, but he keeps pulling me toward him.

"Maybe . . . but"—I choke—"you didn't count on *this!*"

I grab the liquid dish soap and squeeze it all around his feet.

"*Gahhhh!*" Adam loses his balance and releases me.

He does a little slippery jig and falls to the floor with a *thump*.

"What do you think about your cool slick-bottomed boots now?" I taunt.

I rush for the door again but it flies open before I can reach it. Standing on the threshhold are David, Jared, and Luke!

"Luke!" I explode, and rush into his arms.

"Hey." Jared steps in, surveying the mess. "What the heck were you doing in here? My dad's gonna kill me."

"You came back!" I hug Luke tighter.

"I never should have left you, Jenna." He steps back and strokes my hair. "It was stupid and immature."

"You forgot 'self-absorbed with a martyr complex,'" adds David.

"But I'm here now," Luke says, "and I'm not leaving."

Our reunion is quickly shattered as Adam pulls himself up from the floor, looking like a pink-eyed madman. He throws back his head and howls. His body quivers and shakes as if he's about to morph into his wolf self, but before that happens, he maniacally races toward us.

"Let's go," Luke commands, pushing me out the door. David and Jared don't have to be told twice and we all run like we're on fire across the lawn toward the theater all the way to the backstage doors. We hear the great *whoosh* of giant wings and, within seconds, Adam is there at the doorway looking murderous, thunderous, and enraged.

He and Luke stare lethally into each other's eyes.

"Whooaa! How'd he get here so fast?" Jared asks.

Suddenly the back door opens and there stands Mr. Resnick.

"Oh my God! You boys are going to give me a heart attack. Adam! It's the opening number, "Tradition." You're on in two seconds. We don't have time for costumes now. Just go out there!"

Mr. Resnick grabs Adam and pushes him onto the stage, which is all set for the first number, with chorus members dressed as villagers standing at the ready for their cues.

"And you, Luke! What a miracle! A guardian angel is looking after our little show today!"

"I second that," I say.

"It turns out that Dean, our new Motel the tailor," Mr. Resnick continues, "had some kind of sports celebratory dinner last night at Cowboy Clems, ate a bad tortilla, and came down with food poisoning!"

He grabs Luke by the shoulders and looks earnestly into his eyes.

"Now I know you've just had kidney surgery—"

"I had what?" Luke glances over at me.

I motion for him to play along.

"But you look wonderful and we really need you. Will you go on? Will you save us?" Mr. Resnick's voice trembles with dramatic emotion.

"I . . ." Luke stalls.

"Wonderful!" Mr. Resnick exclaims.

"Jebba, quickly, get him into costume. On second thought,

forget the costume for now. You can slip onstage before your lines and get changed later. Tell me, how is your poor little cousin?"

"Little cousin?" Luke looks perplexed.

"Never mind," Mr. Resnick says. "You can fill me in after the show."

Just then the overture begins.

"Ooh, we're starting!" Mr. Resnick throbs with excitement.

A spotlight shines on Mary Beth O'Churney, perched on the scaffold atop Tevye's cardboard house. She plays the violin, beautifully, plaintively. The strings resonate with heartache and hope.

Adam turns slowly, murderously, toward us as we stand in the wings, and a slow, sick, sadistic smile stretches across his mouth and eyes.

"Break a leg everyone," Mr. Resnick gushes in a whisper to the cast onstage. "Oh, heck, break everything you got!"

"Er . . . Mr. Resnick, maybe that wasn't the right thing—" I start, but am ignored as the stage lights go up.

Adam turns his gaze outward to the audience, looking pale, sunken-eyed, and crazy. The audience claps.

But he just stares out, like a supernatural, psychotic madman, and doesn't say or sing a word.

We all stand frozen.

Nothing.

"He has to start his monologue!" Mr. Resnick says frantically. "His monologue about living in Anatevka. About tradition!"

The audience shifts uncomfortably. A few people clear their throats.

Tess plays an opening chord.

Mary Beth plays her violin again. Then stops.

Adam continues to stare out as if he's in a trance.

"Pssst!" Mr. Resnick motions wildly. "Start talking! Start talking!"

The audience begins to whisper. The chorus onstage is frozen with panick.

"A fiddler on the roof." Mr. Resnick prompts him with the first line. "Sounds crazy, no?"

Nothing.

"Sounds crazy, *no*?" Mr. Resnick hisses louder.

Luke, Jared, and I all watch in openmouthed despair.

"Oh my God." Mr. Resnick rocks his head in his hands. "Is he going to stand there all day like a loon?" He motions wildly for Tess to play the opening chord again.

Then suddenly, David Lipski steps forward from the chorus.

"A fiddler on the roof, sounds crazy, no?" he announces.

Mr. Resnick lets out a huge sigh of relief. The audience encourages David with a smattering of applause.

"Isn't that Boy #3? Spotlight quickly!" he hisses to Jared, who immediately communicates this into his headphones.

"Spotlight on Boy #3. Boy #3."

The spotlight swings over to David. Mary Beth plays her violin softly in the background.

"Er . . ." David continues, trying to remember the lines.

"Jebba, you take over prompting him," Mr. Resnick

whispers. "I'm going to put an emergency call in to the chemistry teacher, Mr. Lasinski. Adam's gone apoplectic. I'm going to track down that damn Doogie and get him back here to be Tevye if it's the last thing I do."

"Me?!"

"I have faith in you, Jebba. You're a good little elf," he says, thrusting the script at me and scurrying off.

"But, um . . . here . . . in our little town of Anatevka"— David walks the stage and improvises—"you can say that . . . um . . . ya know . . . we're all . . . just . . . here, and we kind of like it, even though the Cossacks should totally bite me . . . but . . . um . . ."

I flip wildly through the playbook, but it's dark in the wings and the pages are so scribbled over, they're illegible.

"I can't read it!" I say to Luke.

"You're here all the time. You remember it."

"I don't!"

"You do," Luke says gently. "Just calm down and think."

And then, suddenly, I realize that I actually do remember most of it. By heart.

I take a deep breath.

"Every single one of us . . ." I whisper toward David.

"Every single one of us." David does a little dance spin and spreads his arms.

"Is like a fiddler on the roof!"

"Is like a fiddler . . ."

The pendant falls from his pocket onto the floor.

Luke and I gasp.

"Where did he—" Luke turns me toward him and looks at my chest.

"I thought that you were wearing . . ."

"I dropped it on the way to rescuing him. Between the theater and the cable shack. David must have found it when he was escaping . . . It's a long story . . ." I ramble madly.

David gestures to Mary Beth, who bows awkwardly.

"On the roof!"

"Trying to scratch out a tune," I whisper.

"Trying to scratch out a . . ."

David reaches down and picks up the pendant.

"A tune." He grins.

He then turns to Adam, his back to the audience.

"Nyeh!" he razzes.

Suddenly, it's like Adam is reactivated. He turns and starts moving slowly toward David.

"Uh-oh," I moan.

Luke is about to rush onto the stage, but I grab his arm.

"No, wait." I stop him. "Adam won't do anything in front of the audience. It's too risky for him. And David can take care of himself."

David hops away from Adam and continues with his lines.

"Trying to scratch out a tune," David repeats, and then looks to me for the next prompt.

"Without breaking his neck," I hiss.

"Without breaking his neck," David repeats awkwardly,

continuing to dance away from Adam, hopping and weaving around the villagers as Adam slowly stalks him.

"It isn't easy," I whisper.

"No kidding, Sherlock," David scoffs.

"No, say it!" I say.

"It isn't easy." David skirts the cardboard house.

"Why do we do it, if it's so dangerous?" I prompt.

At that moment, Luke takes my hand.

"Because life isn't easy. Especially when you make choices, when you have to find the courage to make choices for yourself.

"Whatever happens tonight, Jenna," he says, suddenly very serious, "I want you to know . . . oh hell, I think too much."

Then Luke, half angel, half hot teenage boy, takes me in his arms, leans over, and kisses me. And I fall heart and soul into his sweet pine scent and tender angelic embrace.

"So why do we do it if it's so *dangerous*, you might ask?" David shouts, and out of the corner of my eye, I see him glaring at me. He continues, "Well, one thing we don't do is make out when we're supposed to be paying attention and saving someone's butt up here onstage."

Reluctantly, I pull away from Luke, just as Adam lunges toward David. In the nick of time, David ducks behind a cardboard mule.

"Sorry," I whisper to David. "Um . . . We keep our balance because of . . ."

"We keep our balance because of . . ." David parrots. *"Oomph!"*

Adam lunges for David with both hands.

Just then:

The entire chorus exuberantly rushes forward, knocking both David and Adam aside, as they sweep into song and dance.

"*Tradition!*" they bellow.

And suddenly it's a swirl of dancers and singers. Tess plays energetically at the piano and the wonky-sounding orchestra kicks in, not to mention Carlo, who is blowing out some kind of low oompah notes on his tuba.

It's a play within a play! Adam drags David around the stage behind the chorus, weaving in and out of the scenery. Tevye's house shakes and Mary Beth atop it shrieks:

"*Ahhhhh!*"

For a moment, it looks as if she's been knocked backward off the roof.

The audience, generally perplexed but going along with it all, gasps, until a few seconds later when she pops back up.

"I'm okay! I'm okay!" she announces.

"*Tradition!*" the chorus belts.

David breaks loose of Adam's grasp and climbs to the top of Tevye's milk wagon.

"You're mine now!" deranged Adam yells. "Give me the pendant and I'll spare your life!"

"Never, evildoer!!" David yells with feeling. He thumps his chest. "For I am a super superhero! I'm a bird, I'm a plane . . . You can *bite me*!!"

The still-bewildered audience offers David a smattering of applause.

"The mamas, the mamas!!" The chorus, also perplexed, keeps singing the lines from the song. *"The mamas!!"*

"Your mama!" David leans down and pumps his finger into Adam's chest.

"Oh my God." I hold my head in my hands.

Without warning, Adam growls deeply, lifts his head back, and howls. And then it looks as though he's literally popping out of his skin. His arms begin to sprout fur.

"Keep singing! Keep singing!" I urge the terrified chorus villagers. "Keep playing!" I urge an astonished-looking Tess and musicians.

"The papas!" the chorus sings. *"The papas!"*

"Oh no," Luke says. "I think David's gone too far."

He rushes onto the stage, grabbing Adam by what's quickly becoming the scruff of his neck and pulling him behind a row of cardboard village houses.

We hear a great scuffling and growls. Wings *whoosh*, and objects crash and break.

Jared rushes over to me.

"What the hell is going on?"

"Quick! Where's Resnick?" I screech.

"He's in the dressing room making phone calls," Jared says.

"Lock him in there!"

"What?"

"Just do it! Now!"

"Okay . . ." Jared is reluctant but agreeable. "Listen, Jenna, I know that Luke's back and everything, but I was wondering if you two were still, ya know, together, and if you had a date for the cast party . . ."

"Yes, we're together. Look, I'm sorry, Jared," I say, taking him by the shoulders and looking him in the eyes. "You're a great kid and a good neighbor. But it's him. It's always been him."

"Oh." Jared hangs his head.

"Don't worry. There are plenty of girls in the neighborhood. We'll find you someone. Now *go!*"

Onstage, everyone's desperately trying to ignore the crashing explosions and crazy noises coming from backstage, not helped by the sudden running and yelling of the butt-crack elves, fleeing down the side stage stairs and up the theater aisles.

"*Whooooaaaa!* Run for your lives!" they scream, flailing their arms as their gangsta pants slide farther down their hips, giving the audience a supergross flash of their butt cracks.

"*The sons!*" David works the stage, rallying everyone to keep smiling and singing and dancing.

"*The sons! Tradition!*" the chorus sings.

Then suddenly the audience gasps loudly. A few of the women shriek. Tess stops playing. The orchestra stops playing. The tuba blows a groaning trailing-off note . . .

"*Traditi* . . ." The chorus voices trail off as well.

"*The daughters!*" David's solo voice rings out and then stops. "What?"

He, and everyone else, turns to gape at the top of Tevye's

house. There stands Adam, dark and sinister. He's bare from the waist up; his sweaty muscles glisten under the stage lights and his gray-black demon-angel wings are spread out full tilt behind him. Facing off against him is Luke, also bare chested, his white-gray wings fully extended, also muscular and gleaming.

"Oh my God, they're both so hot!" exclaims Sarah Johnson admiringly.

"Er . . . I think I'll go now," squeaks Mary Beth, who grabs her violin and quickly scrambles off the roof.

"Holy mother of crap!" Jared is back by my side.

Adam lunges for Luke. They tussle. Then Adam gets the advantage and twists his hands around Luke's neck. He pushes on Luke until he's leaning backward over the scaffold.

And in that moment, I know what I have to do.

"Wait!" I cry, rushing out onto the stage. "Stop!"

I hear Jared on his headphones.

"Spotlight on Jenna. Is anyone still back there?"

A spotlight shines in my face. It's so bright that at first I have to shield my eyes.

"Stop!" I scream up to Adam. "You'll kill him!"

"That's the general idea," Adam yells back, continuing to choke Luke. Adam pulls a dagger from his waistband. He releases his grip for a millisecond, then with one hand he grabs Luke by the hair and pulls him back over the railing so his throat is fully exposed. He holds the blade aloft.

"Noooo!" I scream.

Then:

"David, the pendant. Throw me the pendant!"

David pops up and tosses me the pendant, which, miraculously, I actually catch. Before I can even think, I aim. Throw. Close my eyes. And pray.

For a moment, it's as if time has stopped. When I open my eyes, it feels like I'm no longer on the stage, but alone in a dark void. Everything around me goes quiet. I see that ugly pendant swirling like a tiny Frisbee, glinting under the stage lights, its edges having sprouted deadly sharp teeth. I see Adam's stunned face.

Then. It hits. Adam. Square in the chest.

Adam drops his knife, an expression of pure astonishment on his face. He collapses onto the ground. Luke pulls away. He looks from Adam to me, then looks up, shielding his eyes from the blinding white light of the spotlight.

The audience bursts into applause.

I turn and am blinded by the spotlight that has swung onto me.

"Huh?" I had forgotten that the audience was even there.

Everyone onstage turns to stare at one another. David rushes toward me and actually gives me a hug.

Luke is human again, and Adam has disappeared entirely. A long, black crow leaps from the scaffold where Adam had lain, dripping droplets of blood. But now his body is gone, and the crow flies, squawking, up into the rafters and disappears.

Luke composes himself and I see him slipping backstage unnoticed.

I am still standing center stage and everyone looks to me.

I shoot Tess a panicked glance and send her a mental message to do something and fast. As if reading my mind, she starts playing "Tradition" again. The little orchestra kicks in, Carlo syncopates on the tuba, and Tess prompts the actors onstage to start over. The extremely confused audience offers support in the form of limp applause.

The cast kicks in, along with David, who seems happily right back into the swing of being Boy #3.

I bolt behind the curtain into the wings. Mr. Resnick appears beside me holding a screwdriver, presumably having escaped from the dressing room.

"Thank the angels in heaven," he says. "I was able to get in touch with Doogie's mother and—"

Miraculously, at that moment, Duncan (aka Doogie) appears, out of breath, slamming through the backstage door.

"Okay, I'm here," he pants.

Mr. Resnick spins him around, pulls out a black Sharpie, and starts drawing a mustache and beard on his face. A backstage elf rushes up to me, holding Duncan's Tevye costume, and Mr. Resnick gestures for me to get him into it as quickly as I can.

"I don't really want to be here, but I didn't want to leave everyone hanging," Duncan says.

"Leg in, Doogie." I instruct.

"Besides, it is kind of cool. No one has ever needed me so desperately before," he says.

"Okay, now arms into the vest."

"Usually, people don't even know I'm around," Duncan

continues. "And sometimes when they know I'm around, they even ask me to leave."

"That's very interesting, Doogie," Mr. Resnick says, pushing him in the direction of the stage. "Oh, wait, do you know the lines?"

"Well, I was supposed to be Motel, but I had most of the other lines memorized too. Sorry about that, by the way, but I had a big science test and was under pressu—"

"Good enough," Mr. Resnick says, and pushes him onto the stage.

"Jerry." Mr. Resnick turns to Jared and hands him the screwdriver. "Please go now and fix that dressing room lock before someone else gets stuck in there. It seems to be jammed."

Jared takes the tool and heads backstage.

"This job will kill me yet." Mr. Resnick sighs. "All right, we're back on track. I'm going down to the orchestra pit to mouth the lines to Doogie."

I stand there trying to make sense of what just happened for what seems like forever, but in actuality is probably just a few seconds. It feels like I've fulfilled some kind of spiritual destiny, sort of like how David fantasizes about being a superhero. I, Jenna Bloom, misunderstood, insignificant middle school student, have saved this space-time continuum, or at least the cast of *Fiddler on the Roof* and the residents of Oceanville, from an evil entity. That makes me feel pretty good. And maybe that's the point. When you save other people, you somehow save yourself. Luke steps up beside me. He's already in costume and primed to join the cast onstage.

"I couldn't agree with you more," he says.

"Are you reading my mind again?" I tease.

"Well, maybe just a little. But I promise I'll stop. Scout's honor." He holds up two fingers in a mock oath.

"Okay, well," I respond, "you better get out there, Motel."

He lifts his hand over my head and releases a long cord. My little lopsided heart unfurls and dangles before my eyes.

"It was in the grass," he says. "Don't lose it again."

"Only to you," I say.

"Ooh, corny." He grins.

"I know," I say.

Then he gives my shoulder a squeeze and bounds onstage just in time for his lines.

Out of the corner of my eye, I spot a large black crow sweep across the rafters. A high window slowly opens and what's left of Adam flies out into the night.

Acknowledgments

As always, there are people who deserve my gratitude and thanks: My editor, Nancy Mercado, for her insight and guidance, and the creative team at Roaring Brook Press. My fabulous agent, Michele Rubin, for her wisdom and encouragement, both in word and deed. My mentor, Patricia Reilly Giff, for her heartfelt support. My writing compadre, Mary Beth Bass, for her much appreciated optimism. My dad, for his quick and clever wit. My mom, for her keen reader's eye.

And, as always, my husband, Tom, and my children, Hannah and Rachel, for their untiring affection, steadfast belief in me, and extreme tolerance for my obsession with Halloween.